Secrets in Pink

Secrets in Pink

A Chattertowne Mystery

K.B. Jackson

For my mom, who instilled my love for reading and has always believed in me.

Chapter One

The morning breeze carried an early autumn bite and nuances of manure.

Sergeant Tony Bianchi took in the scene with his feet shoulder-width apart, hands on his hips, and his thick, dark mustache fringing his grimacing mouth. "Ya know they don't even teach cursive in school no more?"

"Hmph. That explains a lot about this Tic-Tack generation," grunted Old Man Brandt. "So, what're ya sayin'? You don't think a kid did this?" He scratched his backside with grimy hands.

"Nah, Zeb, I don't think it's your garden variety vandalism." Bianchi crossed his arms as he surveyed the scene.

"If I may say something."

Both men turned to look at me like they'd forgotten I was standing there.

"I believe the content of the message is more telling than the cursive."

We stood on the fresh black tar of Chattertowne's new parking lot where the brand-new pavement and sidewalks were covered in neon pink graffiti.

"Whydya say that?" Zeb eyed me with curiosity.

"Well, because first of all, as a former cheerleader, I've made my fair share of spray-painted signs for car wash fundraisers and Friday night football games, and I can tell you even those who don't normally write cursive end up linking letters this way because it's easier to make a swooping motion with an aerosol can. Second, I don't think teenagers who tag are super interested in civic disagreements over land sales."

Instead of the artwork of a seasoned tagger or the curse words of a juvenile delinquent, the messages Farmer Zeb had discovered when he'd arrived on his tractor before dawn that Monday in late September were political in nature, targeting Chattertowne's mayor, some city council members, and his own family, who'd sold the land to the city.

Once the site of a thriving lumber mill started by Zeb's grandfather, when that business had finally succumbed to overseas competition and a reduction in federal and state timber harvesting, Zeb had leased the adjacent field to local youth sports leagues for off-site parking during their tournaments and to the city during events such as the annual Kupit Festival, the classic car show, and the Christmas tree lighting on Black Friday which brought large crowds.

At the end of the previous year, a deal had been struck between Zeb and the city to transfer ownership of the six-acre parcel along the banks of the Jeanetta River, including the abandoned mill. The city had finalized purchase of the land a few weeks back and had finished paving the lot less than a week earlier.

The site was well known to have flooding issues each fall with the rains and each spring with the snowmelt. In addition, the valuation of the property between the last official appraisal and the closing of the deal had gone up significantly, leading some citizens to cry foul. After everything that had recently come out about extensive corruption at City Hall under previous administrations, people were understandably skeptical regarding the propriety of the deal.

A major scandal eighteen months prior had rocked Chattertowne's City Hall to its foundations. Confidence in our local government had sunk to an all-time low. Mayor Quincy had been ousted by voters who'd lost confidence in his leadership because, although not directly involved in the scandal, he'd been oblivious to the rampant illegal activity taking place right under his nose.

Margarita Guzman, a member of the City Council, had been elected to take his place by a razor-slim majority. Despite having moved to Chattertowne from California more than a decade prior, she was still considered by many to be an outsider. Much of the campaign waged against her highlighted this, but her commonsense approach won over enough voters to snag her the job.

One of her strongest initial challengers, a local paint store owner named Chet Buchanan, had been disqualified on a technicality when the city records clerk discovered his property sat outside town limits. Chet had asserted owning a business within city boundaries should have offset his home address being on the outskirts, but the council disagreed.

He accused Guzman of dirty politics and accused the council of making a power play to keep him out of city government due to his outspoken criticisms of their decisions. A regular at monthly meetings, Buchanan had a long list of complaints ranging from property tax rates to school bond appropriations to the purchase of the very lot on which we stood.

"Considering Chet Buchanan's hatred of the mayor and the fact he uses his Facebook group to stir up all sorts of anger about the land sale, I would think he'd be at the top of your list of suspects." I rested my right hand on my hip. "I mean, the dude owns a paint shop, for goodness' sake."

"So, we're letting local media determine the course of our investigations now, are we?"

The soft drawl startled me, and I turned to face the man who'd joined our trio.

"I see you've got your ass-kickin' boots on today, Chief Loveland."

He ignored me and instead addressed Sergeant Bianchi. "Looks like somebody decided to spiff up our new project with some artwork."

Bianchi scoffed. "No artwork, Chief. Just politics."

"This sentiment over here…is that even physically possible?" He pointed to a particularly graphic insult.

"My wife and I tried something similar a couple times, but I ain't never considered trying it on the mayor, as suggested. Even though she's damn attractive." Zeb turned to me. "Don't quote me on that. Edna'd kill me."

Cole Loveland closed his eyes, presumably trying to clear traumatizing images of Zeb and Edna's bedroom exploits from his mind. Perhaps he was also reevaluating his reasons for leaving Jackson Hole, Wyoming, to assume the top job in the beleaguered Chattertowne, Washington Police Department. "Mr. Brandt, could you start from the beginning and tell me what happened?"

Old Man Brandt spit out the side of his mouth, his lower lip bulging from chewing tobacco. His unkempt salt and pepper hair splayed out from beneath a John Deer cap, and his face was unshaven. He wore a gray Carhartt shirt and baggy Levi's which had seen more than their fair share of days working the fields.

In addition to owning the lumber mill, the Brandt family had been farming the valley for generations. They opened a produce shack each summer featuring a variety of crops, most notably their sweet corn. In the fall, they mowed the stalks into a haunted maze and gave pumpkin patch tours to preschoolers from all over the region. Zeb dressed as a scarecrow and read stories about blackbirds getting into the garden and the mice who teamed up to keep them out.

"Well," Zeb said. "I was up before dawn this morning feeding the cows. Some of 'em wandered over here. I guess even though it's paved, don't mean they don't still feel entitled to be here. Anyhoo, I drove over here on my tractor to try and wrangle 'em back. That's when I seen all this stuff. I get that kids can be kids, but this here sounds like a threat against my family, and I sure don't like bein' called no hypocrite. I always been a straight shooter."

Cole appraised Zeb. "So, you didn't hear anything last night?"

"Nah. I was in bed by nine-thirty. I have a nightly ritual of melatonin with a whiskey chaser. Thankfully, the Mrs. is down in Tempe visiting her sister before pumpkin patch season starts. I'd hate for her to hafta see this."

Cole turned to Bianchi. "Anybody talk to the mayor yet?"

"Not yet. I got the call from Ms. O'Connell at about 7:30 a.m. Came right down."

Cole finally acknowledged me. "How'd you know what was going on before Bianchi?"

"He doesn't mean me. He means my sister Vivienne. She's your admin, remember?"

"I know she's my admin. Lemme guess, she called to tip you off and you hustled your heinie down here."

His icy gray eyes stared at me from under the dark blonde fringe of his bangs and his cowboy hat. His sculpted jawline was uncharacteristically scruffy, shadowed like the Marlboro Man persona he wore, the authenticity of which I'd yet to determine. He'd been clean-shaven when he'd first arrived in Chattertowne, but he looked to be headed toward a full beard in time for the weather to turn damp and chilly.

I returned his steely gaze with a defiant one of my own. I had concerns he was looking for a reason to get rid of Viv because of his dislike for me, and I had no intention of giving him the ammunition.

"Actually, she didn't. A friend of mine recently turned me on to the usefulness of police scanner apps when dealing with uncooperative law enforcement officers. The call went out, and I jumped right in my car."

Cole snorted some sort of harrumphing sound before turning back to Bianchi. "Let's cordon off the area. The last thing we need is more looky-loos down here."

I giggled at his use of the term looky-loos.

"I guess asking you not to print any of this is useless." He exhaled a deep sigh.

"Why shouldn't we print it? Clearly this land sale is an issue dividing the town. Somebody got angry enough—or drunk enough—to drive down here in the middle of the night to make their feelings known. And you've got the added challenge of proving you can be trusted. You're an outsider coming into an environment of mistrust. Transparency is your friend."

Bianchi had wandered over to the portable toilet. "Hey Audrey, you need a pitcher of this for your article! Come 'n see!"

On the sidewalk, a bright pink arrow pointed straight at the toilet shack, accompanied by the words "Queen Margarita's throne."

Chapter Two

I arrived at my office at *The Chattertowne Coastal Current*, where I'd recently been promoted from "Lifestyles" to lead investigative reporter, eager to get started on my article. Before Cole Loveland and his attitude had shown up on the scene, I'd gotten some decent pictures of the graffiti and a full recap from Zeb.

Since his arrival six months earlier, the new Police Chief had been nothing but a burr in my side. Or was it spur? I didn't know much about cowboy vernacular.

"Ass-kickin' boots," I murmured, smirking.

I couldn't tell if my jab had bothered him or not. He had the best poker face of anyone I knew. I had the worst, so I was sure as I'd said it, I'd worn a self-satisfied expression.

I hadn't meant to get off on the wrong foot—er, boot—with him. He'd first been introduced at the City Council meeting, and I thought I'd make him feel welcome with a little hometown teasing. It's how we showed affection in Chattertowne. Maybe in Jackson Hole, things were more serious.

"Chief Loveland." I'd waved to get his attention from the back of the room. "My name is Audrey O'Connell, and I'm an investigative reporter for the *Coastal Current*. I was wondering…are you planning on making everyone in the department wear a ten-gallon hat, or can they keep their standard caps? Also, will gun spinning and quick draw become part of standard training?"

He'd ignored me and moved on to someone else's question. The next day when I'd gone by the station to take Viv to lunch, he wasn't thrilled to discover his administrative receptionist was my baby sister.

Also, for some reason, Cole seemed more bothered about my tenuous friendship with former City Manager Holden Villalobos than the fact Viv was still in a romantic relationship with former assistant chief—and current WWCC prisoner 436973—Lacey Kimball.

The scandal at City Hall had cost Holden his job, but in exchange for his testimony, his sentence had been reduced to three years' probation and two hundred hours of community service.

When the dust had settled, Holden took a position with Fred Harper's construction company. Their jobs consisted mostly of commercial projects and a few city contracts. It was far beneath his intellectual capacity, but he said he'd found working with his hands brought its own form of satisfaction.

His fiancée Emily had stood by him throughout the legal proceedings, but in the end, their relationship had sustained too much damage. She'd moved to Spokane about the same time Chief Loveland arrived.

Cole's first few months on the job were pretty tame. Even the criminals had seemingly decided Chattertowne needed a break. Theft was down, domestic violence was down, and we'd gone over a year and a half without a suspicious death. That also meant I'd had less to report, so I found myself digging for buried stories. Perhaps that was what Cole found most annoying. I was constantly hanging around, trying to ask questions, and, according to him, making something out of nothing.

This graffiti thing was not nothing, though. It had everything I'd been longing for in a news story: money, criminal vandalism, political intrigue. Nobody had been hurt, which was a bonus. Having seen three dead bodies in less than two weeks during our last crime wave had proved to me I'd never have survived a big city crime beat. I preferred slow-paced, predictable Chattertowne with its boring citizens and petty squabbles.

I loaded the photos I'd taken that morning onto my laptop and zoomed in to examine them. The messages were so oddly specific, there was no way teenagers were responsible. Any kids who cared about civic disagreements weren't out being hooligans on a school night, even during homecoming week.

Whoever had left the graffiti didn't like or trust the mayor and was angry about the land deal. Pink spray paint seemed a strange choice, and I wondered about the significance of it, if any.

I made a note to research any environmental organizations who might have expressed their dissatisfaction with the project, as well as local Facebook groups who'd taken issue with the mayor, the Brandt family, and the city council.

Chet Buchanan was my number one suspect, even if Wyatt Earp didn't care about my opinion. He'd formed two groups online. The first was a Chattertowne nostalgia page. I'd initially joined because I loved the old stories and vintage photographs. Chet ruled the group with an iron fist, blocking those he deemed unfit to participate and setting rules that applied to everyone but him. One of the rules of the group limited posts to nostalgia only, nothing political. Chet was the primary violator of that rule and, when called on it, promptly ejected those he deemed to be stirring up dissent.

His other group, formed because of the blowback he'd gotten about not following his own rules in the nostalgia group, was called Citizens for Responsibility on Chattertowne's City Council, a.k.a CROCCC. They didn't particularly appreciate me pointing out the extraneous 'F' unaccounted for in the acronym, so I stayed mostly a lurker. I'd found it was a good resource for taking the pulse of community sentiment about various topics, but any challenges to Chet and his minions' opinions were met with attacks like a swarm of angry hornets. I'd also observed that, as with hornets, playing dead didn't work. They just kept attacking. Hiding out and re-emerging was useless as well, as they'd lie in wait. Their grudges were fierce and enduring.

CROCCC's manifesto was unclear. They were much better at communicating what they didn't like than what they did. They didn't like the mayor for many reasons, not the least of which, it seemed to me, was either latent or outright racism. Chattertowne was maybe 2% Latinx on a good day. Our new mayor was of Mexican descent, from a state that embodied "otherness" to many residents. CROCCC tended to reject on principle anything they deemed to promote diversity, liberal elitism, spirituality without religion, or tolerance, which they viewed as an "anything goes" way of thinking. They believed California was a hotbed of hedonism and immorality. This, of course, was a skewed perception of the country's third-largest state with the largest economy. It hyper-focused on caricatures of Hollywood, San Francisco, and the like, while completely disregarding entire communities like conservative Orange County, Redding, and basically all the armpit cities.

Even if California was everything it had been stereotyped, it didn't mean Margarita had an agenda to glamorize or "Hollywood-ize" Chattertowne, like that were remotely possible. Besides, the values her detractors seemed so concerned about preserving, I wasn't sure they were as much a part of the fabric of the town as they wanted to believe…what with the murders, government corruption, and drug smuggling that had been perpetrated by homegrown folks for decades.

CROCCC's online litany of complaints—about the mayor, the land deal, the boat launch, etc.—solidified my belief the group was the source of the anger that had led to the vandalism. Whether Chet had his finger on the trigger of the spray can or not, his rhetoric had stoked the fire of hostility, now well on its way to a roaring blaze.

I drove down to City Hall at about noon, my agenda two-pronged. I wanted to take my sister to lunch, but while I was there, I intended to talk to Cole. I needed to find a way to bury the hatchet and get him to warm up to me so he wouldn't be such an obstacle every time I tried to investigate a story. No longer having Holden in the Mayor's Office, the closest I had to an inside (wo)man was Vivienne, and she definitely wasn't in Cole's inner circle of trust. Viv was grateful to still have a job following her girlfriend's arrest and had warned me multiple times she didn't want to give him any reason to push her out.

I passed the lobby front desk where Joan, the receptionist, was in conversation with a man who I recognized to be a cohort of Chet Buchanan's, Hiram Kaiser. Hiram owned a plumbing company and my few online encounters with him had left me with the impression he wasn't the smartest tack. Much of what he said and did seemed to be a parroting of Chet, or at his prodding. I had yet to see evidence he was actually capable of forming his own opinions.

"Hy, I'm not stonewalling you." Joan employed her politely restrained but firm voice reserved for disgruntled citizens. "Mayor Guzman is in a meeting with a state auditor and cannot be disturbed. They're making sure every "i" is dotted, every "t" is crossed these days. I'm sure you understand the scrutiny we're under."

He pounded his fist on the desk. "I'm a tax-paying citizen of this town, and I have every right to speak to my elected officials, whenever I want."

Joan sighed. "You have the right to speak to the mayor. No one's keeping you from doing that. But you'll either have to make an appointment or sit down here and wait for her to be done with her meeting."

I slowed my pace to observe their interaction. Hiram's face reddened. His frazzled gaze darted around the lobby. He certainly behaved like the type who might spray-paint derogatory things. I put him at the top of my mental list with Buchanan. Maybe they'd done it together.

I skirted past Joan and Hy to the passport office and police station's shared waiting room. It was an odd configuration, with receptionists on each side partitioned behind glass, nearly facing off against each other. The chairs between them were filled with a combination of passport applicants and citizens waiting to report crimes. Behind the CPD reception desk, I could see Viv was talking on the phone. A keypad secured the door to her area, so I had to wait for her to be done.

After ending her call, Viv slid the window ajar. "Hey, what's up?"

"Not much. I wanted to take you to lunch."

Viv eyed me skeptically. "Why do I get the feeling there's more to this than a sisterly lunch?"

I opened my mouth to refute her accusation but stopped when Cole walked into the lobby. He took one look at me and shook his head.

"Well, hello again, Chief Loveland. Fancy seeing you here," I called out to him with false congeniality.

"I work here. As does your sister…for now. I'd suggest moving along so we both can do our jobs."

Viv flinched at the implied threat.

"Do you have a few minutes? I'd like to get a statement from you regarding this morning's incident," I said.

He pulled off his cowboy hat, giving me a rare glimpse of his disheveled dark blond wavy hair. He ran his fingers through it while blowing out a frustrated whoosh. "Here's your statement. There was vandalism. We're investigating. You'll know more when we do."

"Super helpful. Thanks."

He placed his hat against his chest and bowed. "Always at your service, ma'am."

I thought I saw a glimmer of mischief in his eye, but as quickly as it appeared, it disappeared, replaced by his ever-present poker face.

"Officer Chen's gonna come watch the phones so I can take my lunch in about 15 minutes if you can wait," said Viv. "Can we go to that new Mediterranean place? I hear their shawarma is smothered in so much garlic tahini it seeps out your pores for days."

"This is a selling point for you?" I asked.

"Audrey, my girlfriend's in prison and won't be eligible for parole for at least a year. I could bathe in it if I so chose, and there'd be no one to complain about it."

I pursed my lips and nodded. "I could have the breath of a dragon, and it wouldn't affect my current romantic situation either. Shawarma it is."

* * *

We nestled into a booth at Mia's Mediterranean Kitchen near a large picture window. Trees planted in pots along the sidewalk partially blocked the view of traffic on Hannah Street, but being late September, the leaves had begun to change, and some had already fallen.

"What's with you and Cole?" Viv shoveled chunks of chicken with saffron rice slathered in garlic tahini and sprinkled with sumac into her mouth. She moaned with pleasure and closed her eyes. "Food of the gods."

"What do you mean? He hates me. What's there to understand?" I ripped off a small piece of pita and dredged it through my bowl of hummus.

"I don't think he hates you. I think he's trying to figure you out, get a read on you. You keep poking at him like you want him to hate you, though.

11

Why?"

I popped a kalamata olive into my mouth, its salty bitterness an appropriate accompaniment for ruminations on one salty, bitter Cole Loveland.

"He brings out the petty in me. I don't know what it is. He struts around town wearing that stupid hat like he's doing it to spite me at this point."

Viv laughed. "You're giving yourself way too much credit. He doesn't strike me as the type to do anything because of someone else."

"I've finally got a juicy story to pursue and he's so tight-lipped it's like they're super glued together. He takes pride in being an obstacle at my every turn. Would it kill him to throw me a bone or two?"

"Look, I need this job, so I'm gonna have to ask you to keep me out of it. The sooner you two start communicating directly instead of through me, the better."

She had a point. I was a big girl, and Cole was a grown man. We were going to have to solve our differences mano y mano. Or was it mano y mana?

Viv wrapped a chunk of chicken and a dollop of hummus into a pita and took a bite. Her cheeks bulged. "So, what's your thought on this vandalism thing?"

"I can't take you seriously when you have tahini running down your chin."

* * *

When we returned from lunch, I asked Viv to buzz me through so I could talk to Cole in person. His door was slightly ajar, so I rapped twice with my knuckles.

"Come in."

When I peeked my head through, Cole looked up. He didn't recoil, which I took as a positive sign.

"Miss O'Connell, what can I do for you?"

"I thought maybe we could find a way to set aside our differences." I rested my hands on the back of one of two cherry wood chairs that sat facing his desk.

"Our differences? Is this another comment on my Western gear?"

"Look, I never intended for that to become a thing. I was only trying to give you a little friendly welcome-to-the-neighborhood ribbing. Viv really needs this job and I'd hate for my bad manners to cause any trouble for her."

He looked at me with curiosity, his head at a slight tilt and his brow arched. "You don't think very highly of me, do you, Miss O'Connell?"

"Why would you say that?"

"You seem to believe I'd act punitively against one of my subordinates because of a personal distaste for her sister."

"So, you admit it. You feel personal distaste for me."

"Ma'am, in all honesty, I don't know you. I'm sure you're a lovely person. You're probably even a decent journalist, but where I come from, everybody knows their place." His gaze intensified.

"As in, I don't?"

Cole chuckled and shook his head. "I've got a whole lot on my plate today. If I have anything that needs to be passed along to the public regarding the vandalism incident, you'll be the first to know. Fair enough?"

"I guess that's my cue."

I waited for him to say more, but instead, he looked at me with both eyebrows raised and his mouth set firm.

"Okey dokey."

As I left the station, my cheeks were aflame with embarrassment, and my hairline burned with indignation.

I'd met infuriating men in my day, but Cole Loveland took the cake.

Chapter Three

Back at the *Current*, I delved into researching CROCCC's members to see who were the most outspoken besides Chet and Hy. One person—who'd chosen to remain anonymous—used the phrase volage-brained to describe the mayor, and I had to look up the term to discover its definition. It meant fickle. I found the combination of anger and eloquence fascinating. The elevated vocabulary dramatically narrowed the list of Chattertowneites capable of composing such a message and I made a note to visit the library and find out who'd been reading Chaucer of late.

A woman named Tammy Milner was a frequent contributor in the CROCCC group, along with Wanda Harper.

"Harper." I said the name out loud.

I picked up my phone and dialed. The call finally connected after several rings, with the sound of wood being sawed and nails being hammered echoing in the background.

"Hey. This is unexpected," Holden said, somewhat winded.

"You sound busy. Am I interrupting?" My face warmed at the sound of his voice.

"I'm in the middle of work. What's up?"

"That's actually why I called. Wanda Harper…she's Fred's wife, right? The owner of Harper Construction?"

"Sure is. Why do you ask?"

"Oh," I hedged. "I'm looking into something."

Holden's chuckle boomed through the phone. "Audrey, you forget. I know you too well. What's this about?"

"Did you hear about the graffiti down at the new parking lot?"

"Nope. I've been on the job site since 6:30 this morning. What happened?"

"Someone who's unhappy about the land sale spray-painted some messages in protest. My money is on the anti-Guzman crowd. Wanda's a vocal supporter of Chet and Hy. Has Fred said anything to indicate his political leanings or opinions?"

Holden sighed. "Audrey, I need this job."

"You're the second person today who's said that to me. Why does everyone think I'm going to mess up their employment status?"

"Maybe because you barrel into situations without stopping to think of the collateral damage you might be causing? Just a thought."

"Great talk, Holden. Let's do it again in another six months."

Hanging up on him wasn't going to ingratiate myself to him or make him super cooperative in situations where I needed information, but I didn't have the patience to deal with another man chastising me today.

It was at this apropos moment my boss, Nicholas Anderson, chose to pop his head into my office. "Audrey, what's the scoop on this vandalism story?"

"Well, I've been to the scene, and I've interviewed Sergeant Bianchi, Zebadiah Brandt, and Chief Loveland. I've got some photos, and I'm working on a couple of angles, but I'll have an article on the preliminary facts ready before I leave today. It can go up on the website tonight."

The *Chattertowne Coastal Current* was a weekly print newspaper but had recently transitioned to a daily digital format as well. The one thing I missed about my old position was it gave me time to thoroughly research my features. With digital, the pressure to beat the Chattertowne gossip tree was immense and often felt like a losing battle. What I had in my favor this time was Cole seemed to be determined to keep certain aspects quiet. What wasn't in my favor? Zeb. That man was both heavily connected and loudly opinionated.

As I shut down my computer for the night, my phone rang from an unknown number.

"This is Audrey O'Connell."

"Audrey, hello, this is Margarita Guzman. Are you available to meet? I've got something to show you."

"Of course, Mayor Guzman. Would you like me to come to your office at City Hall?"

"No, to my home. It appears the new parking lot wasn't the only location visited by our friend with the paint can."

***

I surveyed the side of Margarita's garage. "Do you have any idea when this might have happened?"

"I don't. I didn't hear anything during the night, and this morning, when I left, I had no need to come over here. I found it this afternoon when I went to look for my rake to start working on these leaves."

Mayor Guzman lived alone in a rambler on two acres at the edge of town—the inside edge, unlike Chet's home. Her property bordered the walking trail, which ran along the river at the west end.

Someone had adorned her garage with neon pink epithets, calling her "Mayor Montezuma" and depicting a stick figure lying across a large mound with the caption "Margarita on the rocks."

"That one's definitely an implied threat." I pointed to the body lying broken upon the boulders. "It needs to be reported to Chief Loveland. Any reason you haven't done so yet?"

Margarita rubbed the back of her neck. She had short, silver hair, cut in what I'd always associated with 70s and 80s-era female ice skaters and women with a reputation for asking to speak to the manager. She wore black polyester pants and a leopard print blouse with sensible shoes. Her mahogany eyes looked sad and her normally tan complexion pale.

"As you know, I've been painted as an outsider. There's a perception I'm not looking out for the people who have lived here for generations. How will it look if I immediately go crying to an actual outsider who's been in this town for half a year? In my dealings with you, I've never felt that you have treated me like I don't have the right to be here."

"Of course, you have the right to be here." I paused. "I'm probably not supposed to tell anyone this, media bias and all that, but I voted for you.

However, with all due respect, you *are* an outsider—to these folks at least—and your silence isn't going to appease them, it'll embolden them. One of the things I've learned over the past couple years is this town likes its secrets and will close ranks to protect their own. You'll never be considered one of them. You're better off shining the spotlight on the cockroaches."

She sighed. "I suppose you're right. I keep wanting to believe I'll prove myself to them eventually. I mean, they elected me to the council and then into the mayor's office. I've been here for more than a decade. My pottery store's been open on Third Avenue for nearly that long. My son graduated from Chattertowne High. He was captain of the tennis team, and I was president of the PTA."

"Hey, I'm local, born and raised here, and they still treated me as an outsider when I moved back from Portland. I get it. It makes no sense, and it isn't fun, but keeping quiet about this won't change that. Also, Cole isn't my biggest fan, so you'll be helping me out if he knows I'm the one who convinced you to give him a call."

Margarita pulled out her phone and dialed the station. "Hello, Vivienne. Is Chief Loveland available?" She waited a beat. "Hello, Cole, it's Margarita. I'm here with Audrey O'Connell from the—yes. Yes. Mm-hmm."

I couldn't hear what he was saying, but the low rumble of his voice held irritation.

"The reason I'm calling is I've discovered some vandalism on my property similar to what was found at the new lot." Margarita's face became serious. "I'd appreciate that, thanks."

Less than fifteen minutes later, Cole's gray Dodge Charger pulled into Margarita's driveway. Sunglasses hid his undoubtedly suspicious gaze, but they couldn't hide the smirk on his face.

"Mayor Guzman, Miss O'Connell." He tapped the tip of his hat. "Let's have a look at the new addition to your decorating scheme."

The three of us walked to the side of the garage, and he surveyed the messages quietly.

"I insisted she call you." I felt only mildly embarrassed by the desperate validation-seeking tone of my declaration.

He nodded his head once, but as per usual, he directed his comments elsewhere. "Have you received any phone calls or emails or even a letter you think might be related?"

"Not really." Margarita wrung her hands. "I mean, I catch a lot of flak for all sorts of things from all sorts of people, but it's rarely anonymous. I'd have to go back and look to see if anything stands out."

"Cole, this is an actual threat against her life. It needs to be taken seriously."

He removed his glasses and glared pointedly at me. "Is there a reason you believe I wouldn't take this seriously?"

Beneath his withering gaze, I fought against my instinct to cower. "I didn't say that, but I'm concerned this might be dismissed as a victimless crime or someone blowing off steam."

"I consider threats against citizens to be profoundly serious, especially when it comes to elected officials. Margarita, if you could look through your communications and see if there are similar sentiments in any emails or letters, that would help. Look for common phrasing or tone. In the meantime, would you like an officer positioned here overnight?"

"I have an alarm system. I'm not worried about my safety. Someone is clearly incensed about this land deal."

"It's CROCCC," I declared. "Citizens for Responsibility on Chattertowne's City Council."

"What about the f?" His forehead creased.

I nodded vigorously. "Exactly. But don't ask them about it. They're a pretty touchy bunch. Their ringleader is Chet Buchanan. Hiram Kaiser is his right-hand man, and they've got a few groupies. I'm not sure Hiram has had an original thought in his life. He simply parrots what Chet says."

Margarita reared her head back with a grimace. "Oh, I'm well aware of Chet, Hy, and CROCCC. They started harassing me as soon as I announced my intention to run for mayor. Chet's angry he wasn't allowed to run, and, well, he's angry about a lot of things."

"Somehow, I haven't had the pleasure of making his acquaintance," Cole said. "I guess I should start with him. Do you have his address?"

Margarita shook her head. "Oh, you won't need it to know where to find him tonight. He'll be at the council meeting. Chet Buchanan never misses an opportunity to cause trouble for me."

* * *

It was standing room only at the city council meeting. Word had gotten out about the graffiti at the parking lot, and curiosity brought the locals in droves. I had been to many other council meetings in search of a story, and other than the regular curmudgeons, most of Chattertowne's citizenry hadn't exactly struck me as civic-minded.

I squeezed in through the doorway and around the side to where Cole leaned against the wall. He made eye contact with me, but his face remained impassive. I'd hoped to score some brownie points by getting Margarita to notify him about the vandalism at her house, maybe even thaw the ice between us. I'd have to settle for less overtly disdainful.

I opened my mouth and leaned toward him to whisper a greeting in his ear, but Margarita called the meeting to order with the bang of a gavel.

"Good evening, everyone. I'm thrilled to see so many first-timers tonight. I'd ask what has stirred your interest in the goings-on within the council, but we all know why you're here. There's no need for pretense."

A murmur washed across the room, a crescendo of commentary which grew to a dull roar.

"Seems like you've lost control of this town!" someone yelled above the din.

Cole straightened his posture and jutted his jaw forward. His defensive reaction about the accusation was understandable. After all, he had as much responsibility for how Chattertowne functioned as the mayor did.

"Folks, one incident of vandalism isn't an indicator of anything other than one person exhibiting poor self-control," Margarita said. "Things are on track in every way."

I knew better, and judging by the murmured response of the crowd, they did, too.

"One incident," someone scoffed.

I craned my neck in hopes of spotting who'd made the remark but couldn't identify the speaker with a mid-range voice. It could have been either a man or a woman. While the parking lot graffiti was public knowledge, no one but the mayor, the chief, me, and the vandal himself knew about the second incident. Cole scanned the room as well.

Chet Buchanan stood in the third row. "Sounds like the council's decision to purchase the land with taxpayer dollars needs to be reexamined in light of what has happened. Seems like the people have spoken, and they aren't happy."

"Chief Loveland and I have met to discuss the situation and I have full confidence in the Chattertowne Police Department to expeditiously identify the culprit. In the meantime, the land sale is completed. I see no need to revisit the issue. It's a done deal, Chet."

Margarita's tone held finality. Chet's expression held rage. He slowly sank into his chair, his furious gaze never averting from hers. Whatever Chet had hoped to accomplish at the meeting, Margarita was having none of it.

The council moved on to other topics, such as the Christmas tree lighting ceremony and a discussion on zoning permits for a new strip mall on the east side of town. Hiram leaned toward Chet to whisper something, but he brushed him away like a gnat. If we were in a cartoon, I'd have sworn there was steam emanating from Chet's ears and lasers shooting from his eyes.

It shouldn't have been a surprise, then, when I got the call just after three in the morning that the old mill was on fire.

Chapter Four

Maybe it was the jarring experience of being awoken in the middle of the night. Perhaps it was surprise over the fact the anger I'd witnessed at the council meeting had erupted into actual flames. Most likely, though, it was the source of the call that caught me most off guard.

"Sorry to wake you, Miss O'Connell. I thought you'd want to know the old Brandt mill is on fire."

"Cole?" My voice was scratchy from sleeping next to an open window through which a hint of smoke wafted into the house. Immediately, I was wide awake.

"I hope it's okay I'm calling despite the time. I got your number from Bianchi. I figured you were gonna want the scoop, and you might as well get it from me."

"Wow, um, thank you. I'll be there in about 15 or 20 minutes."

"You might want to hurry. It's going fast. There may not be anything left by the time you arrive."

I scrambled into the jeans I'd thrown over the back of the chair, which I'd so optimistically placed in front of my writing desk when I'd moved into the house. I'd envisioned writing the great American novel while watching the sun rise across the valley. I'd encountered two problems with that. One, I typically ended up writing in bed with a pillow propped under my laptop, and two, I wasn't a morning person. I could count on one hand the number of sunrises I'd witnessed by choice.

I threw on a reasonably clean bra and my oversized Chattertowne High

Cougars hoodie while simultaneously trying to brush my teeth. I pulled my ash-blonde hair back into a long ponytail and swiped some concealer under my hazel-green eyes. A couple pinches and a slap to my cheeks for a little color, and I was out the door.

My unlikely landlord, Renee Washburn, and I had forged a tenuous truce. We'd started off on the wrong foot because of my previous relationship with her now-deceased husband, but after I'd helped solve his murder, she'd agreed to let me rent her home when she moved with their three boys to Toronto for a fresh start. I'd made her clean the place out, of course, as it had been a complete disaster.

I'd offered Viv the option to move in with me, but she'd chosen to stay in the apartment we'd previously shared. She could afford it on her own between her gig at the Police Station and singing weekend nights at Nautilus.

I'd gotten accustomed to living alone. I could cook curry without anyone complaining about the smell, vacuum at midnight, and paint an entire wall lime green on a whim if I so chose. It also meant I wouldn't disturb anyone when storming out of the house at three in the morning for a story.

* * *

The newly paved parking lot was still cordoned off with police tape from the graffiti incident. Bianchi and the Chief stood right on the other side of the line, watching as the CFD made last-gasp efforts to save a portion of the structure. I pulled out my phone and shot a video right as the roof caved in. Several firefighters rushed to move out of the way of embers as they exploded upon impact with the ground.

There was a lot of yelling and running around. The crowd pressed against the yellow tape barrier, a cacophony of shock and distress rippling through the throng. Margarita arrived and was ushered under the tape but kept her distance from the smoldering remains of the mill.

Cole stood with his feet spread wide and his hands on his hips, watching the scene. His fingers loosely held his hat at his side. He crooked his head in my direction, and we made eye contact. His expression was unreadable, but the longer he held my gaze, the more rapid my breathing became.

What was that? I couldn't tell if I was more unnerved by him looking at me or by my reaction to it.

He flung his hat back onto his head.

The firefighters, several of whom were either Norvald brothers or cousins, hosed down the glowing skeleton of the building. The Norvalds, as their Scandinavian name implied, were all blond-haired and blue-eyed. Why they'd all gone into firefighting, I had no clue.

Soon, there was nothing left but smoke, charcoal, and the sizzling of water hitting hot timbers. The smoke began to dissipate, revealing a clear night. Above us, Cassiopeia's M shone like the Bat-signal, the star Schedar blinking as if trying to convey a message in Morse code.

Margarita walked toward me with slumped shoulders. "Can you believe this?"

"It's crazy. What are the odds they'll be able to find any evidence in this rubble?"

She gave a sad shake of her head. "Who knows? There's no doubt it was arson. You can smell the kerosene clear as day despite no fuel being stored here. The mill's been sitting empty for years."

A commotion broke out a few feet away. Old man Brandt was yelling at Cole.

"Now will you take this seriously? This fire coulda spread to my fields, and I woulda lost my entire corn crop, not to mention the maze and pumpkin patch. What are you gonna do about it?"

Cole tipped his chin down and quietly gave his response. The brim of his hat blocked my view of his lips, preventing me from making out what he'd said.

Margarita leaned in to whisper into my ear. "This isn't Chief Loveland's fault. It's important people know that. There's no way he could've known this would escalate to arson."

"Agreed, but I will need a quote from you for the article about the vandalism, the fire, and the rage simmering below the surface, which is now erupting."

"Here's your headline: Mayor offers ten thousand dollars of her own money in exchange for information leading to the arrest and conviction of the arsonist."

Chapter Five

Anderson loved the headline provided by Mayor Guzman, and even more so loved the fact we'd been given the scoop on her reward offer to uncover whoever had burned down the mill. I was convinced the arsonist was also the tagger, but so far, no official connection had been made.

I'd pounded out my story when I got home at around five that morning and submitted it for online publication at eight. By the time I'd gotten out of the shower at nine, views of the article were through the roof, and I'd received ten text messages about it, four from my mother alone.

I stopped at Abigail's to grab a pumpkin scone and a twenty-ounce latte with four shots of espresso in an effort to counteract my lack of sleep. I overheard two different conversations regarding the fire and the mayor's reward. As I was about to leave, a man entered the coffee shop.

As he brushed past me, he grunted my name. "Audrey."

It was one of my high school boyfriends, Levi Scott. Levi and I had dated during our senior year for about four months. He looked to have grown an inch or two since graduation, standing at about 5'10. He was still slim, still had a full head of black hair, and still wore a smirk that bulged with Skoal chewing tobacco.

He'd been my first serious boyfriend. More accurately, I'd been serious. He wasn't.

Levi captained the swim team, rode motorcycles, and had soft brown lying eyes that peered at me from under long dark bangs that he constantly swept to the side with a flick of his head. His chew habit was revolting, but he made up for it with his slow, sexy smile, which only occasionally had tobacco peeking out between his teeth.

I was the goodie-two-shoes, and he was a bit of a bad boy.

While not a guy I considered romantic, he'd asked me on a date for Valentine's Day. I'd spent hours getting ready and anxiously sat on the sofa in my parents' living room, awaiting his arrival. He hadn't arrived by six, so I called his house. No answer. By seven, I'd entered a full-blown panic, and by eight, I'd resigned myself to the fact he wasn't coming. Humiliated and devastated, I'd thrown on baggy sweats and scooped out a giant bowl of Rocky Road ice cream to drown my sorrows.

When he'd shown up two days later, my mother led him into the living room with a sour look of disapproval on her face. He tossed something into my lap. The dented heart-shaped box of convenience store chocolates with a bright orange 50% off sticker had been the final straw in our flawed relationship.

I'd run into Levi at a bar six years after graduation on a visit home for Thanksgiving.

Clumsily leaning toward me with one hand on the bar counter to hold him up he'd slurred into my ear, "They say looking good is the best revenge, and you sure got me."

His breath had smelled like chewing tobacco and beer. Today, he smelled like chewing tobacco and Axe Body Spray.

"Hey, Levi, how are you? You here for one of Abigail's scones?"

"Nope, just a coffee. Meetin' some friends to talk about some stuff."

"Ah, I see."

I didn't see, not until Chet Buchanan and Hiram Kaiser walked through the doorway, and suddenly it became crystal clear. The men greeted each other with nearly imperceptible nods and grim-set mouths. Whatever they were meeting to discuss, the mood was solemn.

"See you around, Audrey."

Levi went to the counter to place his order. Chet stared at me as he and Hy settled into a corner table. His focus left me feeling like a bug under a microscope. Something to keep an eye on, possibly to squash.

After exiting, I tried to casually peek into the coffee shop through the window but all I saw were the three men huddled closely.

"Still spying on people, I see."

I whipped my body to face the man whose words thrummed in my ear.

"Holden! You scared the crap outta me."

"Maybe if you stopped skulking around, you wouldn't be so skittish."

His dark brown eyes glinted with humor, and he gave me that broad smile of his which always left me weak in the knees. Despite it being nearly October, he still had a deep tan from working on building projects all summer.

"I'm not skulking. I'm investigating."

He glimpsed through the window. "That's one unholy trinity."

"I didn't know Levi was in cahoots with Chet and Hy. I lost touch with Levi after graduation. I guess I don't really know what kind of man he turned out to be."

Holden crossed his arms, which caused his impressive biceps to bulge. "Levi isn't quite as vocal about politics as the other two, but I had my fair share of visits from each of them during my time at City Hall."

As he spoke of his former career, he winced slightly. Seeing him in grubby jeans and a sweatshirt instead of a polo shirt with khakis elucidated how different his life had become. It was certainly better than prison orange, however.

I was proud of him for staying in Chattertowne. It would have been easier for him to leave and start his life over where no one knew anything about him or his past. Small towns can be brutal for remaking one's image. They never let you forget who you used to be or who they believed you to be. I'd experienced this firsthand.

"Doesn't surprise me that Levi didn't talk much. He was yet another boyfriend of mine where conversations were intellectually painful, but his looks made up for it." I sighed. "It's been a pattern."

"Who are you seeing now?"

I met his gaze before looking away. "I'm too busy to date. Too focused on my job. I couldn't even fit in a coffee date these days."

He scoffed. "That's a cop-out."

"How do you figure?"

"Audrey, just because we're both single now doesn't mean I plan on pursuing you. You don't have to preemptively make up excuses."

"Just because we're both single doesn't mean I assumed you would. Or would want you to."

"Glad we're on the same page."

"Ditto." I pinched my lips.

He sighed, rubbing the back of his neck. "You're a real pain in the—"

"So I've been told. I was still hoping you'd answer my question, though."

He furrowed his brows. "Which question was that?"

"The question I asked the other day about Fred Harper."

"You mean about his political leanings? He's never said much. Honestly, he's never said much about anything. He's a pretty quiet guy. His wife's a loudmouth, though."

"I've seen some of her online posts. She seems to be of the same mindset as Chet and Hy, and apparently Levi, so I'm guessing Fred agrees with her. He's kind of in my sights right now."

"Based on what?"

"I'm looking at everyone associated with CROCCC. Fred's listed as a member on Facebook, even if he's not an active commenter. Maybe he's flying under the radar to avoid suspicion. Sometimes it's the ones you least suspect..."

"Look, Audrey, like I told you, I need this job, and I have no intentions of risking it, but I'll see if I can get a read on Fred. Levi, too, since he's a subcontractor for Harper Construction. Is your working theory that whoever spray-painted the parking lot is in construction because it's similar to the paint we use to mark out projects?"

"Something like that." I toggled the zipper on my hoodie.

He surveyed my face. "What aren't you telling me?"

"I forgot you're able to read me like a book."

"I think it's more that you have the worst poker face ever." His mouth twisted to the side.

"Yeah, so, we aren't talking about one graffiti incident. There's a second location. Margarita Guzman's garage. And then there's the fire at the mill."

Holden blew out his breath in a slow whistle. "You really think the two things are connected? It's a long leap from vandalism to arson."

"Yeah, well, it was a leap from parking spot thief to criminal mastermind, but I proved Peter Chatterton was both."

"Criminal mastermind is a pretty generous description. What are you thinking in terms of the arson and the graffiti?"

"I've been looking into the CROCCC crowd. Say that ten times fast." I snorted my laugh and then covered my mouth and nose with embarrassment. "Anyway, I believe that group is the source of this activity. I'm not sure if it's a lone wolf tangentially affiliated with them who's become radicalized by their rhetoric or if it's Chet or Hy or one of their more prominent and vocal members. But the messages are clear. They're angry about the land deal, and they don't like Mayor Guzman."

"Audrey, please be careful. If they've escalated from spray paint to blowtorch, their next step may be to target people in their homes or cars they've deemed to be adversaries." He started to reach out and grab my arm but pulled back before making contact.

"I appreciate your concern, Holden. I do." I checked my phone. "I've got to get to work now but give me a call if you find out anything. And I'll keep you in the loop as much as I can."

As we parted ways, his hand grazed mine, and I felt my heart jump the tracks. Some feelings stick with a person no matter how hard they try to will them away.

* * *

I sat at my desk researching everyone associated with CROCCC's Facebook group, but my mind kept wandering to my earlier encounters with Levi and Holden. Though Holden had never been my boyfriend, we'd nearly kissed once while he was still with Emily, and like my ill-fated relationship with Levi, our attraction was indicative of my propensity for drawing in emotionally elusive and/or unavailable guys.

There was Rick from my gym back in Portland, who'd asked me to dinner but then spent the evening chewing on a parsley sprig and stared at me dead-eyed for what felt like an interminable amount of time without uttering a word.

Chew. Blink. Chew. Blink.

Seriously, who chews on parsley? It's a garnish, not a side dish.

In the glory days of high school, Rick had been the star of his hockey team and had kept the mullet in tribute. He'd peppered what little conversation he mustered with the word wicked the way my father seasoned the discount steak he sometimes bought from the trunk of some guy's Buick in the local hardware store's parking lot, meaning an exorbitant amount intended to disguise poor substance.

There was the newly single guy, Ira, who'd asked me out on the recommendation of my dental hygienist, Angie. If I remembered correctly, he'd managed an office supply store, but it could've been a dollar store that sold office supplies. Angie had said he was her go-to source for paper clips and sticky notepads. She'd said if she weren't already married, she'd snatch him up. Once, when I was getting my teeth cleaned, Angie's Neanderthal-like husband had come in with her forgotten lunch. I should have realized in that moment her taste was questionable.

My first clue it wasn't going to be a fantastic first date? Ian had suggested we meet at Denny's. Now, I love a two a.m. Grand Slam breakfast after a night out dancing as much as anyone, but Eggs Over My Hammy in a sticky red pleather booth didn't exactly scream romance.

Ira spent an hour talking about his ex-wife, followed by twenty minutes of light sobbing. Occasionally, he'd stopped to blow his nose and apologize. I'd reassured him I understood.

Between crying jags, he'd left the table to suck down a cigarette out in the parking lot. When the bill had arrived, he'd stared forlornly out the window until I pulled my wallet from my purse. I didn't send Angie a Christmas card that year.

Of course, none of my terrible dating experiences would ever be topped by the brief period where I'd accidentally almost dated my distant cousin.

My phone rang, startling me out of my self-pity stupor.

"Audrey O'Connell."

"Hello, Ms. O'Connell." Cole's drawl was becoming more familiar to me with every passing day.

"Hello, Chief Loveland. Everything okay? I can't imagine you're calling me for fun."

"Why would you assume that? Perhaps I'm calling to invite you out for coffee."

"You don't drink coffee."

"How would you know that? Have you been researching me?"

"No!" My cheeks flamed with embarrassment that he might think I'd paid him that much attention. "Viv mentioned it."

He chuckled. "Your reaction's more telling than I think you realize."

I cursed my inability to cloak my thoughts and feelings and, of course, my aforementioned terrible poker face. At least he couldn't see me through the phone.

"How can I help you?"

"I got a call from a trail runner who noticed another spot that's been tagged. I planned to have a patrol officer check it out, but with the ongoing arson investigation and a scheduled training this afternoon, I don't really have the manpower to spare on this. Any chance you can go look around a bit? Maybe take some pictures? I'd go myself, but I have to lead the first half of the training."

That explained the niceties. "Wow. I just had to pick my jaw off the floor. You need me."

"Don't make this more unpleasant for me than it already is. Consider it an opportunity to prove yourself, which may lead to other opportunities down the road. If I feel you can handle this with discretion, I'll be more inclined to include you on other investigations. Fair enough?"

"Oh, I can handle it, all right. Where am I going?"

* * *

Cole directed me to a structure next to the trail about five miles outside of town. The gray-slatted building, which housed public restrooms, had a partially covered courtyard with picnic tables adjacent to a small parking area.

There were enough spaces for five cars but mine was the only one in the lot. The crisp air aided the maple trees in their initial stages of shedding vivid red and orange leaves all over the paved trail.

The west side of the building could be seen from the road, the east side from the parking lot. The sheltered portion of the patio faced south and likely saw the bulk of trail traffic. For many walkers and joggers, the landmark acted as a turnaround point to head back into town. Cyclists and those who ventured further north wouldn't necessarily get a good glimpse at the north side of the building where I stood taking in a third defacement.

The paint, the same hot fuchsia color, and looped script as at the parking lot and Margarita's house, had one singular message: *Mayor Guzman es un mentiroso*. A quick search on my phone revealed *mentiroso* translated to "liar" in Spanish. I took several photos before walking around the building for any other messages but found none.

Returning to the message, I stared at it for several minutes. I'd taken French in school, not Spanish, but I was almost certain it should have read *una mentirosa*.

A vehicle drove by, the first since I'd arrived. It slowed as it passed. The windows were nearly as dark as the vehicle, a nondescript SUV, so I couldn't see the driver. They continued about a quarter mile before turning right onto a side road.

I began walking the trail north in the direction the car had gone. A stiff breeze picked up. I pulled my jacket tighter. The trees created a canopy over my head which protected me from most of the fat raindrops which had started to fall, thumping onto the remaining leaves. The more the wind swirled, the more debris pelted the path. Tiny pinecones bounced around me while needles, dehydrated from the unusually blazing-hot summer, fluttered like confetti. The air smelled fresh despite the trees going dormant.

About a quarter mile down the trail, the snap of a twig stopped me in my tracks. I strained to listen for unexpected movement through the rustling of trees and rushing winds. Exacerbated by the dark clouds which had moved in and the shade of the woods, the whole scene suddenly felt spooky.

After a minute of stillness, I began to walk again, but stopped once more with the next crackle of a branch. My heart thumped loudly, making it impossible to identify subtle noise or movement in the brush.

"Hello?" The hovering trees and whooshing winds swallowed the sound of my voice.

No one answered. I hadn't really expected them to do so, and I'd have likely peed my pants if they had, but someone was there. Watching. Stalking.

The air felt like it was being sucked from the area, forcefully pulled out as the winds swelled. I struggled to catch my breath. The rain intensified, and the canopy no longer provided protection. I pulled my hood onto my head and started walking briskly back toward the parking lot. The swish of my nylon jacket blocked out any possible sounds of someone following. I picked up my pace until I was practically running, which I did…headlong into a dark figure holding a large black umbrella.

Chapter Six

"Oh, my gawd!" I shrieked, pushing myself away from the hard body into which I'd collided.

"Audrey, what in the heck are you screaming about?"

"Cole! You scared me half to death! What are you doing here?"

"I got done with my training and decided to come meet you. Why were you running?" He squeezed closer to shelter me with his umbrella.

"To avoid being killed."

"Lemme guess. Death by rain-soaked hairstyle?"

"Ha. You're hilarious. No." I brushed my hair from my face and considered how bad it must look for him to have brought it up.

"What then?"

"A dark, blackish SUV slowed when it drove past me. I'm not sure what kind, midsize or larger. The windows were tinted, so I couldn't see who was driving but I had the distinct impression the person was checking me out. They drove a little way and then turned down either a street or a driveway, so I walked up the path to see where they went but got spooked when I heard noises further into the woods. I'm fairly sure the driver of that car got out to stalk me."

He reached his arm around my shoulders and guided me back to the trail rest stop. The rain began to deluge so we took refuge under the portico. Cole shook his umbrella, sprinkling water onto the cement.

"Did you get any decent photos of the graffiti?"

"I got a couple. Cole, this is Chet or one of his cohorts. It has to be."

"That's a strong allegation and an even bigger leap. Just because someone posts opinions online, it doesn't mean they're going to take it into the real world and do something about it. In fact, most keyboard cowboys are all hat, no cattle."

I couldn't contain the laughter which bubbled from my gut. "You're literally wearing a hat and own no cattle."

He arched a brow. "Actually, I do. My family has a ranch back in Wyoming, and I'm part owner. However, you're completely missing the point of the metaphor."

"No, I got it. It just struck me as humorous and a bit ironic. My bad. You really are a legit cowboy."

"Regardless, we have no direct evidence Chet has taken his online rantings into the physical world."

"He still needs to be held accountable. Either he himself is committing these crimes, or his minions are. Also, whoever did this one," I pointed at the building. "Isn't as clever as they think. If you're gonna insult someone with a racist, xenophobic sentiment, at least get it right."

"Why do you say that?"

"The translation's wrong. They used the masculine form instead of the feminine."

Cole arched his left eyebrow and shifted his posture.

"What?"

"Hmm?"

He pretended he hadn't heard me, but all the signs were there that he had and was unsuccessfully trying to act nonchalant. He tensed his shoulders. He twisted his mouth. He increased his blinking and fluttered his eyelids like a hummingbird's wings.

I tilted my head and crossed my arms. "Out with it. What aren't you saying?"

"Follow me back to City Hall. We should talk to Mayor Guzman together."

* * *

Cole had a designated spot in front of City Hall, while I had to look for street parking. I circled the block for the second time and was surprised to see him waiting for me at the entrance. A minivan began backing out of a spot on the opposite side of the street. I pulled my dark gray Volvo into it.

The rain had increased to a steady downpour, so I dashed across the street.

"You could have gone inside. No need standing out here in the rain."

"That's not how my mama raised me." He opened the door and gestured for me to go ahead of him.

Joan was perched at her desk in the lobby. Cole tipped his hat to her, and she giggled. She'd never struck me as the giggling type, but apparently, Joan was a sucker for a little old-fashioned cowboy chivalry. I understood the appeal myself, but I wasn't about to admit that fact to anyone, least of all Cole.

I followed him back to the police station waiting area, where my sister sat at her desk behind bulletproof glass. Viv eyed us with her mouth agape. She raised her hands into the air with her palms up, the international sign for asking *what's going on?* I shrugged my shoulders in response and grinned.

Cole keyed in the door code, and we headed down the hall to his office.

"I thought we were going to see Margarita," I said.

"We are. I need to pop in on the training session and update Bianchi. I'd like him to go back out and see if he can locate the vehicle you spotted. If we can eliminate it as belonging to a local resident watching you out of curiosity, then we can refocus our efforts back to what we already know. You seemed pretty worked up out there, and I trust your instincts. If something seemed suspicious to you, it's best to follow up."

"Wow, thank you for that. I'm not used to people validating my intuition. I've actually struggled much of my life to trust my own gut."

He tilted his head to observe me. Whatever conclusion he came to, he kept to himself. "Hang out here. I'll be back in a few minutes."

I took a seat in the burgundy leather chair opposite his desk. Having only been in the position for six months, his office was sparsely decorated. Behind the desk, two poles flanked a large cabinet, one American flag, the other a Washington state flag. The wall behind the cabinet had been painted dark gray and above it hung the Chattertowne city seal.

The circular seal featured a blue ring surrounding a portrait of town founder Jonathan Chatterton overlooking the Jeanetta Valley and the Jeanetta River. 1861, the town's charter year, was embossed at the top with *Ceterorum Domantur Deserto* below. In typical colonizer mentality, Jonathan had chosen a Latin phrase which roughly translated to *Wilderness Tamed*, a wanton disregard for the Coast Salish People who'd inhabited the land for hundreds—if not thousands—of years.

The only noticeable personalization in Cole's office was a photograph of an older man and woman standing under an archway constructed entirely from elk antlers. My lids began to grow heavy as I tried to count how many animals had contributed to the display.

"Audrey. You ready?"

My eyes flew open at the sound of my name. I hadn't been asleep, but it had been a long day following a short night.

"Yes, sorry. Just relaxing for a moment. I think my morning coffee wore off."

I stood from my chair and wiped the corner of my mouth in case I'd drooled. His slight smile was visible through his ever-thickening facial hair.

We took the elevator up to the second floor. As we exited, I glanced to my left to room 204, the office Holden no longer occupied. Cole turned right toward the mayor's office, room 226, on the opposite end of the hall.

Holden had preferred keeping his distance from his former boss and Chattertowne's former mayor, Patrick Quincy. That way, he could actually do the job while the mayor played the role of figurehead.

Margarita did the job very differently, much more hands-on than Mayor Quincy. She also hadn't chosen a replacement for Holden as city manager, choosing instead to consolidate the two positions.

"I hear you've got a new development in the vandalism case." She indicated for us to sit on the sofa which abutted the large picture window overlooking the river and took the high-backed armchair opposite.

"We've discovered a third location," Cole said. "It's more remote, on the trail outside of town, so there's no way to know exactly when it happened. It could have come before the other two incidents, or it could be the most recent. Audrey went out to the spot earlier and took a couple photos." He nodded at me.

I pulled my phone from my pocket and pulled up the first picture. "We aren't dealing with a genius here. Anyone who's taken a foreign romance language in school would know this is wrong." I passed my phone to Cole, who handed it to Margarita.

Pigment drained from the mayor's freckled fawn skin as she scanned the picture. She looked up, first at me, then at Cole, her expression pained.

"Have you told her?" Margarita asked, her voice barely above a whisper.

He shook his head. "No, ma'am. That's not my story to tell."

"What are you talking about?" I looked between them for clarification.

Margarita sighed. Her rich brown eyes had developed bags underneath them. Her lids hung heavy, drooping, like her troubles weighted them to nearly closing. "This isn't someone being ignorant. It's someone being - cruel." Her voice caught in her throat. Trembling fingertips reached up to quell the quiver of her lips.

"Take your time," I said.

A tear ran silently down Margarita's cheek.

I'd always envied her prominent cheekbones. Most days, I struggled to locate my own on my full, round face before ultimately resorting to creating them by contouring.

Cole pulled a folded cloth from his pocket and handed it to her.

She dabbed his cheeks. "When Chet decided I was his public enemy number one, he began doxing me."

"Doxing?" I leaned forward. "In what way?"

"He created a campaign to harass and humiliate me and others by exposing private and personal information in as public a way as possible. He posted my private home phone number online and dredged up old rumors supposedly heard from my former acquaintances. He obtained, through both legal and illegal means, and disseminated some of my financial information and medical records. This has become Chet and his cronies' favorite pastime. They don't only go after elected officials with whom they disagree, either, but also citizens who publicly support us online."

"Kinda like what Marcus did." I turned to Cole. "Maybe it's unrelated, but what happened to all the files containing this type of information that were in Marcus Washburn's home office? When I moved into the house last year, they'd already been cleared out. Did the Chattertowne PD take them? The FBI?"

Prior to his murder, Marcus had accumulated stacks of files with both public and private information in his office. He'd been a conspiracy theorist who made outlandish accusations against local government officials and prominent citizens and had aggregated evidence against each of them. Much of his speculation proved to be accurate, although sometimes the information told a different story than the one it appeared to tell.

"I have no idea," Cole said. "That was before my time. I can ask Bianchi when we're done here."

"What about CROCCC?" I asked.

"What about 'em?"

"Was Marcus a member? That group seems right up his alley."

Cole shrugged. "Again, a question for Bianchi."

"I apologize for interrupting, Margarita. Sometimes, I get caught up on tangents. Please, continue."

"It's fine." She gave me a sad smile. "This isn't a topic I particularly enjoy discussing, but it sounds like I have no choice. Until now, he's kept his word to keep the information under wraps. Apparently, that's no longer the case. In the course of his doxing campaign, Chet uncovered something about me that isn't public knowledge, at least not in Chattertowne. It must have been more than he'd bargained for because he actually called me to talk about it. He promised me at the time the information wouldn't see the light of day. He said while he disagreed with some of the actions I've taken as a government official, he wasn't trying to destroy my life." She emitted a guffaw. "You could have fooled me."

"What was it he discovered?"

Margarita's fingers fumbled in her lap. "I wasn't born Margarita Guzman."

"I didn't think you were. I always assumed it had been your married name since your son's last name is Guzman as well."

"No, you don't understand. My last name has always been Guzman. It's my first name that's been changed. I was born Florencio Jr., after my father."

She stared at me, unblinking.

"I don't—"

"Audrey. My biological sex at birth was male."

Chapter Seven

Whatever I might have expected Margarita to say, it wasn't that she'd been born biologically male.

"I…I had no idea."

My immediate concern was that my surprise over her announcement might in itself be offensive, but Margarita was gracious in her response.

"It's okay. Most people don't. On the one hand, being part of the transgender community, or any marginalized group, carries with it an inherent responsibility to represent well. The way I've lived for the past twenty-five years, especially the past twenty since I came to Chattertowne, I can't say I've represented well, nor have I represented poorly. I haven't represented at all. On the other hand, it's no one's business. I made the choice to live my external life authentically to who I am on the inside, and in many ways, it felt like I'd simply exchanged one inauthenticity for another by choosing not to reveal I'd transitioned. But is it fair to expect every trans person to put the most private aspects of themselves on display for the world to denigrate? Is it not enough I live my life as an advocate for all marginalized people without revealing every way I am one?"

"I can't speak to what anyone else should or shouldn't do, especially when I don't have the lived experience to inform my opinions. I will say, I believe each person has the right to decide for themselves how much of their story they choose to tell. I can only imagine the pressure you must feel to lay yourself on the altar of a cause that directly impacts you, but I also fully respect your right to privacy, especially residing in a place with a history of small-minded mentality such as Chattertowne. I wish I could say otherwise, but I'm not sure how you would have been received, as crappy as it feels to say that out loud about my hometown. You've already faced discrimination for being an outsider, a woman, a Latina at that."

She nodded. "Yes, I've experienced discrimination regarding all three of those things."

"I'm curious, though. How did Chief Loveland come to know this about you?"

Margarita looked fondly at Cole. "When Chet told me what he'd discovered, I had concerns about how the information might be used for extortion and whether it was a liability for the city. I had an instinct I could trust Cole, and he proved me right. He met with Chet and got his reassurance he wouldn't use it against me or Chattertowne."

I looked at Cole. Because he'd come from Wyoming, I'd assumed he'd be provincial in his thinking. Regardless of his personal opinion, which I still didn't know, it sounded like he'd proven that his integrity dictated his actions.

"Margarita, rest assured, I'm doing everything I can to solve this case. Obviously, I need to speak with Chet Buchanan. If he's the only one who knew, then he's gotta be our culprit. On the graffiti, at least."

Margarita exhaled. "What about the fire? Anything new there?"

"I'm still waiting for Chief Norvald's investigator to complete his analysis of the evidence. I think it's important to refrain from making any assumptions about a connection between the two, but in my view, it defies logic to believe the vandalization of the parking lot the day before the mill fire on the same piece of property was merely a coincidence. Property, I might add, which was part of the controversial land sale specifically mentioned in the graffiti."

"I've been looking into the other members of CROCCC," I said. "Chet's the face of the group, which leads me to believe he's too obvious a suspect, but even if he's not directly involved, or even tangentially involved by directing the actions of someone else, he's certainly inciting this kind of behavior through his rhetoric. He has accountability for his words and what people do because of what he's said."

"The law is dicey here. It's imperative for me to protect free speech, especially when the optics portray a narrative that I'm trying to silence dissenters." Margarita wrung her hands.

Cole nodded. "I agree, Madam Mayor. I've already looked into these statutes in Washington and frankly, standing is unclear. In my mind, the First Amendment should always take precedence." He turned to me. "You, of all people, should be in favor of protecting First Amendment rights."

"Of course I am." I folded my arms. "What I'm saying is people's words aren't without consequence. You have the right to speak out against the government without threat of imprisonment. However, an employer can fire you for making racist social media posts because they no longer want to be associated with you. Those are the consequences of speech. If a person provides information that they know has the potential to motivate an unstable person to an act of violence, how can that be protected? It seems to me they'd be considered an accessory, at least because they lit the fuse."

Cole shook his head. "You're gonna have to ask a lawyer about that."

"Audrey, I have someone you can talk to. His name is Todd Wainwright. He's a civil rights attorney in Tacoma. I haven't used him, but we've chatted in the past and I know some who have. I'll text you with his info." Margarita rose. "Thank you both for coming to me directly with this. I'd appreciate it if you kept me in the loop. If my secret's out, I'd prefer not to be blindsided."

"Of course." Cole stood and reached out to clasp her hand. "We're going to get this handled quickly and discreetly."

Once we were in the elevator, I stared at him.

He looked back at me with furrowed brows. "What?"

"Nothing. I'm just trying to process everything. I'm actually pleasantly surprised."

"By?" The portion of his forehead not shadowed by his hat creased.

"By you. You handled her...situation with a lot of sensitivity and deference."

His gaze bore through me. "Audrey, I know you think I'm some yee-haw hick from flyover country, but I'm not. I attended Nebraska on an academic scholarship. I trained for two years in Phoenix and spent a year on the force in East St. Louis, Illinois. Having Midwestern values doesn't mean I'm a racist or a homophobe; it means I treat every single person with respect. The reason folks back home are so resentful of the so-called coastal elite is assumptions like this from people like you."

Feeling chastised, I lowered my head. "I'm sorry. I know I can be judgy. Someone once told me it's my superpower, but I think they meant it more like a supervillain's power. I'm trying to do better, to be better."

The elevator doors opened on the ground floor, and Cole waited for me to exit ahead of him.

"I'm going to go pay Chet a visit," he said. "Let me know what you find out from talking to the attorney."

"I will. And Cole?"

"Yeah."

"I really am sorry for making assumptions about you."

He nodded his head but kept his mouth closed in a firm line. I didn't know why it mattered so much that he was unhappy with me, but it did.

I was determined to fix it.

Chapter Eight

The Law Office of Wainwright and Associates in Tacoma wasn't quite what I'd been expecting. Margarita had texted Todd's contact info to me, and I'd set up an appointment to meet with him the following day.

I didn't want to drive all the way down there, but his paralegal had infeed me he wouldn't give any legal advice to new clients over the phone.

Instead of a posh office building, Todd had hung his shingle in a nearly abandoned strip mall that had once housed a K-Mart. The discount department store vibe still permeated the 24-hour gym and non-denominational church that shared the building.

In addition to the law office, the rest of the complex was comprised of a teriyaki joint with two stools, a liquor store, a nail salon, and a tattoo parlor. The architectural style of concrete and 70s-era garish orange brick with brass light fixtures and single-paned windows gave the complex a dated and run-down appearance.

I pulled into a parking spot right in front of the office, marked by a solid oak door with the firm's name etched on a brass plate. The row was nearly empty, save for a silver convertible Mustang, a tan minivan, and a MINI Cooper emblazoned with the Union Jack on its roof. The MINI's license plate was personalized. It read LOTTIE.

A bell rang above me as I entered. A voluptuous brunette with cherry red lipstick sat behind the oak reception desk. "'Allo, what can we do you for?"

Judging by her accent, she was Lottie, the owner of the MINI.

"Hi, I spoke with Mr. Wainwright last night, and he said if I came down, he'd be able to squeeze me in."

"Sure 'nuff, luv. Take a seat right over there an' he'll be wit' you shortly." She lowered her voice to a conspiratorial whisper. "He's meetin' wit' a radge at the moment."

I had no idea what a radge was, but I didn't want to offend her, especially since she'd already confided in me. I nodded knowingly, even though I was clueless.

The waiting area smelled of stale cigarettes and cloying perfume. I pulled Google up on my phone and found that "radge" was slang for "crazy person." I needn't have bothered, however, because I soon got my answer when a plump middle-aged woman wearing two different shoes rushed into the lobby from the inner hallway, her wide-open, crazed gaze darting around, her cheeks flushed. She turned around to yell in the direction from which she'd come and pointed her finger.

"I'll have you disbarred!" Her voice cracked between the last two syllables of her declaration. When she got no response, she wagged her trembling finger at both the receptionist and me before storming through the doorway.

"Mr. Wainwright can see you now."

I stared at Lottie. She'd already returned to typing on her computer.

How could she be so calm after what had transpired?

I stood hesitantly. "So, do I...?"

She pointed her red stilettoed index fingernail down the hallway. "First door on the left, luv."

I snaked through a gauntlet of metal filing cabinets in the hallway.

The *radge* had left without completely shutting Wainwright's office door, so I pushed it lightly, and its hinges creaked as it opened.

"Mr. Wainwright?"

"Come in, Ms. O'Connell." The voice inside the room boomed, a rich baritone.

Like the hallway, the office was also filled with file cabinets. Stacks of manila folders were piled on top of them. The remaining furniture was sparse and utilitarian, atypical of law offices in my experience. Most of the firms I'd visited had chesterfield sofas and cherrywood built-ins with a faint whiff of old books and arrogance.

Todd Wainwright sat behind a solid oak desk cluttered with paperwork. His red hair was slick and thin on the top, longer in the back. He wore three gold chain necklaces, which were visible because his blue collared shirt was unbuttoned to the third button. His thick gold watchband sat upon his bare wrist where the cuffs had been rolled up twice. The room smelled like robust cologne, half-smoked cigars, and sticky pomade.

He stood from his chair and reached out to offer his hand. "Call me Todd. Margarita let me know you'd be getting in touch. Please, have a seat." He gestured to the chair opposite his desk.

"Are you sure you don't need a minute? I can wait if you need to recalibrate after…" My voice trailed off, and I pointed toward the hallway through which the woman had made her dramatic exit.

He looked momentarily befuddled. "Huh? Oh, Stephanie. Yeah, she's a little unhappy about how well I represented her ex-husband in their divorce."

"Divorce? I thought you were a civil rights attorney."

"That too. Most of the time I'm working pro bono on those kinds of cases. Divorce pays the bills. So, how can I help you?"

"I'm trying to understand what the legal culpability might be for someone who incites another person into committing a crime. Your name came up because I told our town mayor I think this guy who's been running an online hate campaign against her should be held responsible for three incidents of nasty graffiti. Also, it's possible the graffiti artist may have set a fire that destroyed an abandoned building. If not the actual perpetrator, his rhetoric likely inspired the criminal actions. The Chief of Police insists the dude's well within his First Amendment rights, but he's from Wyoming, so he's not yet clear on all the nuances of Washington State law."

Todd leaned back in his chair, which squeaked in protest. He opened a side drawer, pulled out a toothpick, and stuck it between his teeth. "These cases are tricky. Obviously, you've got to prove a connection between your inciter and your incitee, as it were. But let's back up a bit. What makes you think the graffiti incidents and the fire are related?"

"The first messages were on the freshly laid asphalt parking lot adjacent to the old mill that used to operate there. There's been a lot of arguing about the project. The mill was burned to the ground within 48 hours of the graffiti being discovered."

The toothpick flicked in his mouth. "You're right; that doesn't sound like a coincidence. Okay, so, what connects the vandalism to this harassment campaign?" He dug his finger into his ear, twisted it, and pulled it out to examine it.

"Oh, uh, well, the graffiti messages were similar in content and tone to online postings by a group protesting the city's purchase of the land from a local farmer. They specifically mentioned the mayor, the family who sold the land, and the city council. The second message we found was on the side of the mayor's garage."

The flutter of the toothpick sped up as Todd processed what I'd said. "Isn't it possible someone who possessed similar sentiments to your online instigator took matters into their own hands? Maybe the tagger and the arsonist are two different people. Those are two distinct M.O.s in my experience."

"I'm aware of that, but I believe the investigation will bear out my theory. If it does, at that point, the question becomes, can the dude who lit the metaphorical match be held accountable alongside the person who lit the literal match?"

"Assuming all that's true, and you can definitively draw direct lines between the incidents as well as the perpetrator's connection to your purported inciter, there's still a high bar to prove liability. It can be done. There are rare exceptions to First Amendment protections regarding freedom of speech, and direct incitement of a crime is one of those exceptions. However, the primary argument of the defense will almost always be that simply because you ask someone to commit a crime, doesn't mean they have to do it."

"Could you give me a specific example?"

"Do you remember the movie *Christmas Vacation*?"

"Of course."

"So, Chevy Chase…sorry, I can't remember his character's name."

"Clark."

"Oh, yeah. Clark. He tells Cousin Eddie he wishes his boss were wrapped up under his Christmas tree so he can tell him off about the crappy jelly of the month club he'd given instead of the expected Christmas bonus. Cousin Eddie goes and kidnaps the boss. Is Clark legally responsible?"

"I wouldn't think so," I said. "He didn't really mean it. He was venting his frustration."

"You would be correct. The incitement needs to be proven to be an intentional directive from one party to another with a reasonable expectation the order would be carried out, as well as it needs to be an imminent precursor to the criminal activity. My guess is you're not going to find text messages between the two parties where one overtly directs the other to commit the crime. I'd look for social media postings less than 24 hours preceding the first incident from your inciter. See who liked the posts and who commented. Complaining about the land deal and the mayor isn't a request. You'd need something along the lines of someone should burn the mill to teach them a lesson, or, at least, you need to make your anger known by whatever means is necessary for people to start paying attention. Something like that."

"That makes sense. So, then, what would the possible charges be if a link can be established?"

"There are a few different crimes this could fall under. Solicitation requires a direct request. It doesn't necessarily involve payment like when someone hires an assassin or a hooker. This is probably the closest to your scenario, but like I said, the bar is pretty high, and the wording of any perceived request will be a factor. Another area of culpability is if they planned the crime together, but only one carried it out. That's conspiracy. Finally, you've got your old-fashioned mafia boss dictating criminal activity. That would be racketeering, like your Chattertowne City Hall scandal, and it's prosecuted under the federal RICO statute."

"I don't think the last would apply. There don't seem to be any financial stakes involved other than frustration over how taxpayer money is being utilized. These messages are rooted in a specific ideology with a healthy dose of racism on the side and possibly…" I paused, not knowing how to address the bigotry without divulging Margarita's secret.

"Possibly what?"

"It's difficult to determine how much of the anger is because of the land deal and how much is an inherent dislike of the mayor. The arson is frightening because that kind of escalation in such a short period of time is irrational and dangerous. That's why I keep coming back to the idea the inciting rhetoric is putting them into a frenzy, either because they're so incensed about the deal, or their hatred of Margarita has pushed them over the edge. Maybe they're trying to impress Chet."

"Chet? You don't mean Chet Buchanan?" He sat upright in his chair, head tilted, eyes wide. "And Margarita Guzman?"

"Yes, Chet's the ringleader of the anti-Guzman crowd. You know him?"

Todd fiddled with his gold nugget ring on his right hand. "I'm sorry, Ms. O'Connell, but I'm going to have to end our meeting." He stood and proffered his hand for me to shake. It took a moment for me to catch up with his abrupt change in mood.

"What? I don't understand. Is something wrong?"

I had yet to stand up, and Todd shifted from one foot to another. The motion wafted his musky scent toward me.

"This morning…" He stopped himself. "Well, all I can say is any *ex-parte* conversation regarding Chet Buchanan without him being present would be a conflict of interest."

Chapter Nine

I slammed my satchel onto Cole's desk. "Welp, we've been scooped."

"Audrey, what the heck?" He pushed back from his desk and thrust his palms out face-up.

"Sorry, I'm super annoyed." I plopped myself into the chair opposite his.

"And you thought you'd spread the annoyance around?"

"Yes." I crossed my arms. "So, Todd, the lawyer dude Margarita suggested I speak with about First Amendment law?"

"Mm-hmm?"

"Guess who hired him this very morning?" I stabbed my index finger on the top of his desk for emphasis.

Cole's brows arched. "Who?"

"Chet!"

"Really." His voice and expression gave away only a hint of surprise.

"That's all you have to say?"

"Well, unlike some people, I usually process information thoroughly before I spew my opinions on it."

I scowled. "Just when I was starting to like you."

This time, he allowed the extent of his surprise to appear unchecked. "You were?" He quickly recovered and replaced it with a smug smile. "Will wonders never cease."

I groaned. "I'm trying to help you here. The least you could do is not make our interactions unbearable."

He tilted his head. "You find being around me unbearable?"

I shifted in my seat under his lasered focus and then looked down at my lap as I fiddled with my car keys.

"I didn't say that…exactly." I raised my head to meet his gaze. "Can we stay with the topic at hand, please? How in the hell did Chet know to hire a lawyer in Tacoma—who just so happens to be the one Margarita recommended I contact—on the morning I'm set to meet with him?"

"So, the lawyer told you Chet hired him? I thought they couldn't reveal stuff like who their clients are."

"He started to tell me, but then stopped short of saying it flat out. It's all so suspicious."

"You make it sound like there's some sort of conspiracy happening. Coincidences do happen, you know."

I stared at him as if a horn protruded from his head. His condescension triggered my own patronizing response.

"You're not from around here, so let me explain a couple things. First, Tacoma is a minimum of an hour's drive away, and that's on a Sunday night around eleven. You're typically looking at two-plus hours. Second, there must be hundreds of attorneys between here and there he could have hired. Third, he hired him today. Today, Cole. A year and a half ago, I didn't believe in widespread conspiracies or that someone might infiltrate my email and social media accounts to spy on me, but guess what? They did. I used to believe in coincidences. I don't anymore. Chet is highly intelligent and diabolical. There's no telling what he's capable of. Frankly, I think he's the puppet master, so he can keep his hands clean. Plausible deniability."

Cole leaned back in his chair and placed his hands behind his head and his feet upon his desk.

I'd always interpreted that type of posture as a power pose, a way for men to communicate their dismissiveness of the person sitting in front of them. The less cynical side of me left room for the possibility it was simply a comfortable position in which to process information. Cole didn't seem to be ushering me out of his office, so I made the charitable determination he should be given the benefit of the doubt.

After a moment of silence, he said, "I see where you're coming from. I'll grant you it's odd. Something definitely spooked Chet into hiring a civil rights attorney. That's not a normal thing people do."

"Right? I mean, even if Todd is the best civil rights attorney in the area, which I highly doubt based on my experience today, he's certainly not the only one. But what keeps nagging at me is, how did he know his activities online might require legal defense, and why Todd?"

"Couldn't say. I'm guessing Todd didn't tell you."

"At the mere mention of Chet's name, he shut down the meeting."

"I guess that means he's at least an ethical attorney."

My phone buzzed. I looked at the screen. Holden had texted asking me to call.

"Everything all right?" Cole asked.

I waved my hand dismissively. "Yeah, it's fine. An old friend wants to talk."

He scanned my face. "Old friend or old boyfriend?"

"It's complicated."

"I can tell."

I wrinkled my forehead. "What do you mean?"

"Your reaction when you saw the message. It was like watching the full spectrum of emotion play out in ten seconds. Surprise, followed by curiosity, then concern, a little hint of anger, some sadness, and ultimately stoicism."

I attempted to clear my face of any emotion.

"Whatever you're trying to do now, it isn't working. You should never play poker."

I sighed and grimaced. "I'm fully aware.

* * *

Salty wind assailed me I stepped out of the City Hall building and I gave an involuntary shudder. Seagulls cawed as they hovered in the sky above the marina waiting for someone to drop a morsel.

Months of therapy had helped abate my lifelong aquaphobia, but it hadn't completely erased the fear of water, which started when Viv almost drowned as a toddler on my watch, or the additional trauma from the night in the marina I'd nearly lost my sister for the second time.

I pulled my phone from the pocket of my jacket and called Holden. Rather than get in my car, I started walking up Oakwood Street, Hoping it might disperse some of the nervous energy I felt.

"Hey there." Holden's voice dripped like molasses through the receiver. It had a richness which reached into my soul, grabbing it until my heart and lungs constricted. His effect on me was like a Donny Hathaway song combined with a hearty glass of wine, full-bodied and inhibition-lowering.

"Hey," I managed to choke out. "What's up?"

As per usual, I lost all ability to play it cool when it came to interacting with him. I cursed myself, wondering if I'd ever be fully immune to his...whatever it was about him which left me undone.

He lowered his voice. "I can't talk freely, but I wanted to give you a heads-up. I overheard something today I thought you might find interesting."

"Oh yeah?" I trudged up the street. Its slope became more pronounced, as did my breathing.

"Are you okay?"

"Yeah, why?" I huffed.

"You sound...breathless." There was an intimacy to his tone.

I felt a zing move through my body to my toes and back again.

"I'm walking up Oakwood from the marina. This hill is a bitch."

"Ah. I thought perhaps you were flustered to be talking to me. My mistake. So, this morning, when I got to work, Fred was talking to a couple guys over by the trailer. One of them was your boy Levi."

"He's definitely not my boy. He hasn't been for a very long time. What were they talking about?"

"When they saw me, all of 'em got real quiet." Holden paused. There was a rustling sound and muffled voices in the background. "Sorry about that. I'm not supposed to be on a break right now, but I didn't want to miss your call."

"They got quiet when they saw you and then what happened?"

"There was something about the way they looked at me. It riled my suspicions, so I went around the backside of the trailer to see if I could hear what they were talking about. With all the construction noise, it was difficult to make out everything, but it sounded to me like they were discussing the graffiti. Levi mentioned something about the pool."

"The pool?" My breathing became even more labored as I nearly crested the hill.

"The Chattertowne Public Pool. It's been closed for two years waiting on funding for the remodel. I think it may be their next target."

"Holden, this is huge! We already know Levi is connected to Chet and Hiram, and now we've definitively linked Fred to them, beyond being a member of their social media group. Now we can catch them all in the act!"

"Whoa, Audrey! I'm not sure what you're thinking, but it sounds like instead of doing the responsible thing and calling the authorities, you're planning on ambushing an organized militia."

"I have no intention of ambushing anyone. But that doesn't mean I can't be there in the shadows taking their photos."

Chapter Ten

I pushed the button on the side of my car seat in order to recline it into a more comfortable position. I had a blanket wrapped around me to stave off the chilly fall night, along with a tall thermos filled with coffee. I'd watched enough police dramas to have a sense of what being on a stakeout was supposed to look like and had tried to anticipate any potential issues that might arise. What I hadn't expected was the quiet tap on my passenger window. My ensuing scream most definitely alerted everyone in the area to my presence.

I pressed the button to unlock the door and scowled at Holden as he slid into the seat next to me.

"Are you trying to give me a heart attack?"

"I did you a favor." He shut the door.

"How do you figure?"

"If you didn't see me coming, you won't see anyone coming."

"Alright, I'll give you that one."

"How's it going so far?"

I tightened the blanket around my shoulders. "Well, it's dropped about twenty-five degrees since sundown. I already ate all my snacks, and I have to pee. Well, I did have to pee, but then you knocked on my window, so… problem solved."

Holden threw his head back in laughter. "I'd feel bad if I actually believed you. I should have brought wine. I just discovered this amazing Portuguese Alicante Bouschet. You should definitely give it a try sometime."

"Sounds good."

"So, any sign of hooligans and miscreants?"

"Nothing yet." I indicated the run-down building we were scouting. "It's sad to see it in this condition. I used to come here in the summers."

"Really? But you're terrified of water." He shifted in his seat to face me.

"There was a boy…"

"I should have known," he chuckled.

I swatted at him. My fingertips grazed his sweatshirt, and it took all my willpower to not rest them on his arm. If I rolled up his sleeve I was sure to find soft skin and bulging muscles and the last thing I needed was that distraction. I was already struggling to keep myself together with his musky scent infusing the car.

"My best friend Meryl and I would walk down here in our platform flip-flops and pay the three bucks to sit in the vicinity of the pool and watch him. His name was Phillip McKenzie. He had curly brown hair, which he'd lightened on the tips. His entire wardrobe consisted of Ed Hardy t-shirts and cargo shorts, but I thought he was the most amazing human specimen I'd ever set eyes on."

"I'd give you a hard time, but during that same era, I was obsessing over Corinne Davis, who wore nothing but Juicy Couture terrycloth sweatsuits."

"Ah, the follies of young millennial love. The fact I was so enamored with that little twerp that I was nearly able to overcome my deepest phobia is truly a testament to the power of lust."

A heavy silence fell over the car. His smile gleamed through the dim lighting.

I squirmed in my seat. "What?"

"I've missed you."

My breath caught at this unexpected and uncharacteristic declaration of emotion. "I've missed you too."

"Can I ask you something?"

"Of course."

Insecurity flashed across his face. "After Emily left…why didn't I hear from you?"

I released a whoosh of air. "I didn't know if I should. I mean, you'd recently gone through all your legal stuff, and I wanted to give you the space you needed to decide what you wanted. *Who* you wanted. I felt like I got my answer."

"How do you figure?"

"You didn't reach out to me either." I shrugged.

"Fair point. Like you said, I needed time and space to sort it out. I mean, I had years invested in my relationship with Em, and I owed it to her, to me, and frankly, to anyone else I might end up with, to explore every possible solution to our issues."

"That's why I backed off. After she left, I waited for any sign you wanted me in your life. I got none."

Holden's laugh was without mirth. "And there you have the reason we could never be in a relationship. You gave me no indication there was anything to pursue. Have there ever been two people who were worse at communicating than us? I've heard of couples who literally don't speak the same language but managed to figure out how to express their feelings better than we ever have. Why do we suck so badly at it?"

Something about the look in his eyes triggered me to lurch across the center console and kiss him. It was as if his gaze had unleashed months of pent-up passion, hurt, desire, frustration, and a strange feeling that sort of resembled love. I retreated to my side of the car, humiliated by my impulsive actions. He sat silent, and my shame grew exponentially with each passing second of perceived rejection.

"Audrey."

"I'm sorry, I shouldn't have done that."

"*Audrey.*"

I hung my head in embarrassment. "I was out of line. I'm still learning about boundaries and—"

"Audrey!" He said my name for a third time with an urgent hiss.

I looked at him, startled by his intensity. "What?"

"Look." He pointed out the windshield.

I followed his eyeline and his index finger to the scraggly, overgrown rhododendron adjacent to the pool building. A hooded figure rustled in the bushes and appeared to be spray-painting the wall. From a distance, it was difficult to judge height or whether it was a man or a woman because of their slim build.

"What do we do?" I whispered.

"Did you bring a camera?"

"Only my phone."

"It's gonna be hard to get a good shot. You should have brought something with a long lens."

"Well, I see that now. I'm not a staff photographer, and I can't do anything about it at the moment."

"We're gonna have to get closer."

He carefully opened the car door, and its creak echoed into the darkness. The figure froze in place. I held my breath. The culprit took off like a shot, and Holden raced after him. I sat wondering whether I should join the chase or stay put. I considered following in my car, but by the time I'd pushed the ignition button, Holden had already reappeared.

I called out to him. "Did you lose him?"

He nodded, hands on his hips as he walked in circles to catch his breath. I got out of the car and walked toward him. He was only slightly winded by the time I reached him. "You're still pretty fast. All that jogging has kept you in shape."

"Thanks. He—or she—was fast. I'll give them that."

"They had a head start."

He smiled at me. "Thanks."

"For what?"

"For always building me up, giving me the benefit of the doubt. Other than that time, you accused me of murder, of course."

"Of course."

We grinned at each other, and for the first time in a long time, I believed maybe we could get past our complicated history and have something akin to friendship.

More than that, well, we would have to see.

We turned our attention to the side of the building where the hooded figure had been. Through the dimness, one fuchsia sentence glowed:

Shame on Mayor Guzman!

"Well, so much for deterring a crime."

Holden put his hands out to indicate I should be quiet. "Do you hear that?"

"No, what?" I craned my neck and tilted my ear toward the sky.

"Listen."

Sirens wailed in the distance. I picked up my phone and opened the police scanner app.

Through the crackle of static came a female voice. "All units on route to structural fire at 15400 Jeanetta River Road please be advised. A witness on scene says the roof collapsed."

Chapter Eleven

When Holden and I arrived at the Brandt farm, the blaze had already engulfed the entire barn. Three fire trucks, two police cruisers, one sheriff's vehicle, and an aid car blocked the crowd from getting closer.

"That's a relief." Holden let out a deep breath.

I pulled the car off to the side of the road. "What's a relief?"

"It's not the house."

The night sky glowed from the flames. We got out of the car and walked to the edge of the crowd who'd gathered to observe the mayhem. Watching infernos was getting to be a regular pastime around Chattertowne.

"This was no accident," I declared. "Do you think they used spray painting the pool as a distraction to make sure we were nowhere near this area?"

Holden shook his head. "I don't think so. They didn't seem to be purposely trying to get me to overhear the information. They stopped talking when I approached the area. I only found out what I did because they didn't know I could hear them. Besides, why would there be any reason for them to think I would pass the information on to you or to the CPD? It's pretty much common knowledge I don't run in the same circles anymore."

I spotted Cole and waved. He gave a slight nod of his head before shifting his attention to Holden. His posture stiffened. He said something to the firefighter standing next to him and then made his way toward us.

"I don't know why I'm not surprised." Cole pulled his hat off and rubbed his scalp, ruffling his hair in an insufferably adorable fashion before returning it to his head.

"Surprised I'm here? I mean, it is my job."

He didn't acknowledge my question, nor did he clarify what he meant. "Mr. Villalobos." He nodded his greeting.

"Evening Chief Loveland." Holden returned the head nod. "Looks like somebody's keeping you busy."

"Sure are. What have you folks been up to tonight?" Cole spread his legs into a wide stance and placed his hands on his belt. It reminded me of those nature documentaries where the birds positioned themselves to preen for a mate and intimidate rivals.

I shuffled my feet in the dirt.

Holden let out an exasperated sigh and mumbled, "Tell him."

"Tell me what?" Cole's gaze narrowed.

"Well, see, Holden overheard something at work, but we weren't completely certain that he heard what he thought he had, and…"

"Audrey." Cole was losing patience with my aww shucks routine.

"We were on a stakeout when we heard the sirens."

Cole's face contorted, both amused and annoyed. "A stakeout of who?"

"Whom." I regretted correcting him as soon as the words escaped my lips, and his face flashed irritation.

"Sorry, bad habit. We were watching the old Chattertowne Pool building."

"May I ask why?"

Holden shifted next to me. "I overheard my boss and a couple guys talking about the vandalism this morning, and it sounded like maybe the pool was the next target."

Cole indicated the flaming barn. "Guess you misunderstood."

His tone was a little condescending, and I felt my hackles rise on Holden's behalf.

"As a matter of fact, he didn't misunderstand. Someone *was* there, and Holden chased them off. However, they did manage to put up one phrase on the side of the building."

"Oh yeah? What was that?" Cole asked, shifting his weight from one foot to the other.

"Shame on Mayor Guzman."

"Did I hear someone say my name? My ears are buzzing." Margarita walked up to the three of us. She was bundled in a thick gray wool shawl-collared cardigan.

"*I* wasn't saying shame on you. That's what was spray-painted on the side of the old Chatterton Pool building tonight."

"Lovely." Margarita pursed her lips. "So, did they vandalize the pool and then come here or vice-versa?"

Cole cleared his throat. "Actually, I don't think it could be the same person. Based on the timeline these two gave me, the vandal ran off from the pool right before they heard the fire sirens."

"This town is breaking my—" before Margarita could finish her sentence the few barn timbers still standing began to fall.

Holden grabbed my hand and dragged me across the street, nearly sending us both into the ditch on the other side. The tall jointed goatgrass that lined the road poked through my jeans and scratched at my ankles.

There was yelling and chaos as the firefighters retreated. Officers frantically pushed the crowds further away from flying embers and billows of charcoal smoke. People shrieked in disbelief as the hundred-year-old landmark crumbled, sending plumes of ash and sparks into the air.

Holden hooked his arm through mine as we stood shell-shocked, observing the pandemonium on Old Man Brandt's property. Cole had his arm around Margarita as he ushered her to a spot out of the fray. Within minutes, the barn was nothing but a hill of smoldering rubble, save for the random crackle of glowing cinders.

Cole placed his hands on Margarita's shoulders. He patted them a couple times in reassurance before re-entering the throng of people. The crowd couldn't seem to decide which direction to go. Cole flapped his arms in an attempt to corral them like sheep into a pen, but not everyone was cooperative. One of those people was Chet Buchanan.

I leaned against Holden and whispered through gritted teeth, "Are you seeing what I'm seeing?"

Holden lifted his chin and scanned the scene. "Ah, our good friend Chet is in the mix."

A police officer yelled at Chet while gesturing for him to move back. Chet waved his hands, pointing at various people around him, and shook his head in belligerence.

Something inside me snapped. I broke free of Holden and marched toward the man who'd been sowing the seeds of division in Chattertowne, fertilizing them with his rhetoric, poisoning them with his hate. I'd had enough of his attitude of entitlement and antagonism.

"Audrey, wait!" Holden called after me.

He could have caught up with me to prevent me from reaching Chet if he so chose, but he didn't even try. His booming voice did, however, catch Chet's attention. Chet appraised me as I approached him. He sported his typical sneer on his face.

"You seem like a woman with a purpose." His words dripped with honey-coated arrogance and contempt.

I reached where he was standing and tempered my desire to simply punch him in the mouth and walk away. At some point, it would probably be a good idea for me to address my latent violent fantasies, but as I was still able to harness a modicum of self-control, I counted it as a moral victory. There was no doubt Chet was itching for someone to retaliate against him in such a way as to paint himself as the victim, not the instigator. He was a master at gaslighting and manipulation.

"Audrey O'Connell with the *Chattertowne Coastal Current.*" I said this to indicate I was speaking with him in an official capacity, not because he wasn't well aware of who I was. "Mr. Buchanan, do you have a moment to comment on the recent rash of property destruction and hate speech in light of your campaign of anti-governmental rhetoric?"

He smirked at my characterization. "That doesn't sound like an unbiased assessment of the facts to me, but then again, why should I be surprised? It's par for the course with the lamestream media."

"Mr. Buchanan, this is your opportunity to comment on the desecration of public and private property. Given that many of the sentiments expressed by the vandals mimic statements you've made on your social media forums, I assume you want to set the record straight and denounce such behavior."

"Is this on the record or off the record?"

His question caught me by surprise. "I'd prefer on, but if you're willing to speak off the record, that's fine."

"Alright, Mizzzz O'Connell." He emphasized the pronunciation. "On the record, CROCCC stands behind public statements we've made against the mayor, the city council, and the land deal. However, we bear no responsibility for any actions which might be taken by those who are like-minded." He bobbed his head back and forth as he spoke, daring me to challenge him.

"Did your lawyer advise you to say that?"

His face was impassive, save for one arched eyebrow. "Any information related to legal counsel I've procured for my own protection and conversations connected with that are subject to privilege. I do have a question for *you*, though, Mizzzz O'Connell."

"Oh yeah? What's that?"

"You said vandals, not vandal. What makes you think more than one person is involved? After all, every message has been consistent with the others, and, of course, they've all been pink."

I scanned his face to see whether he was baiting me or was actually concerned I might know something. The darkness didn't help me in getting a clear read on him.

"Also, in your journalistic endeavors," cough-cough, "did it occur to you to investigate whether this was a false flag operation designed to create sympathy for the actual perpetrators?"

Chet gestured toward Cole and Margarita standing with Fire Chief Gunner Norvald.

The Chief was saying something to them I couldn't quite make out over the sound of water hoses. Cole shook his head while Margarita stood with one hand covering her mouth.

"Listen, Chet, I'd like to continue this conversation later if you have any information to actually back up your insinuations, but right now, I need to go see what's going on." I walked toward the group with Chet right on my heels. "I didn't invite you to follow me." I practically snarled the words over my shoulder.

"I have as much right as you do to listen to their conversation."

I didn't have it in me to argue with him. I reached the somber circle. "What's happened?"

Chief Norvald stayed silent. I looked to Cole, who was tight-lipped.

Finally, Margarita spoke. "Oh, for the love of Pete, they're going to hear it anyway; might as well hear it from us." She turned to me. "Zeb Brandt is missing."

"What do you mean, missing?" I looked at the concerned faces of the mayor, the police chief, and the fire chief. My stomach dropped. From behind me came a strangled yelp. I turned around to look at Chet, who appeared to be as stunned as me by the information.

Cole sighed. "No one has seen him. The call that came into dispatch was from a neighbor. She said Mrs. Brandt is still out of town, but Zeb should be home. By the time fire and police arrived, a crowd had already gathered and continued to grow as time went on. Everyone assumed Zeb had been in the house when the fire started, and he must be somewhere in the horde. As if he doesn't always make his presence fully known."

"I went to knock on the door, but there was no answer, and it was locked. I went to the back door, same thing. After peeking into the windows, the place looks locked up tight." Chief Norvald wiped sooty grime from his forehead with the back of his sleeve.

"Maybe he decided to go to his sister-in-law's house after all. I wouldn't blame him, with all the craziness that's been happening around here." I clung to my last shred of hope.

Cole shook his head. "Yeah, that's not how it works, Audrey. Farmers don't up and leave their fields unattended right before harvest. That corn is tasseled and nearly ready."

I opened my mouth to ask him how he knew so much about farming but decided to leave the question for later.

Holden approached the huddle. "Hey, I know I'm no longer helping to run this town, but am I allowed to know what's going on? Y'all look like someone stole your lunch." He eyed Chet. "And if he's allowed to be here, I most certainly should be."

Chet guffawed. "Disgraced corrupt politician says what?"

"Grow up, man." Holden glared at Chet.

I turned to Holden. "As much as I'd love to watch you kick Chet's ass, this is serious. No one knows where Zeb Brandt is. Did you see him milling around out here when they were working on the fire?"

"I saw what you saw. It's hard to tell who's who with so many people clustered together and the lighting out here so limited. I was trying to catch a glimpse of our hooligan graffiti artist, but there were several people wearing dark hoodies." He nodded his head at Chet, "Including you."

Holden sized Chet up and down. Chet's tall, thin build and black hooded sweatshirt could make him the vandal but that would mean he wasn't the arsonist, a possibility I wasn't yet willing to concede.

"Has anyone checked with Edna Brandt?" Margarita's voice cracked.

She looked at Norvald, who looked at Cole.

Cole shrugged. "Not me."

Margarita pulled out her cell phone and pressed a few buttons before putting it up to her ear. "Edna? Hi, it's Margarita Guzman." She paused to listen to Edna's response. "I apologize for calling so late. I was wondering if you've spoken to Zeb tonight?" Her face turned from cautiously optimistic to rumpled with concern. "Oh, he did?"

She closed her eyes and placed her palm across them, as if to shield herself from a reality she didn't want to face. Her jowls sagged and my stomach dipped like I'd crested the hill on a roller coaster and was barreling downward at Mach 1.

Margarita moved her palm from her eyes to her forehead. "Well, I'm looking for him. I need to ask him about something, so if you do hear from him, please have him give me a call. It's quite urgent. Uh-huh. Right. Okay, listen I have to go but I will be in touch very soon. Take care of yourself, Edna."

She disconnected the phone and dropped her head. Tears plopped onto the asphalt ground at her feet. Cole once again placed his arm around her to give comfort. An eerie stillness washed over the six of us, despite the echoes of firefighters shouting over the din of their trucks and equipment.

"That didn't sound encouraging." Chief Norvald was grim-faced.

One of his crew jogged over, pulled him aside, and whispered something in his ear.

Margarita stumbled over her words, trying to get them out. "Edna…she said Zeb was w-worried the barn might be a target of the 'P-pink Panther' as he'd come to call the perpetrator of the graffiti slurs."

Chet mumbled, objecting to her characterization of the messages. We all turned to glare at him. He raised his hands in mock surrender.

Chief Norvald finished his conversation with the firefighter and returned to the group. "I don't even know what to say. I'm stunned and speechless."

"You found a body." I could barely get the words out.

Cole jerked his head to look at me and then to Norvald. Margarita sucked in a sharp intake of air and let her head drop, heavy with grief.

Chief Norvald's shoulders sagged. "We did. We found a body."

Chapter Twelve

I t's an odd sensation when bad news is dropped like a bomb in the midst of a group of people, causing them to face it all at the same time, together. It becomes a shared experience, and even if one doesn't like the people they're with in that moment. It becomes an immutable tie that binds.

For example, my summer camp cabin mates who were with me when it was announced Princess Diana had died. Becky Greenblatt was annoying as hell, but she'd always have a special place in my heart because we'd cried together and then spoken in fake British accents throughout our entire last day while waiting for our parents to arrive to take us home.

Now, six unlikely people stood shoulder-to-shoulder in stunned grief and silence. The mayor and the man seeking to destroy her. The new police chief who'd been brought in to clean up the mess left behind by the former City Manager who at that moment stood next to him. The Fire Chief, and me, the woman who kept finding myself in the thick of all of it.

Margarita was the first to speak. "Chief Norvald, has the coroner been called?"

"Yeah, I told my guy to get her over here. Shouldn't be too long. I already called in the investigator. I assume, Chief Loveland, you're gonna want to get your people in there at some point." Chief Norvald nodded toward Cole.

"We don't really have much in the way of experienced arson investigators. Other than the mill fire, the most I've had to deal with since I've been here is a couple of unauthorized bonfires. Now that this is a homicide, I'll definitely want to be kept in the loop on anything the fire investigator comes up with."

Cole turned to me. "Please don't run with this story yet. Not until there's been an official ID and notification of next of kin. We need to get in touch with Edna regardless, because it's her barn that's been torched, and the last thing I want to deal with is this town's rumor mill."

"I'll be shocked if someone doesn't beat you to the punch with Edna, but you don't have to worry about me," I said. "I mean, obviously, I'm going to report on the fire and the new graffiti. Everyone knows there's been a fire, so it would create more suspicion if I didn't post something about it, but I can use the standard *details are forthcoming* and *still under investigation.* I certainly wouldn't comment on there being a dead body inside or speculate on who it might be. That would be irresponsible."

"New graffiti?"

Holden shifted his whole body to give Chet a look of incredulity. "Like you didn't know."

Chet held up his hands in innocence. "Wasn't me."

"Even if it wasn't, which I'm not convinced is true, it was definitely somebody in your group." Holden poked his finger at Chet without physically making contact. "And that makes *you* responsible."

"According to my attorney, it actually does not." Chet's smug face begged to be smacked.

"Attorney?" Margarita looked from Chet to me with a wide-eyed gaze.

"Oh, yeah, I didn't get the chance to let you know I met this morning with Todd Wainwright."

Margarita looked uncomfortable at the mention of Todd's name. I sensed she feared the proverbial cat was about to be let out of the bag.

"Couldn't get much information out of him, though, because right before I arrived, he'd been officially retained by one Chester Buchanan." I crossed my arms.

Margarita tilted her head toward Chet, looking like she wanted to knock his block off. She'd have to wait in line.

Cole cleared his throat. "As fascinating as this is, time is of the greatest import right now. Chief, let's go talk to your guys."

Norvald nodded his head, and the two walked over to the firefighters sitting on the back fender of one of the trucks.

"I think you're right about Edna. I'm going to go home and give her a call." Margarita gave a vague wave to the remains of the group as she walked away.

"And then there were three." Chet flashed a smirk at Holden and me.

"No, and then there was one." Holden pulled me away from Chet and toward my car.

I let out a sigh. "My mother would kill me for being that rude, but I don't feel even the slightest bit bad about it. Are you parked over by the pool?"

"Yeah, I was a few cars behind you on the street."

We drove in silence back to where the evening's journey had begun. I pulled alongside Holden's black Lexus.

He placed his hand over mine on the steering wheel. "Audrey, about earlier..."

"You really don't need to say anything. I don't know what I was thinking. I wasn't thinking. You looked so handsome, and your eyes—"

He laughed. "If you would stop talking long enough for me to get a word in."

"Fine, fine. I'm sorry. What did you want to say?"

"You don't need to apologize for kissing me. It was a surprise, albeit not an entirely unpleasant one, but there's a lot more conversation to be had before anything like that can happen again. I'm gun shy about hopping into anything yet, especially with someone I care about so much. I'd hate to start something that goes badly because the timing's off, and then we don't even have our friendship at the end of it all. Know what I mean?"

"I do. I would add that I'm enjoying this new copacetic phase of our relationship in contrast to the way things have been."

He laughed again. "Copacetic, huh? Isn't that a fancy way of saying it's sorta alright?"

"Maybe. I mean, I'm hoping to keep things drama-free. It's calm right now."

"Other than the fact we're embroiled in another murder investigation."

"Yes, that. Okay, well, have a good night. I'm sure we'll be in touch soon."

"Take care, girly." He lightly punched my upper arm as he got out.

I crept my car past the pool so I could get another look at the wall that had been defaced. It didn't look like the other messages to me. Instead of being looped together, the letters were all in block caps, printed separately. The only exception was the As, which in this case were written in lowercase two-story, like a typed "a" instead of a written one with a circle and line on the right side. I snapped a photo of it. If I could match the handwriting to anyone in Chet's group, we'd at least be able to nail one of the vandals.

* * *

The next morning, I sat in my office at the *Current*, looking through the photos I'd taken over the course of several days. I paid particular attention to the ones of the graffiti. As I'd surmised the night before, the message on the pool building looked markedly different from the others. The photos taken at the parking lot seemed to indicate at least two people had done the painting. At the time, it wasn't noticeable. Comparing them all side by side, however, the most heinous and obscene messages sprayed onto the asphalt were all in capital letters. It was a small discrepancy that hadn't stood out at the time because there was so much to take in, including several graphic depictions.

At least two people were responsible for the set of messages found at the parking lot. Maybe there were three of them, if the pictograms were the sole contributions of a lewd cartoonist. One of the original vandals—the one who wrote in cursive—was also responsible for the messages on the side of Margarita's garage and the back of the trail building. I believed the person nearly caught by Holden the night before was not the same one who'd tagged the parking lot. At the pool building, all the letters were capitalized except for the As, which were two-story lowercase. Also, the printing at the lot used a standard Z, while the vandal at the pool had a diagonal line through the middle of the Z.

The question which weighed heavy upon me was who, then, was responsible for the fires? Was it an opportunistic pyromaniac taking advantage of the distractions provided by the vandalism, or was it one of the vandals themselves who'd decided to escalate the situation to arson?

My thoughts were interrupted by a tap on my office door.

"Come in."

Cole poked his head through the gap. "Are you sure?"

"Well, I guess that depends. Are you coming with good news or bad news?"

He shut the door behind him. "A little bit of both. Which would you prefer first?"

"Bad news. I like to get it out of the way and then soften it with the good news."

He leaned against my file cabinet and draped his arm over the top. "Daphne Pierce over at the county coroner's office has already compared dental records. We have a confirmed identification. It was definitely Zeb Brandt who perished in that barn."

My shoulders slumped, and I blew out a long breath. "Even though I knew it would be, it's still heartbreaking to hear."

"I know what you mean. Poor guy thought he'd catch someone in the act and bring this whole series of incidents to a close. Instead…"

"So, what's the good news?"

"The good news is I'm coming to you first, and you get the exclusive."

My mouth pulled into a frown. "Somehow, getting to be the first to report on the death of a beloved citizen doesn't feel exactly like good news, but I appreciate the courtesy. What spurred this conciliatory act?"

Cole pushed away from the cabinet and sat in the chair across from me. "I've decided if I can control the information being put out, the gossip mill won't be muddying up my investigation."

I blinked rapidly and sat back. "It's honest, even if it does smack of censorship. You do realize I'm not beholden to disseminate the information you provide to me, nor am I constrained to report only the official line. This isn't state-run media."

"Of course, but I want you to consider something else."

"Which is?"

"There are certain aspects of every significant crime scene we purposely withhold from the public. These are details known only to the perpetrator and those investigating. If you're willing to work with me on this, I believe we can bait this guy into revealing himself without him even knowing he's doing it."

I contemplated his proposition. "I'm willing to give it a try, but I believe you're underestimating how invested the people of this town are in the business of its residents. Gossip is currency here, and those who peddle in it won't take kindly to having their streams of revenue brought down to a trickle."

"I don't doubt that, but I still think it might work. So, who would you say is the Bill Gates of Chattertowne's information superhighway?"

"That would be my mother, and you're in luck. She'll be in attendance tonight at the retirement party of our town historian, Mildred Driscoll. It's at the library, an open house from six to nine."

"I'd heard about that but wasn't sure if I would attend. Sounds like I should. I don't suppose you'd be willing to accompany me. Unless, of course, you already have a date with Holden." He shifted in his seat.

"Are you—are you asking me on a date?" I tilted my head and raised my eyebrows.

"I should be insulted that you sound so horrified at the idea. However, I meant in this new spirit of cooperation we're fostering; perhaps we could take advantage of this opportunity to question attendees under the guise of small talk. I'm not quite as comfortable in social settings as you seem to be, and I figured if we tag-teamed the conversations, something might shake loose or spill out. You know more about this town and its people and are therefore more likely to catch subtleties I might miss."

"I suppose you're right. So, we're kind of going undercover."

"How do you figure?"

"No one needs to know we're not really on a date. They'll be more likely to talk freely if it feels sociable and not interrogative. I'll put on a dress and heels and a little makeup, and you're gonna stand at my side all night looking like you adore me. I know that will be a challenge, but do your best."

Cole leaned forward and looked me square in my face. His mouth tipped to the right in a lopsided grin. "Challenge accepted."

Chapter Thirteen

The library was lit up both outside and in, the rare after-hours event temporarily transforming it from public utility to reception hall. Strands of illuminated globes hung across the entrance while white twinkling lights draped each boxwood topiary. In the lobby, Cole assisted me in removing my coat so it could be checked and told me he'd meet me inside.

Folks holding punch-filled cups gathered in clusters to talk between the low bookshelves and leather reading chairs. The focal point of the room was a maple and stone fireplace topped with an Art-Deco-arched bas-relief sculpture of a forest.

I scanned the room until I located the woman of the hour. Mildred wasn't wearing her standard cardigan, but instead was dressed in a sage-colored wrap dress and low gray heels. Her lips were pink, as were her cheeks, flushed with the pleasure of the fawning affection she was receiving.

"Looking for someone?" The timbre of Holden's voice in my ear sent a shiver down to my toes.

"Hey. I was, uh," I struggled through a swallow. "Looking for the guest of honor."

"She deserves all of this and more." He tipped his cup toward Mildred.

"She really does."

"Looks like Dudley Do-right left his cowboy hat at home tonight." Holden jutted his chin in the direction of the bar where Cole chatted with the bartender. "He cleans up surprisingly well. For a country boy."

"Okay, first, Dudley Do-right was Canadian. Second, Chattertowne isn't exactly what I'd call cosmopolitan. In fact, Jackson Hole is pretty ritzy for a western town. He probably thinks we're the country bumpkins."

Cole approached us with two drinks in hand, passing one off to me. "Evening, Holden. Audrey, I have your claim ticket. Would you like it, or should I hold on to it for you until we're ready to leave?"

"You can keep it," I mumbled, sipping my drink and avoiding eye contact with Holden, who stiffened next to me.

"Is there an actual ceremony or anything?" Cole looked around.

"I believe it's an open house. Maybe someone will make a toast when they wheel the cake out." I took another sip.

"I'm going to go give her my regards." Holden marched toward Mildred without even a glance back in my direction.

"What was that?" Cole mused, like he had no idea the interaction had gone exactly as he'd intended.

"I could ask you the same question."

"What do you mean?" Cole gulped his punch and observed Holden interacting with Mildred, who was giggling like a young girl.

"Are you saying you weren't making a show of the fact we're here together?"

"That's the whole purpose of tonight, remember? Convince people we're on a date so they'll be more likely to let something slip in casual conversation."

"Not with Holden, though. He's not who we're trying to convince."

"You seem pretty concerned with what Holden does or does not believe about you and me."

I turned to face him. "There is no you and me." I gestured between us. "There's a *you*, and there's a me, and there's the you and me we're pretending to be."

Cole smirked. "That rhymed."

I let out a frustrated growl. "Look, this is prime time to talk to people. The room is full. Nobody's leaving until after the cake, so let's make the rounds. Where do you want to start?"

"How about I leave that up to you? You know these people better than I do."

I spotted Tammy Milner and her husband, Gabe, speaking with another couple I didn't recognize. I indicated the foursome. "Let's start with Tammy. She's an active poster on CROCCC's page."

Cole gave an "after you" gesture. We walked over to the two couples, who stopped speaking as soon as they saw us approach.

"Evening, Chief Loveland." Gabe nodded at Cole.

"Evening, Gabe." Cole reached his hand out to Tammy. "I don't believe we've met. You must be Gabe's better half."

Tammy's cheeks turned crimson, and her hand fluttered against her neck. "Oh," she tittered and held out her hand. "Yes, I'm Tammy."

Cole shook her hand. He turned to the other couple. "Cole Loveland." He reached out his hand to the man, who offered his own.

"Of course. I'm Don Whitehead. This is my wife, Blakesly."

Cole made a quarter-bow. "Blakesly."

She smiled at him, and he shook her hand as well.

"I assume you all know Audrey O'Connell?"

Blakesly sniffed and tilted her head back and forth. "We know of her."

Don chuckled. "I believe, Audrey, my wife sees you as her competition."

I looked at Blakesly, who was shooting daggers my way. "How so?"

"I have an online news blog called the *Chattertowne Clarion*. I cover area happenings from a less biased viewpoint than the *Current*."

Her statement caused me to jerk my head back in surprise. "Excuse me?"

Cole's hand rested on my lower back.

Tammy sneered. "We've read your account of the graffiti and the fire. It's clear you've bought into Mayor Guzman's lies."

I sputtered. "What in the world—"

"Oh look, Audrey, there's your mother. Let's go talk to her." Cole pulled me away from the group and dragged me toward the entrance of the library.

I looked around. "I don't see my mother."

"I have no idea what she looks like. I just didn't want our mission for tonight to be derailed because you got into a hair-pulling match with Tammy and Blakesly."

I inhaled and gave a deep exhale. "What was that all about? I'm not biased. Am I biased?"

Cole shrugged. "How would I know?"

"Are you saying you've never read my articles?"

"I don't need to read the news. I experience enough of it firsthand."

Halfway through a stellar eye-roll, my mother indeed walked through the doorway.

"Audrey Jeanne, how many times have I told you rolling your eyes is classless?"

She was dressed to the nines, as always. Her blonde hair, courtesy of Travis at Salon du Monde, was perfectly coiffed into a chignon even Doris Day would have envied. Her hazel-green eyes sparkled under freshly-applied mink lashes and a swipe of lilac eyeshadow—matte, not shimmer. One of her beauty regimen no-noes was mica based makeup for any woman over forty, saying it highlighted wrinkles and aged them.

"Cole Loveland, this is my mother, Claudine O'Connell."

She held her hand out the way she'd learned from watching classic films starring Grace Kelly and Rita Hayworth. "Chief Loveland. I've heard so much about you. Should I apologize for your having to put up with not one but two of my daughters?"

Cole's expression was one of sheer confusion with a hint of horror. "Pardon, ma'am?"

Her laugh was delicate and thin, like the sound of a wind gust blowing through a crystal chandelier or the plinking notes of a tiny music box. "Somehow, despite my best efforts to raise my girls to be demure, they're both stubborn as mules."

Cole looked between us. "Oh, I don't know. I'd take a woman who knows what she's about over a doormat any day. From what I've seen, they both know how to stand their ground. That's an important quality when dealing with the ornery public the way they do on a daily basis."

Heat rose from my toes through my scalp. I'd never seen anyone put my mother in her place so deftly, and to hear what could only be construed as praise from him was stunning. Her gaze widened, but she quickly regained her composure.

"Well, of course, you're right. I should be proud to have two very tenacious daughters, even if they are a little rough around the edges."

I was used to her disappointment that I was less debutante, more pococurante, and apathetic toward her attempts to groom me into what she deemed acceptable. Cole, on the other hand, was not, and there was a good chance he was about to say something that would bring out my mother's uncooperative side.

"Dad didn't want to come out tonight?"

"You know how your father is. He hates stuff like this."

"Mom, we were hoping to get your insight into some of the rumblings around town regarding the graffiti and the fire."

She wore a smug smile. "You're usually chastising me for, as you like to call it, running the switchboard at gossip central. Now, you want me to spill what I know?"

Cole rocked back on his heels. "Audrey mentioned you have your finger on the pulse of the town, specifically their sentiments regarding council decisions."

"I've cultivated relationships with some of the chattier Chattertowneites, as I like to call them. It's an art, really. There must be an exchange of information which is perceived to be equally valuable, otherwise they'll start feeling like they're being taken advantage of, and they'll peddle their tidbits elsewhere. There's also an unwritten rule regarding sharing with outsiders."

Cole blinked at her a few times. "Perhaps you'll make an exception in my case. I have something to share which hasn't likely reached your circuit."

This time her laugh was a disingenuous "hahaha."

He raised his eyebrows. "Come on, now, Claudine. Don't let an opportunity like this slip through your fingers. This is the kind of morsel which will solidify you as the go-to for years to come."

Her eyes glinted, and she looked around to see if anyone was watching. "Okay, let's have it."

He lowered his voice. "It's about the fire."

Claudine ran her middle fingertip across her pearl choker. "I'm not sure what you could tell me about the fire I don't already know. Ingrid Norvald told me all about it this morning over coffee. She said Gunner was a mess when he got home around two in the morning. He told her the barn was a total loss. Poor Edna Brandt. To be all the way in Arizona, completely helpless to do anything, while hooligans destroy their property. I sure hope you've got a lead." She caught me pulling my mouth. "What? What's that unpleasant face about?"

Cole cleared his throat. "It wasn't only property which was destroyed. Mr. Brandt thought he might try and catch the taggers in the act. Edna told Margarita Guzman he'd planned to sleep in the barn last night."

Realization dawned across my mother's face like an ominous sunrise. Her knees buckled and Cole reached out to support her by the elbow. He led her over to a bench, and she sagged down onto it. I excused myself and went into the area where the reception was being held. I grabbed a bottle of water off the table and brought it back to her. She guzzled the entire thing in about thirty seconds.

After dabbing her mouth with the back of her hand, she looked up at Cole with red-rimmed eyes. "What would you like me to do?"

Chapter Fourteen

After my mother had regained her composure and Cole had given her instructions on her mission for the evening, the three of us reentered the party. Holden glanced at me, but quickly turned his head. I spotted Mildred and made my way toward her with Cole in tow. My mother slinked her way through the crowd with the intention of dropping gossip breadcrumbs to see who would take the bait.

"Audrey! I'm so glad you were able to make it."

Mildred pulled me in for a hug. I used restraint for fear if I squeezed too hard, I might crack her frail bones.

"I wouldn't miss this for anything."

Cole leaned in to give Mildred a kiss on the cheek. "Congratulations on your retirement."

"Why thank you, Chief Loveland." She turned to me and leaned in to whisper in my ear. "I thought for certain you would be here with Holden Villalobos. I hear he's officially back on the market."

I pulled back so she could see my expression of chagrin. I shrugged my shoulders. Cole observed our nonverbal interaction with curiosity.

"Mildred." I placed my comparably giant hand on her tiny forearm. "Remember how much you enjoyed helping solve what happened to Marcus Washburn?"

"Oh, yes. It was like I was Watson to your Sherlock."

Cole choked down his laughter, and I glared at him. He held up his hands in a mock apology.

"This is your big night, and we don't want to do anything to take away from that, but I was wondering." I paused when Cole cleared his throat. "*We were wondering* how you'd feel about a little diversionary kerfuffle in hopes of flushing out the perpetrators of our recent string of vandalism incidents."

The twinkle of excitement in Mildred's eyes gave her answer before her lips formed the words. "We're getting the gang back together!" She clapped with glee. "We'll have this thing solved in no time."

A few of the partygoers eyed the three of us with curiosity.

"Gang?" Cole wasn't thrilled with the idea. "I can't have you putting yourself in harm's way. We wanted to make sure you were aware of what was going on, and that you're okay with our plan."

Mildred's face fell, and I scrunched mine disapprovingly at Cole.

"I think what Chief Loveland means to say is…" I scowled at him once more. "This first phase is more of an intel gathering than anything else. We're about to drop a bomb, and we need to see how the people gathered here react to it."

Mildred winked at me and then again at Cole. "Gotcha. So, what's my objective?"

Cole sighed and rubbed the back of his neck. "When word gets out, and people begin to respond, I think we need to be spread out to be able to observe as many folks as possible."

"Let's split the room into quadrants. Mildred, you take that section over there near the banquet table. I'll go over by the bar, and Cole can take the section near the entrance. That will give him visibility of the room."

"Quadrants implies four people, not three," Cole mused condescendingly.

I looked at him and raised my eyebrows. He scanned my face. He must have finally understood what I meant because his look of confusion was replaced with irritation.

"No."

Mildred looked between the two of us. "What am I missing here?"

"Cole doesn't want to include Holden in the plan."

"Poppycock," she said. "Holden was a great help in solving our last case."

"You mean the case for which he's currently on probation because he was a participant in the criminal conspiracy that nearly destroyed this town?

That case?"

"When you put it like that…" her voice trailed off.

"What will it hurt to have him keep an eye out? He's already aware of…the news," I said.

Cole sighed again. "Fine."

"I suppose I should ask what this big announcement is, seeing as how it's about to blow up my party."

I looked at Cole, who looked back at me and grimaced.

"Maybe we should go to the ladies' room. That way, your reaction won't draw too much attention before we're ready, and it will give Cole time to update Holden on what we need him to do."

Mildred nodded her head, and I followed her out of the room.

After I'd broken the sad news and Mildred had cried herself out, she dampened a paper towel and blotted her face.

She freshened her lipstick, puckering and popping her lips a couple times, and turned to me. "Let's nail the S.O.B."

Cole was standing near the entrance to the party when we returned. "Everything okay?"

I nodded. Mildred had her game face on. She gave one bop of her head and joined the crowd grazing at the buffet. I looked at Cole, who returned my stoic expression. As I walked to the bar area, I sensed both Cole's and Holden's gazes on me. From my station, I caught my mother's attention and pulled my right earlobe. She nodded her head in recognition of the signal.

My mother stood in a circle with two city council members, the owner of one of five Mexican restaurants in town, and a woman I only recognized because every time I drove to the grocery store, I saw her out jogging. It didn't matter the day or time. I wondered if she ever stood still. I had my answer, as she currently was stock still, enthralled by the story my mother was telling.

A gasp went up from within the group, and it was almost as if you could visibly see the news ripple through the crowd. People began pulling out their cell phones to read the *Current's* website, where my headline story about the murder of Zeb Brandt had been posted only a few minutes earlier.

Blakesly craned her neck in order to hear what my mother was saying, her flamboyant hand gestures waving wildly as she told the story. The color drained from her cheeks as she turned to look wide-eyed at her husband, Don, and Tammy and Gabe Milner. Tammy's gaze darted across the room to Wanda Harper, who was huddled with Fred near the shrimp cocktail display. Nearby, Holden eavesdropped while pretending to be fascinated by a mini sausage wrapped in caramelized bacon on a toothpick.

I inched my way along the edge of the crowd until I was behind the two couples. Wanda muttered something under her breath to Fred. Fred's head jerked up, and he looked over at the Whiteheads and Milners. He jutted his chin to indicate they should look behind them. At once, the foursome turned to look at me.

I froze in place. "I hear there's cake?"

Judging by their expressions, not one of them believed my ruse.

Lucky for me, something diverted all their attention away from me: the arrival of Margarita Guzman.

Chapter Fifteen

Margarita sure knew how to make an entrance. Of course, she had no way of knowing about the cockamamie plan Cole and I had concocted with the aid of Mildred and my mother, or that she'd be arriving right after the who's who of Chattertowne had been informed of the tragic death of one of their own.

Though he was more comfortable mucking stalls wearing overalls than hobnobbing in a monkey suit with Chattertowne's social elite—such as they were—the truth was Zeb Brandt was probably worth more than every person in that room…combined. His family had farmed their land for generations, and they owned a lot of it.

Now he was dead, and all because of an unpopular land deal he'd negotiated with the woman who was late to the party in every meaningful way. All eyes were on her as she removed her coat, and conversations had ceased.

"Hey, Margarita!" shouted Don Whitehead. "What do you have to say about Old Man Brandt?

Margarita's gaze cut to Cole and then to me. Immediately I had a sinking feeling. We should have let her in on the plan so she wouldn't be ambushed. Cole must have realized it as well because he jumped right into the fray.

"Mayor Guzman is not running this investigation. I am. If you have any questions, you can direct them to me. The information in Audrey O'Connell's article is, sadly, an accurate account. Last night, the Brandt barn was burned to the ground. Unfortunately, according to Edna, Zeb had planned to sleep in the barn hoping to catch the person or persons responsible for the graffiti in case they returned to his place to vandalize his property. These supposedly harmless acts of protest have escalated from misdemeanor vandalism to homicide."

A sharp collective gasp rose from the crowd, followed by murmuring.

"So, what, we've got two outsiders running this Keystone Cop investigation?" Blakesly scoffed.

"Might I remind you all, it was longtime Chattertowne residents who perpetrated our previous outbreak of criminal activity," my mother said. It was completely out of character.

"Your liberal media hack of a daughter has gotten to you, huh Claudine?" Blakesly sneered at me.

Before I knew it, Holden was standing next to me, speaking through gritted teeth. "Don't let her get to you. The whole point of this is to bait them into showing their hand."

I heaved a deep sigh of resignation but otherwise kept my thoughts to myself.

Mildred clapped her hands three times. "Ladies and gentlemen! You've all come out here tonight to wish me well and thank me for my many, *many* years of service to this town. We've got a huge cake over here with my name on it. It's my party, and I say we take this opportunity to celebrate with memories of our good friend Zeb. Let's get our tears out tonight so when Edna gets back into town, she doesn't have to deal with all our blubbering. We're gonna pull ourselves together and do what this town does best. We're gonna rally around Edna and show her how much she means to us, how much Zeb meant to us. In the meantime, let us eat cake!"

More murmurs snaked their way through the crowd, but people began moving toward the cake table. Mildred sliced each piece and addressed each person with a smile and a "thanks for coming" as she handed it to them.

Cole spoke with Margarita and then walked over to Holden and me.

"I'm not sure we accomplished what we'd hoped," he said, placing his hands on his hips and spreading his feet apart.

"Do they make you practice that pose at the academy, or does it come naturally to you?"

"Holden!" I elbowed him in the ribs. "Don't be rude."

Cole ignored him and instead addressed me. "You about ready to go?"

"Yeah, these past few days have been exhausting." I turned to Holden. "If you hear anything, you'll let me know?"

Cole interjected. "You mean, he'll let *me* know."

"How about this? I'll meet you both at Audrey's office tomorrow around noon, and I'll let you both know what I overheard tonight."

"Can't," I said. "I have to cover the Homecoming Cavalcade. Can we do ten instead?"

"Works for me." Cole looked at Holden expectantly.

"Sure. Ten. Night, Audrey." With that, Holden turned on his heel and left the party.

"Has he always been so…I don't know…petulant?" Cole asked.

"I've noticed only certain people bring out that side in him."

* * *

At half past nine the next morning, there was a knock on my office door.

"Come in."

The knock repeated.

"I said, come in."

Through my door, a muffled voice said, "Can't. My hands are full."

I got up and opened the door to find Holden standing there with a white pastry bag in one hand and a cardboard cup holder containing two cups of coffee in the other.

"If your hands are so full, how'd you knock?"

"Elbow." He entered my office and set the items down on my desk.

"I thought we said ten."

"We did, but I wanted to chat before Dudley got here."

"Are one of those for me?" I indicated the coffee.

"Yep. Irish cream latte for you, black for me." He handed one of the cups to me. "Extra whip, just like you like it."

"You know Cole's coming. You didn't get one for him?"

"He can get his own coffee." Holden sat in one of two chairs opposite my desk.

"He's not a bad guy, you know."

I opened the lid and licked a dollop of whipped cream off the top before realizing he was watching me. I chuckled, embarrassed and a little self-conscious under his intense gaze.

"I'd hope he's not a bad guy. He is the chief of police, after all, and he was brought in to clean up the department."

"What's in the bag?"

"Crullers."

"Going for sainthood, I see." I reached for the bag, opened it, and inhaled. "I think I've decided crullers are my favorite."

"You think you've decided? Or you've decided?"

"I've decided you're incorrigible."

"You decided that a long time ago." He winked.

"It's crazy how they get these to be as light as air." I took a bite of the donut. "So, what did you need to talk to me about before Cole gets here?"

"Nothing in particular. I just know the guy despises me, and I'm a little concerned it's gonna rub off on you. I want to make sure we're still… copacetic."

"In case you haven't noticed, I'm not the kind of woman who can't make up her own mind."

He laughed. "Very true. How's Viv? I never see her anymore.'

"She's as well as can be expected, considering the love of her life is a two-hour drive away, across a giant toll bridge, behind cement walls and iron bars."

Holden blew out a breath. "I can't believe how close I came to that being me. I'm grateful every day for my freedom."

"I'm thankful you've been able to make a fresh start. I heard rumors that Emily might be headed to Spokane, but I figured there was a good chance you'd go with her and get out of this fishbowl of gossipy busybodies."

We exchanged regretful smiles and looked at each other with the unspoken understanding that comes from having been through an ordeal together. A sharp rap on the door interrupted the moment.

"Come on in, Cole."

Cole walked into my office and gave a surprised glance at Holden. He checked his watch. "Didn't we say ten? It's not even nine forty-five."

Holden shifted in his seat and crossed his legs. "That would make you early as well."

Cole took the chair next to Holden. "What was the upshot on last night?

"Actually, we hadn't gotten to that yet. We were catching up on personal stuff."

A smug smile appeared on Holden's face, while Cole's remained blank.

"I wasn't able to hear much of Fred and Wanda's conversation," Holden said. "I didn't want it to look too obvious I was listening, especially because I need my job. Wanda whispered something in Fred's ear, which caused him to alert the others to Audrey's presence. Before that, I thought I heard Wanda harping on Fred—no pun intended—about Jenna."

"Who's Jenna?" I asked.

"Jenna Doyle. She's our company bookkeeper."

"Any chance there's something happening between them?" Cole asked.

Holden's mouth pulled to the left. "Maybe? I mean, she's like twenty-five and he's in his forties at least. Not to mention, she's way too hot for him. You never know, though. That old *boss boinking the secretary* tale is as old as time."

Classy," I said. "From what I could see, Blakesly seemed pretty upset. I'm not a great reader of people, but her expression looked like she'd realized the way they've been stirring things up could actually have real, dire consequences. Tammy's reaction was more of a CYA."

Cole tilted his head. "CYA?"

"Cover your ass. She acted like someone in containment mode. What about you? Did you hear anything?"

Cole shrugged his shoulders. "Turns out, even without a uniform, people clam up around the Chief of Police."

"Imagine that," Holden said drily. "Even with your highly trained observational skills you came up with nothing?"

"I wouldn't say that exactly," Cole said. "If there's one thing that became crystal clear last night, it's that those three couples are thick as thieves."

Chapter Sixteen

After Cole and Holden left my office, I had about an hour before I needed to leave for the parade, so I decided to pull up Blakesly's website. If she viewed the *Current* as her competition, I wanted to know what we were up against. The *Chattertowne Clarion's* website had a subtitle, *Speaking Truth Since 2015.*

Blakesly's bio stated she'd developed a love for journalism at Chattertowne High under the tutelage of my boss, Nicholas Anderson. It was ironic, considering she believed the newspaper he edited to be the source of the muddied misinformation her site purported to clarify.

Her masthead contained a menu for the categories of news articles she'd posted: Crime, Government Corruption, Politics, Probes, Opinions—as if it weren't an entire web page of her opinions—and, oddly, movie reviews. I clicked on the movie tab out of curiosity. Her review of best picture nominees for the previous year indicated a fondness for war epics, mixed feelings about a Nazi with a heart-of-gold story—she seemed less perturbed by the Nazi part, more by his crisis of conscience which she deemed forced— and a complete rejection of the indie art film she saw as a propaganda piece.

Under the government corruption tab, she explored everything from local issues to a coverup of aliens and the existence of Bigfoot.

Her latest post was on the graffiti incidents. It had been posted prior to the fire.

Recently, Chattertowne has experienced a string of vandalism incidents which have left the citizens of our town feeling uneasy. I purport to you that is exactly the intention of the person responsible. We must all ask ourselves, who benefits the most from this?

I'd say it's the person using it to gain sympathy, Mayor Margarita Guzman. It enables her to paint herself as a victim, meanwhile the real victims—the taxpayers—continue to foot the bill for her backroom deals and shady politics. Why hasn't Chief Loveland questioned the mayor on her whereabouts during the times the incidents occurred? Why does he always give her the benefit of the doubt? Is it because they're both outsiders, and don't have the best interest of Chattertowne at heart?

This publication, as well as CROCCC, tried to warn you all, but you insisted on electing a Californian set on reshaping our beloved Chattertowne to forward her own agenda.

Use your heads, people! This is a farce designed to take the heat off the mayor for her abuse of office and mismanagement of public funds. It's sleight of hand. Legerdemain. Don't fall for her schemes. Keep Mayor Guzman accountable!

I emailed the article's link to Cole and Holden, making sure to send them separately. The last thing I needed was to be in a group email with the two of them.

I found Blakesly's social media accounts and stalked her photos. She had the typical random assortment of posts. She'd linked her blogs, a few articles from other sources to support her point, pictures of events throughout town, a meme here and there, and an occasional diatribe, which, ironically, was almost always immediately preceded by some inspirational quote about spreading love.

What really caught my eye were photos she'd posted a few weeks earlier, which showed Blakesly and her husband Don walking on the trail. In the background of the selfie was the very building on which the comment about Margarita, in Spanish, had been painted. I took a screenshot of it.

It didn't prove anything other than that, like many other people in Chattertowne, Blakesly, and her husband took advantage of the walking trails outside of town, but I couldn't shake the feeling it was significant somehow.

* * *

The Chattertowne High School's Homecoming Cavalcade had been a tradition for more than a hundred years, even before cars had become commonplace on Main Street. The parade's starting point was right in front of the school, and the route was a circuitous loop through town. The streets were already lined with business owners popping out for a peek, homeowners standing on their front porches, and supportive townspeople waving at the kids as they got into formation.

Chief Norvald arrived with a couple fire trucks. As was tradition, senior football players wearing their jerseys over street clothes climbed up for the ride while the cheerleaders piled into the back of a pickup truck. Their pom-poms glittered in the early Autumn sun.

Next to the bushes, one lone cheerleader hunched over a metal trashcan. Her back and shoulders heaved as if purging something awful from deep within her tiny body. I'd heard through the grapevine a raging bonfire party had taken place the night before in someone's field north of town. My guess was she was hungover.

"Welcome to the consequences of your actions, my dear," I murmured.

The rest of the students were decked out head-to-toe in Chattertowne High School's colors of green and blue. Technically, they were supposed to be called emerald and sapphire, but I always felt that came off a bit pretentious for a town known for its grungy riverside docks, crop fields, and antique stores. Also, our school nickname was Cowpie High.

The band tooted horns as they prepared to march. Some practiced the school fight song, "Roll on Chattertowne," which I still knew by heart from my days as a cheerleader.

Roll on Chattertowne, the Cougs are here to prove
We will fight for victory, the Cougs are on the move
Roll on Chattertowne, the Cougs are here to play
Cheer for our boys, the Cougs will win the day
Roll on Chattertowne, for the glory of our team
Shout the praises of the Sapphire and the Emerald Green!

It wasn't the greatest song ever written and still harbored echoes of misogynistic days gone by, but the local folks had dug in their heels any time changes were proposed, so it stood.

Carter Yip—quarterback and captain of the football team—was perched atop the first fire truck with his legs dangling. He held the Chattertowne homecoming trophy. Every year, during the crowning of the homecoming queen at halftime, the trophy was awarded to the student who'd exhibited the most school pride and spirit throughout the week. On the base, a plate listed names going back more than fifty years.

"Hey, Carter! Can I get you and your buddies to move a little closer for a photo? And lemme see that trophy. Hold it high."

Carter triumphantly thrust the bronze cougar statue over his head. His teammates leaned in and made various poses and gestures. Several of the boys had their tongues sticking out, which I'd found at last year's Kupit festival was a popular thing for teens to do in their pictures. One gave a peace sign, one the horns, one made a hang loose symbol with his thumb and forefinger, and one gave me the bird.

"Could you please tell your buddy on the end there if he doesn't knock it off, he'll be looking at a front-page photo of all his friends, but he won't be there because I'll crop him out?"

Carter leaned over and flicked the kid's shoulder, and he sheepishly jammed the offending hand into his letterman jacket pocket.

"Thanks. Now smile!"

I took a few photos and then walked in the direction of the cheer truck. Blakesly was attempting to tame the curly blonde hair of the young woman I'd seen vomiting in the trashcan. The girl swatted at her with a white-gloved hand.

"Mom, stop!"

"Regan, hold still." Blakesly made one more pass at some flyaway strands before backing up.

"I heard Bigfoot was spotted rummaging through the dumpster at Chuck's Chowder Grotto. Maybe you could go fix *his* hair." Regan turned back to her friends.

Blakesly's head reared slightly in embarrassment at her daughter's disrespect. She looked around to see if anyone had witnessed. She spotted me observing her, and a look of mortification washed across her face, followed by a snarl. She stomped toward me.

"What are you doing here?"

"My job."

"Does your job include spying on people?" She crossed her arms.

"I'm not spying. I'm taking photos of the event for my feature story."

She snorted. "You mean like you weren't spying at Mildred's party last night? Eavesdropping?"

"For someone who claims to be in the media, you sure seem to take issue with its function."

"Audrey, I do not now, nor would I ever consider myself, part of the media. I am a truth seeker and a truth-teller. You're merely a cog in a giant wheel of misinformation you may not even fully comprehend the ramifications of."

I bit my tongue in order to prevent myself from addressing her dangling preposition. "If you're on the side of the truth, then we're on the same side."

Blakesly scoffed and then hissed, "You wouldn't know the truth if it bit you on the a—"

"Audrey. Blakesly," Cole said. "Hello."

"Chief Loveland." Blakesly slapped on a broad, fake smile.

"Did I hear your daughter say something about Bigfoot being spotted at Chuck's?"

"Oh, that." She waved her hand dismissively. "Regan likes to tease me. She says I'm a bit of a conspiracy theorist. You know how teenagers can be. Always trying to embarrass their parents." She flipped her hair over her shoulder and gave a forced laugh. "Are you marching in the parade?"

"Not officially. I'm here to walk alongside and make sure everything goes smoothly." He gestured between Blakesly and me. "Everything okay here?"

"Nothing I can't handle," I said.

"We were just discussing the dearth of objective journalism these days."

Cole looked at me and then back at Blakesly. He opened his mouth to say something but was drowned out by the wail of fire trucks, indicating the parade was underway.

"Mother!" Regan stood in the truck bed with her hands on her hips. "Stop making a fool of yourself. You're already married and way too old for him. Come here. I need more lip gloss. Hurry!"

Color crept up Blakesly's neck. "Like I said. Teenagers." She hustled over to her sullen child, while simultaneously digging in her purse.

Cole attempted to speak, but once again was thwarted by sirens. He gestured toward the back of the parade line-up. I waved a quick goodbye and jogged over to my car. My plan was to get to a position near the end of the parade route in order to catch the participants as they came around the last bend and onto Main Street.

The cacophony of firetrucks and trombones quieted the further I got from the group. I located a spot about three blocks northeast of Main and parked. As I walked toward the final leg of the parade route, I spotted Levi, Fred, and another guy I didn't recognize across the street and standing in front of Louden's Tavern.

Fred's face was purple with anger as he jabbed his finger in Levi's face. For his part, Levi kept his demeanor calm; no small feat when your boss is screaming at you. The other guy, a weaselly dude with grimy clothes, took a long drag of his cigarette.

I stopped for a moment, unsure if I should get involved. I didn't particularly want to find myself on the receiving end of Fred's ire, but the situation seemed to require some sort of response on my part. I decided to play dumb.

"Hey, Levi! Are you coming to the game tonight?"

Fred stopped his finger in mid-jab and turned to look at me. The color in his cheeks lightened a bit, but not completely.

"Oh, hey, Fred. I didn't see you there. How nice of you all to come down to watch the Cavalcade and support the kids."

"Hey, Audrey," Levi said. "Yeah, I'll be at the game. Nothing like trying to relive the glory days at your high school homecoming."

I forced a laugh. "You know it! See you there."

I lowered my chin and walked with purpose to the corner where the parade would arrive shortly. I had no intention of looking back at the group of men, no matter how curious I was about what had made Fred so angry.

Apparently, I'd lowered my chin too far because I ran smack dab into Chet Buchanan. "Oof!"

"Hey! Watch it!" Recognition flickered across Chet's face. "Audrey. You really should look where you're going."

"I'm so sorry. I was a little distracted by…" I looked over my shoulder at Fred and his gang.

He followed my gaze. He shifted his feet and cleared his throat. Fred's face turned the color of beets as he narrowed his gaze like a laser on Chet.

"Oh, hey, listen, I gotta get going. I've got an appointment." Before I could even respond, Chet was gone.

I looked back at Fred, Levi, and the weasel. They were all staring in the direction of Chet's hasty escape, and none of them looked happy.

I couldn't help but wonder, had a crack formed among the members of CROCCC? Which one of them had taken things a step too far?

Chapter Seventeen

If Chattertowne knew how to do one thing well—in addition to spreading gossip—it was Friday night lights. Chattertowne High School football games were *the* place to be on chilly fall evenings. Not only for students and their families, but the whole town turned out. It probably didn't hurt that large crowds also satisfied the gossip mongers. Inevitably, at least one juicy tidbit would be revealed, whether it be a new couple spotted making out behind the bleachers, a tipsy confession made following the imbibing of spiked hot cocoa from a thermos, or simply the congregating of so many townsfolk in one place enabling information to be disseminated faster than usual.

CHS's teams were always fairly competitive. Several district title banners hung from the roof of the stadium, along with one prized state championship banner from the seventies, faded and frayed. Our sole advantage came from fielding a team full of boys who'd been raised baling hay before dawn, unloading cargo off boats at the port, and spending long summer days feeding cattle or digging trenches. Even on game days, many of them were up early for harvest in the fall. A dock man or farmer's workout made for tough competitors.

The student section had already exceeded capacity by the time I arrived about a half hour prior to kickoff. Because it was homecoming, the rest of the stands were filling in rapidly as well. Elementary school-aged children ran around unsupervised while the middle school kids skulked and tried to play cool. On the track adjacent to the field, a platform had been constructed for the court of princesses and the crowning of the homecoming queen.

The air held a whiff of popcorn and concession stand hotdogs, and I couldn't help but feel nostalgic. I hadn't been to a game in years, but the smells took me right back to my own days at Chattertowne High.

Even though it was annoying, I couldn't change shampoo brands without everyone in town finding out, there was something to be said for being part of a tight-knit community where traditions were held sacred and nearly everyone was invested in what happened there. I hadn't found that while living in Portland and I hadn't realized how much I'd missed it until I returned to Chattertowne two years ago.

I leaned against the railing at the east end of the stadium behind the goalpost and scanned the crowds. I spotted Tammy, and Gabe Milner huddled in the stands next to Blakesly and Don Whitehead. Wanda Harper stood on the end by herself. She looked around, like she was trying to find someone. Maybe Fred was on his way back to his seat with snacks.

I soon got my answer when a voice boomed out over the loudspeakers.

"Hello Chattertowne Cougars!"

The crowd cheered.

"I'm Fred Harper, and welcome to homecoming night!"

More cheers erupted.

"Would you please rise for the presentation of colors?"

The throng rose to their feet as a group of uniformed teenagers with the American Flag, the Washington State flag, and what appeared to be rifles marched to the middle of the field.

"Before the band plays the national anthem, let us bow our heads and have a moment of silence for our dear friend Zeb Brandt, who tragically lost his life in a fire this week. Zeb was a proud alumni of Chattertowne High School and a valued member of our community."

"Alumnus," I muttered.

A woman standing behind me made a shushing sound. I threw a glance over my left shoulder. The shusher was one of my former teachers, Madame Prendergast. Mme. Prendergast—Susan—wasn't more than ten years older than me. She still wore her hair in a short, sassy bob which she swished back and forth constantly.

She hadn't been teaching long when I'd had her for French my freshman year. She also taught drama, liked to wear miniskirts, and flirted with all the boys like she was the embodiment of the sexy teacher trope in a Van Halen song.

She'd given me my worst grade, which I'd always believed was out of spite. *Très mesquin.* Very petty.

The crowd noise dimmed to a low murmur. Men removed their ballcaps and lowered their chins. After about a minute, the band began to play the anthem. Hands were placed across hearts, and mouths opened, although it was difficult to make out any actual singing over the sound of intermediate musicians honking their brass instruments.

"Let's gooooo, Cougars!" Fred yelled and a large blast sounded about twenty feet from where I stood, followed by the siren's wail of the ambulance parked in the northeast corner of the stadium.

"What the—" I screamed and jumped.

I'd forgotten the explosion of a cannon punctuated every kickoff, along with every touchdown. If I were going to keep my hearing, I'd need to find another lookout point.

I turned to leave the vicinity just as Chet walked with purpose in my direction.

Great.

Only, he wasn't looking at me, but at Susan Prendergast. She greeted him with a big smile and an even bigger hug. He caught me staring, so I jerked my head and looked away.

Now facing the crowd in the stands, it was impossible to miss the intense gaze of Wanda Harper. She wasn't looking at me either. She was focused on the couple embracing next to me. I followed her sightline back to Chet and Susan, who giggled and looped her arm through his. She nuzzled her head into his neck as they ambled away.

When I returned my attention to Wanda, her face was pinched and scowling.

She looked like she wanted to kill somebody.

* * *

At the end of the first quarter, the game was tied 10-10. The second quarter would have ended with the same score if it hadn't been for a long bomb from Carter Yip to Cooper Vargas for a touchdown. Over the loudspeaker, an unfamiliar voice called the play and subsequent extra point attempt, the last of the first half.

Midway through the halftime festivities, Blakesly and Don Whitehead stood next to their daughter Regan as she awaited the announcement of homecoming queen. Regan had left the game midway through the second quarter to change from her cheer uniform into a white gown and tiara. Four other girls stood with their parents on the platform in similar dresses, all with rose-colored "princess" sashes. It looked like a fashion show for child brides.

After much fanfare, the queen's crown was placed on the head of the one girl I hadn't expected, the one who wore glasses, whose ghostlike pale skin indicated she hadn't gone to the tanning booth like the other girls, and whose thin frame barely held up the heavily beaded gown.

"It's pretty sweet, isn't it?" Holden's voice was recognizable without me having to turn around.

"What's the story?" I asked.

"Dana's got leukemia. She's been battling it for a couple years now."

"I hadn't heard."

"When she was first diagnosed, there was a fundraiser. I think that was before you moved back from Portland."

I turned to take in the full picture of him. "I see your letterman jacket still fits."

He smirked and gave a shoulder shrug, but it was obvious he felt proud to wear it. He'd been a three-sport athlete. Football in the fall, basketball in the winter, and track in the spring. I'd been a cheerleader, but my jacket was a bit too snug to wear in public these days. For kicks and giggles, I'd attempted to pull on my cheer skirt. In addition to not buttoning, the lower half of my rear end peaked out from underneath it. Not safe or appropriate for public viewing.

Something caught Holden's attention, and I turned to see what it was.

Down on the track Blakesly looked to be throwing a tantrum, waving her hands, and yelling at her husband. Next to her, Regan appeared mortified. She slunk away, leaving her parents to hash out whatever had gotten her mother so upset.

"Holden, have you heard anything about Susan Prendergast and Chet Buchanan?"

"In terms of what?"

"They seem to be chummy, perhaps even romantically so."

Holden pulled his mouth into a grimace. "I don't see the appeal, but I guess since Chet's positioned himself as the leader of this anti-Margarita movement, he's likely to have stans."

"Stans?"

Holden blinked at me a couple times. "Stans."

I shook my head and held my hands up. "What does that mean? Like a fan?"

"This is why you need to join the rest of us in this millennium. Your outdated music tastes and current pop culture ignorance are doing you no favors."

"No good music's been created since the early 90s. I'll die on that hill."

Holden sighed. "A stan is more than just a fan. It's someone who becomes a little obsessive."

I returned my attention to the scene below, but the Whiteheads were no longer on the sidelines. They weren't in the bleachers either. The row where they'd sat with Wanda Harper and the Milners was empty. On the platform, a few students looked around, confused. One of them, a tall boy wearing blue and green striped overalls and face paint, seemed to be yelling at a cheerleader. She shook her head and shrugged her shoulders in response.

The cannon blast announced the beginning of the second half, and when the voice came on over the loudspeaker a moment later, it still wasn't Fred Harper.

"Third quarter action is underway. I'm Jermaine Pope filling in for Fred

Harper. Trey McClain with the kickoff return for about eight yards. The Cougars will start on their own twenty-three yard line."

I turned back to Holden. "It's kinda weird that Fred left the game at halftime, don't you think? And now all Chet's CROCCC cronies are gone." I indicated the stands. "Did I miss some creepy bat signal in the sky calling them all to a secret sedition meeting?"

"Maybe they were only here for the crowning ceremony, but now that's over, they took off."

"Or maybe they're going out on a vandalism spree."

Cole walked up with a hotdog in his hand. "Ms. O'Connell. Mr. Villalobos. Great game, huh?"

"Off-duty tonight?" I asked.

"I'm never a hundred percent off-duty. Did I hear a mention of vandalism?"

"Audrey's conspiracy theories getting the best of her." Holden chuckled.

"It's not a theory when the conspiracy's already been established as fact." I tried not to let my defensiveness undermine my point. "The members of CROCCC are clearly engaged in a plot to—"

"To what?" Holden asked. "Nothing's been established as fact other than that Chet and his cohorts despise Margarita and are unhappy about the land deal. There's no definitive proof they're behind the graffiti *or* the fires."

Cole nodded. "I've got to side with Holden here. There's nothing to officially connect Chet to the rash of destruction."

Overhead, the announcer's voice echoed. "Cooper Vargas with the sack on the Knights' quarterback." He paused. "Chief Loveland, please report to the courtyard. Chief Loveland, please report to the courtyard."

The three of us looked at each other.

Cole pulled his cell phone out of his pocket. "I missed a call from Bianchi. I guess I couldn't hear it over the crowd noise. I left my walkie home tonight."

He headed toward the courtyard with Holden and me hot on his heels. We got some curious looks from people as we rushed past them. The courtyard of the school was in the center, where the gymnasium and cafeteria intersected with the science and math wing. The focal point was a concrete fountain with a bronze cougar atop a mountain peak.

Water sprayed out from the fountain in an atypical way, drenching the cement surrounding it. Bianchi had already set up a crime tape perimeter, and a crowd had begun to form.

I gasped and covered my mouth at the sight that greeted us. Zeb Brandt's death may have been an unfortunate yet unintended byproduct of vandalism, but there was no mistaking this for anything but intentional.

Chet Buchanan was draped face-up across the back of the cougar while water from the fountain washed blood from what appeared to be a massive head wound.

Chapter Eighteen

"I'll bet you're really glad right about now that you took this job. You could've been directing traffic on a cattle drive."

Cole didn't seem to appreciate my sarcasm. "Despite what you might believe, I have experience with violent crime."

"But not like this, right? I mean, come on. You have to admit Chet was your number one suspect in the graffiti and the fires. Now he's been *murdered*. That just took this thing to another level."

"I have to admit no such thing."

"Any idea on the murder weapon?" Holden asked.

"Not yet. Something heavy."

Cole walked over to Bianchi and said something quietly to him. Bianchi nodded his head, took one last glance at Chet Buchanan's dead body, and left.

"Hopefully, he's sending Bianchi to talk to the members of Chet's cult. Oh! That reminds me." I strode in Cole's direction.

"Audrey…" Holden's voice held a warning as he followed close behind me.

Cole observed my approach and heaved a sigh.

Unnecessary. "The theatrics are a bit much, don't you think?" I asked. "I'm coming to give you some information I just remembered."

"What's that?" He crossed his arms and spread his feet apart in his standard tough guy pose.

"Earlier tonight, I witnessed an interesting interaction between Chet and Susan Prendergast."

"Who's Susan Prendergast, and what do you mean by interesting?"

"She was my high school French teacher sophomore year. Still works here. Kind of a floozy. I think they were involved." I raised and lowered my eyebrows suggestively.

"Involved beyond CROCCC?"

"She isn't a regular commenter on CROCCC. If she were, I would have noticed. I wasn't a fan of hers, and she wasn't a fan of mine either. One day, we showed up wearing the same skirt, and that really seemed to irritate her. Maybe she was embarrassed she got exposed for shopping in the junior's department. After that I could do no right in her eyes. She gave me a C minus even though she'd known I had mono for three weeks, and I did extra credit to make it up." The repressed indignance of my fifteen-year-old self rose within me.

Holden made a face. "You got mono when you were only a sophomore? Who were you kissing?"

"That's a myth. I got it from my best friend Meryl, who got it from her sister. Her sister got it from kissing her boyfriend, but I'd put money on her boyfriend having gotten it from Bella Andrade. Bella had it twice that year, and she wasn't above using her ample bosom to lure other people's boyfriends into the back seat of her Volkswagen Beetle. It was a red one with a black roof and eyelashes to make it look like a ladybug."

"I didn't know it was even possible to get mono twice." Holden cocked his eyebrow.

"I didn't think so either, until it happened. The rumor, ironically, was Bella got it the second time from the *new* boyfriend of the girl whose ex-boyfriend had gotten it from Bella in the first round, which is what had led to their breakup in the first place."

Cole cleared his throat. "As fascinating as this Jerry Springer-esque walk down memory lane has been, Audrey, I can't even remember what you were trying to tell me in the first place."

"Oh, uh, Susan and Chet. They seemed very cozy."

"Okay. And?"

"Nothing. I thought you should know. She might have been the last person to see Chet alive."

"Noted. Anything else?" Cole observed me fiddling with my car keys. "Clearly, there's something else. You always fidget when you have something to say but aren't sure how it will be received."

I gave a look of surprise. "I didn't know you paid that much attention."

"I'm a trained observer. It's my job to study everyone. Spit it out."

"Well, I'm not a trained observer, so I hesitate to bring this up because I may be totally off-base."

Cole flung his head back in impatience.

Holden put his hand on Cole's shoulder and gave it a quick pat. "Welcome to the club, man."

"What club might that be?" I put my hands on my hips.

"It's more of a vaudeville routine, really. The Audrey O'Connell Show: a one-woman act in nine parts. I believe we've come to the part where Audrey makes a lot of assumptions while simultaneously dismissing them. Actually, it's more of a circular thing. If you give her long enough, she'll talk herself out of it without you having to say anything at all."

I blinked at Holden. His teasing seemed almost hostile.

Cole cleared his throat again. "Sounds like maybe you two have some things to talk out privately. In the meantime, Audrey, what was it you wanted me to consider?

I didn't want to cry in front of these two men, or the crowd which had gathered. I widened my gaze in an effort to hold back the tears and took a deep breath.

"Holden's right. I probably need to think it through a bit more before I recklessly cast aspersions on anyone. I'm, uh, I'm gonna go. Let me know what you find out, okay?"

I turned on my heel and rushed across the corridor. Holden's voice calling my name echoed across the courtyard. I didn't stop.

* * *

I'd schlumped onto the sofa and pulled the blanket over my head when the doorbell rang. I heaved a sigh and pulled it off again.

"Go away, Holden!"

"Audrey, come on. Let me in so I can apologize properly."

I closed my eyes for a moment, torn about how I wanted to respond. On the one hand, I hated having unresolved conflict. On the other, I tended to have less emotional bandwidth for difficult conversations on days when I've seen dead bodies up close. I'd come to know this about myself.

"Audrey, please." His voice had softened enough to break my will.

I stood and walked from the sofa to the front door. I was greeted by Holden's remorseful face.

"Look, you don't need to apologize. I get why you still resent me. I jumped to conclusions and accused you of murdering one of your oldest friends. That's not something which can be easily forgotten or forgiven."

"May I please come in?"

I ushered him into my living room and indicated the sofa. I flipped the fireplace switch, and immediately a warm glow cast across the room.

"I can't believe this is the same house. The place was a disaster when Renee and Marcus lived here."

How could I forget? It had been the stuff of nightmares. "I keep reminding myself they had three young children with all their toys and stuff. It's only me, and I'm still eating off disposable plates at the kitchen counter. One of these days, I'm going to have to invest in some furniture."

Holden sat on the sofa and patted the cushion next to him. I eyed him suspiciously.

"I don't bite."

I laughed. "I don't believe you." I sat next to him anyway.

"I was out of line tonight. I was teasing, but I heard myself say some pretty unkind things, and I'm sorry. You didn't deserve that."

"I appreciate the apology. Like I said, though, I don't blame you for still being hurt."

"That's just it. I think there's more to it than some hurt feelings about you accusing me of murder. After you left tonight, I sat in my car trying to understand why I acted like such a jerk to you. I think I've figured it out."

"Are you going to let me in on it?"

He rubbed the back of his neck. "I've told you this before, but I'm not someone who's super comfortable talking about feelings. With you, well, I thought you understood that about me and were able to read me better than most. So, when you accused me of murdering Marcus, it was like you didn't know me or understand me at all. After the anger subsided, I guess the residual hurt is a little stronger than I'd realized."

"That's totally understandable. I wish I could take it back, undo the pain I caused you. My gut told me you weren't capable of hurting anyone, much less your friend, but I was confused, and I got a little turned around. At that point, I didn't know who to trust."

"I know. It doesn't make rational sense for me to be upset with you when I was caught up in the very situation that had led to Marcus's murder. I'm gonna keep working through it. I needed you to know what I'd figured out, and I'm sorry I embarrassed you in front of Cole."

I furrowed my brows. "What does Cole have to do with it?"

"Really, Audrey?"

"Really, what?"

Holden chuckled. "There's obviously something brewing between you."

"The man can barely tolerate me."

He shook his head. "For someone so smart, you sure can be clueless sometimes."

"In the interest of keeping the peace, I'm gonna take the compliment part of that statement and ignore the insult. You're welcome."

He clapped his hands together. "I'm gonna let you get some rest. The way things have been going around here lately, we all need to be our most alert selves."

"Now that Chet is dead, maybe things will settle down."

"That's a great thought, except you're forgetting something."

"What's that?" I asked.

"Chet, the leader of the movement to undermine Margarita, is dead, and his position is about to be filled by someone else, maybe even his killer. There's always someone waiting in the wings to take a leader's place, and oftentimes, the replacement is even worse."

Chapter Nineteen

By the time I hit Abigail's for coffee around ten-thirty on Saturday morning, word had already gotten out about Chet. The post-homecoming night win glow, which usually permeated Chattertowne had been dimmed by a morose haze of grief, despair, and unease. Regardless of where people stood regarding Chet and his antics, no one had wanted him dead. Except, of course, his killer.

Vivienne came bounding into the café about ten minutes later like a woman on a mission, that mission being less than the fifteen minutes late for our meet-up. I wasn't known for my punctuality, and I gave grace for anything up to that point, but I considered anything over fifteen minutes late without a good reason to be rude, and my sister was well aware of that fact.

"You took that corner like you were on a roller coaster."

She was winded. "I would have been on time, but I ran into Jenna Doyle walking her dog, and she filled me in on what happened to Chet. She said Fred Harper called her first thing this morning to say he'd had an official visit from Cole Loveland."

I looked around to see if anyone was listening. "I have questions, but I don't want to ask them where someone might overhear. Can we take our coffees to go?"

"I suppose. I was kind of hoping to do a little people-watching, but I guess I can do that as we walk. Ooh! I know. Let's walk down to the gazebo."

Once we had our cups in hand, we strolled over to the walkway, which paralleled the Jeanetta River. I rarely used the path, but it was surprisingly busy for a dreary day, with rain threatening at any moment. The gazebo itself, however, was empty. Inside, it had benches where we could sit and look out at the river.

Twice a year, the Jeanetta rolled at its peak. In the spring, the mountain runoff swelled the river to nearly overflow, and in the late fall, often around Thanksgiving, heavy rains brought flooding to the valley. That was one of the reasons CROCCC was so unhappy with the land deal. The new parking lot would be underwater at least once each year.

"So," Viv said. "You have questions?"

I shifted on the splintery bench. "How well do you know Jenna?"

"Oh, uh, I would say more than an acquaintance, not quite a friend."

"What does that mean?"

"She was a freshman or sophomore when I was a senior, but she was the kind of girl who got invited to upper-grade parties, if you know what I mean."

"Not exactly." I took a sip of my latte.

"She's pretty, for one thing. Also, she liked to have a good time. I think she might have even dated a college guy when she was a sophomore."

"So, she's into older guys. That is interesting."

Viv's gaze narrowed at me. "What does *that* mean?"

"You said Fred Harper called her first thing this morning. Why?"

"Because he got a visit from the Police Chief."

"Yes, I know, but why did he call her? On a Saturday?"

"What are you implying?"

"I'm wondering if perhaps there's more going on there than boss-employee."

"Maybe, I don't know. What does that have to do with Chet Buchanan being draped across the fountain like cheap lingerie flung over a lampshade in a seedy motel?"

I tilted my head to look at her, my left brow arched.

"What?" Her cheeks tinted pink. "Too much?"

"I've never heard you use similes, particularly tawdry ones."

Viv shrugged her shoulders. "With Lacey…unavoidably detained," she began.

"I wouldn't exactly call her detainment unavoidable, but go on."

"It's a turn of phrase. Anyway, I've got a lot of time on my hands and some sexual feelings which aren't getting satisfied anytime soon."

I put my palms over my ears. "Lalalalalala. I can't hear my baby sister talking about sex."

She rolled her eyes. "Grow up, Audrey. I'm nearly thirty. As I was saying, I've decided to take up writing romance novels. I've read through pretty much every lusty book at the grocery store, and I've come to the conclusion I think I can do it better."

"Really! I didn't know you liked to read, much less write."

"I didn't have a lot of confidence in that area growing up. It was always your thing. I kind of figured there could only be one writer in the family. I've surprised myself, though. I'm actually enjoying it."

"Good for you! I'm not a good fiction writer, so I find those who can create something out of their own imagination to be impressive."

Vivienne's blushing pleasure at my compliment crept from her hair's part to the base of her throat, which she cleared.

"Thank you. Let's get back to Jenna and Fred, though."

"Right. Well, Fred does the announcing at the football games. He did the first half, and when they were back for the second half, after the homecoming queen was crowned, someone else was in the booth calling the play-by-play. Chet was found dead in the third quarter. Fred doesn't have an alibi."

"I still don't get what that has to do with Jenna, even if they were having an affair."

"It doesn't, necessarily, but the possibility of an affair came up in my meeting with Holden and Cole. I initially thought she was too young for him, but maybe not."

"I guess him calling her could indicate a closer relationship than normal boss-employee. I wouldn't expect to get any early morning call from Cole unless it was an absolute emergency that required me to do something. So, you're leaning heavily in the direction of Fred as a suspect, and so must Cole. Why?"

"I can't speak for Cole, but I ran into Chet yesterday afternoon during the Cavalcade. I'd just passed Fred, Levi, and some other guy I've taken to calling the weasel."

"Because…?"

"Because he looks like a weasel. I don't know who he is. Fred was really angry and yelling at Levi. I bumped into Chet—literally I ran smack into him— and when he caught sight of Fred across the street the vibe was not friendly. Which is weird, I think, since Chet was the ringleader of CROCCC, and Fred and his wife are active members."

Viv sat up straighter. "So, Fred gets mad at Chet about something, and he kills him. Maybe Chet made a pass at Jenna, and Fred got jealous."

"Maybe. There are a couple other things to consider. Last night, Chet was with Susan Prendergast at the game. There seemed to be something going on between them."

"Eww. Do you mean the Drama teacher who thought it was cute to make flirty comments to students?"

"She taught French, also."

"Oh yeah. You took useless French instead of Spanish like everyone else. How'd that work out for you?"

"Trilling your Rs when you order margaritas at Los Frijoles doesn't exactly justify your three years of Spanish either, Viv."

"Touché. That's French, right?"

* * *

After my hangout with Viv, I decided to go see Cole. Unfortunately, he wasn't at the station. The weekend receptionist, Charlotte, used to have Viv's job but when it was time for her to come back from maternity leave, she'd decided she didn't want to be away from her baby that much. Charlotte's husband had agreed to watch the baby while she worked a couple short shifts on Saturday and Sunday.

"How's the baby?"

Charlotte smiled broadly. "Believe it or not, she's practically a toddler. She's been walking for a few months now, getting into everything. I'm sure poor Kyle is in over his head, but he's her father. He should be able to handle her for a few hours a week."

"Amen. Do you have any recent photos?"

She pulled out her phone and scrolled. "Do I have photos," she scoffed. "Oh, I have photos. Here's one we took at the sunflower fields a couple weeks ago. It's a little blurry, but you should be able to tell how big she's gotten." She held up her phone for me to view through the Plexiglass.

I squinted at the picture of Charlotte holding her daughter in what looked to be a sea of giant golden blooms atop thick green stalks. Next to her was a man I assumed was Kyle, her husband. Beady eyes punctuated his long face.

"Is that Kyle?" I asked.

"Yes. He was a good sport that day. It wasn't his preference to spend his day off from work tromping through muddy flower fields, but he humored me."

"I feel like I recognize him. Could you zoom in a little bit?"

"Oh, sure." She zoomed in the photo and held it up again. "Maybe you've seen him around town. He's a roofer with Harper Construction."

I'd seen him in town, alright. Kyle was the weasel who'd been hanging out the day before with Levi and Fred.

Chapter Twenty

"Y ou've reached Chief Cole Loveland of the Chattertowne Police Department. I'm unavailable to take your call. If this is an emergency, please dial 911. Otherwise, leave me a message, and I'll get back to you as soon as possible." Beep.

"Hey, Cole, it's Audrey O'Connell. I stopped by the station, but you weren't there. I heard you paid a visit to Fred Harper this morning. I think I have some information you might find helpful. I'm headed down to the new parking lot to look around again. Give me a call when you get a chance."

I drove down Main and took a right onto Jeanetta River Road. I hadn't come this way since the fire had taken Zeb's life. I pulled into the parking lot where the collapsed mill lay in ruin. Further down the road were the remains of the Brandt barn, along with a makeshift memorial of signs, cards, and flowers.

My mother had told me Edna was unable to fly home in her emotional state, so she was still in Arizona at her sister's. She'd directed Kohler's mortuary to cremate Zeb. In a brief macabre thought, I'd wondered whether that was even necessary, considering he'd died in a fire. I decided some questions were best left unasked and unanswered.

I pulled into a parking spot close to the entrance. Although the lot was completely empty, when I got out, I instinctively locked my car. I walked the perimeter looking for evidence or clues, even though there had been two separate incidents investigated by police and dozens of people had crowded the area a few days prior to watch the mill fire burning. I wasn't even sure what exactly I expected or hoped to find.

Mostly what I found was garbage. Cheesy puff wrappers, dented aluminum soda and beer cans, and a used diaper. Sometimes I really wondered about what went through people's heads when they did stuff like that.

Closer to the river, the debris looked less like litter left behind by a crowd, more like remnants of a fishing expedition. A few hooks, an empty bait package, and a couple half-drunk water bottles had sunk into crevices between the rocks. Blackberry shrubs clung to their booty of fabric scraps which had been snatched from the clothing of passersby.

Just as I was about to move along, a small beam of sunlight broke through the overcast and reflected off something metal deep inside the sticker bushes. I leaned over, trying to see what it was, most likely another aluminum can. I got down on my knees to get a better look, but the sun had disappeared again behind the clouds, and the underbrush became heavily shadowed. Not wanting to actually crawl into the thorny vines, I lay flat on my stomach and hung my head over the edge of the pavement to carefully retract the shrubs.

A car pulled into the parking lot. Awkwardly, I tried to crane my head around to see who it was, but from my angle I struggled to make out anything other than it was a dark SUV. The car drove slowly and stopped behind me. My heart began to beat wildly.

The driver rolled down their window.

"Looks like I got here just in time." Cole gave a low, rumbling laugh.

I rolled over onto my back and sat up, resting my palms behind me. "Very funny. You could have called me back. You didn't have to come down here."

"And miss the show? What were you doing, may I ask?"

"I thought I saw something in the blackberry bushes and was trying to extricate it without tearing up my arms. New car?"

"Mine's in the shop for maintenance." Cole turned off the car's engine and opened the door. "What did you find?"

"There's a decent amount of trash out here, so it's probably nothing."

"You're doing it again."

"Doing what?"

"Talking yourself out of something you believe to be true. I've noticed you do it a lot, even before Holden mentioned it last night. You need to learn to trust your own instincts."

"I'm a work in progress on that front, I'm afraid. Anyway, I thought I might have seen a spray paint can."

Cole looked skeptical. "We've done a pretty thorough search of this lot. Twice, actually. Once on the day of the graffiti and then after the mill fire. I'm sure my guys would have found evidence if it were here."

"I realize that, but this is pretty far down in the bushes, under lots of thorns. I only noticed it because there was a brief moment of sunlight which reflected off the metal."

"Probably a soda can, then."

"Could be." I shrugged and wiped the asphalt off my hands. "That's what I was trying to determine when you arrived."

Cole reached into the SUV and pulled out a large, heavy flashlight.

"Let's have a look, shall we?" He got down on his hands and knees, shining the light into the thorny abyss. "Well, what do you know? Audrey, can you reach into the glove box and pull out a latex glove?"

I stood and leaned into the car, draping myself across the driver's seat and center console in order to reach the compartment. "I think this may be the first time I've ever retrieved actual gloves from the glove box." I wriggled my way back out of the car and turned around to see Cole watching me.

"That was a sight to behold."

I dropped the glove into his lap. "How about you keep your focus on the task at hand and off my derriere."

Cole blushed and cleared his throat. "Right. Sorry. Totally inappropriate." He pulled the glove onto his right hand and rolled back onto his stomach. "Do you mind holding the flashlight for me?"

I got down on my knees next to him and took the flashlight. "Is this good?"

"A little to the left. Actually, could you move in closer?"

I leaned in until I was right above him. I tried to control my breathing, so it didn't sound like he had a predator hovering over him. He strained to reach the item, grunting as he did so. If anyone happened upon the scene, it would be pretty tough to explain.

"I've…just…about…got it. It's right beyond my fingertips."

I leaned closer and tipped my upper torso forward, trying to get a better look. Unfortunately, I leaned a smidge too far and found myself toppling into the thicket.

"Ahh! Cole! Ouch!"

"Audrey!"

He reached out to grab my hand, but as he tried to pull me out, the thorns dug in deeper.

"Ouch!"

"Sorry."

I tried to lift my head, but it was as if talons had gripped my ponytail, holding me into place. "Get me out of here!"

"I'm trying! Hand me the flashlight."

I did as he asked. He pulled again at my arm, but only succeeded in causing my legs to drop further into the bushes.

"I'd always imagined if I were going to be swallowed up by the earth, it would be in quicksand."

Cole stopped pulling on me and dropped his face into his forearms, trying to suppress a laugh. He didn't succeed. Soon, we were both laughing, mine interspersed with cries of pain whenever I got poked.

"I think you're going to have to call for help."

He nodded. "I think you're right. Wait here."

I guffawed in response. Like I had a choice.

He let go of my hand, and surprisingly, I didn't fall too much further. The toes of my shoes touched the ground.

Cole spoke into his car radio. "Dispatch, this is Chief Loveland. I need assistance at the new parking lot on Jeanetta River Road. I have a female who needs extrication from some blackberry bushes."

The radio squawked. "This is dispatch. Did you say extrication from blackberry bushes?"

"Yes, ma'am. Probably a ladder truck will do."

"Putting out the call now."

There was some rustling, and then a shadow came across me. Cole stood over me and dropped something. It was a latex glove.

"Since you're already down there…"

* * *

CFD Chief Norvald thought the whole thing was hilarious. He'd ridden along in the ladder truck so he could see firsthand the predicament I'd gotten myself into. They'd called in the utility crew to trim away the shrubs until I was able to break free and onto the rocky beach below. I'd managed to grab the spray can, which was indeed hot pink construction spray paint. Cole had bagged it in an evidence container in hopes it might have fingerprints. Although it had rained pretty heavily a couple times since the first graffiti incident early in the week, the can had been protected by the bushes.

The medic looked me over and declared me mostly injury-free, save some nasty scratches. He advised me to buy an extra-large tube of antibiotic ointment and to keep an eye out for any signs of infection.

The fire truck and ambulance left, but Cole and Sergeant Tony Bianchi remained.

"You look like you got into a scuffle with a bobcat." Tony shook his head. "Let me rephrase that. You look like you lost a scuffle with a bobcat."

I grimaced. "I'd consider it a success. After all, I was able to retrieve what could turn out to be a key piece of evidence."

Bianchi bobbed his head. "We'll see."

"Audrey, in your voicemail, you said you had some information to share about the investigation?" Cole said.

I smacked my forehead and winced. "Ow. Yeah. So, when I went to see you at the station earlier, I was hoping to get some insight on why you'd gone to talk to Fred Harper this morning."

"Yeah, how did you find out about that?" Cole rubbed his chin.

"I had coffee with Vivienne this morning. She told me she was running late because she'd run into Jenna walking her dog. Jenna said Fred had called her to tell her you'd paid him a visit."

"That's interesting. Maybe the idea of Fred and his bookkeeper being romantically involved isn't completely absurd."

Bianchi's dark brows furrowed. "What's this now? Harper and Jenna Doyle?"

"Maybe. It was one of the things that came up as a possibility." I shrugged. "It might have a totally innocent explanation, though."

Bianchi turned to Cole. "So, what, you don't run things by me anymore, you run them past the media first? I thought you didn't trust her. Now, it seems you trust her more than me."

I interrupted before Cole had the chance to respond. "It wasn't like that. Holden and I—"

Bianchi's laugh was hollow. "Villalobos? Lemme get this straight. You're discussing case theory with a two-bit reporter and her criminal boyfriend, but not your top detective?"

Cole jerked his head to look at me at the word *boyfriend* before turning back to Bianchi. "Tony, you're right. I should have done a better job of keeping you in the loop. It won't happen again."

"Wait, so that's it? He calls me a two-bit reporter, and you're gonna act like it's no big deal?"

"Audrey…"

"Nope."

I marched over to my car and got in. I gave them one last glance before driving out of the parking lot. I used enough restraint not to make an obscene gesture, but I might have stuck out my tongue. Just a little.

Chapter Twenty-One

I stomped around my house rage-cleaning, ranting to myself about how infuriating it was that all I was trying to do was help, but because Cole insisted on keeping everything close to the vest and controlling all the information, Bianchi had thrashed me, and Cole had done nothing to defend me. I piled three full bags of trash next to the front door and marched upstairs to start on the bathroom. As I scrubbed my tub, I mumbled an angry diatribe against stupid boys' clubs and their stupid egos.

"Two-bit reporter? I'll give you two bits of advice." Scrub-scrub. "How about, never trust a man in power, and, while you're at it, develop a good poker face?" Scrub-scrub. "How about, if you can't join 'em, beat 'em?" Scrub-scrub.

The front doorbell rang. I wished I had one of those high-tech doorbells which sent me video of whoever was on my front porch so I could decide if I wanted to open it or not. Instead, I had to tromp down the stairs and look through the peephole. Two very contrite-looking men stood on the other side.

I yanked open the door. "I became a human pin cushion in order to help you solve this case. I don't deserve to be disparaged because I happen to be standing in the crossfire of your poor workplace communication."

Bianchi bowed his head, and Cole nodded.

"You're right. We've both come here to tell you we're sorry. Right, Tony?"

Bianchi raised his chin to look at me with a sheepish expression. "I was frustrated, it had nothing to do with you."

Cole pointed to my living room. "Can we come in?"

"Fine."

I led them into the house.

Bianchi looked around. "Damn! It's like a whole different place since the last time I was here." He scrunched his nose. "It smells like bleach, not rotting bananas." He plopped himself onto my sofa and rested his arm across the back. "Look at me. I can sit without moving laundry or worrying about what's hiding underneath the cushions."

The last time Tony had been to the house was before I'd moved in, during the Marcus Washburn murder investigation when Marcus's wife Renee had gone missing. I'd helped Tony rifle through their hoarder's mess to try and find information that would result in solving the case.

"When I'm upset, I tend to clean." I indicated the trash bags next to the front door. "I don't usually have trash piled up. I was just about to take it outside."

"Let me help you," Cole said.

"It's fine. I can do it myself."

"Audrey."

I blew my hair out of my face. "Fine."

Cole and I carried the trash bags through the front doorway and to the side of the house. The area didn't see much sun, so the walls were covered in moss and mildew. Cole hoisted one of the bags into the gray bin.

"I try to avoid coming over here. I probably should have someone out to clean it. Is that something a landlord should be doing? I've never rented a house before, only apartments and those landlords were pretty useless."

As Cole was about to launch a second bag into the bin, he stopped, cranking his head in bewilderment. "Shh."

"You did not just shush me. I mean, I know I talk a lot, but—"

"Audrey, I'm not insulting you. Do you hear that?"

Straining to hear what had garnered his attention, a quiet but high-pitched shrill noise echoed nearby. "That screeching sound?"

"Yes." He began looking around for the source.

"I hear it now. What is it? And where's it coming from?"

We followed along the side of the house until we reached the back corner.

The sound grew louder.

"What *is* that?" he asked.

"I think it's raccoons."

"How can you tell?" His tone was skeptical.

"Because." I returned his condescension. "It's definitely not cats, and 'possums hiss."

Growing up, opossums would try to shelter in our garage over the winter. I'd had more than my fair share of opossum encounters, including a standoff with an adolescent in our root cellar. He'd been perched on a can of Campbell's chicken noodle soup, hissing at me like I was the one invading *his* space.

Cole looked around and grabbed a pole, which looked to be the vestige of a disintegrated rake. He whacked it against the house. A ferocious growl emitted from the crawl space. Both of us hightailed it out of there and into the driveway.

"Holy sh—" Cole stopped himself from cursing. He bent over at the waist to catch his breath.

"I'd be making fun of you for running away if I hadn't peed a little myself. It's like the bowels of Hades has opened underneath the house. I'm calling my mother. They've dealt with this before. She'll know what to do."

My parents were remnants of an era when people still used home phones. "Hey, Mom, I need your help. I have a raccoon problem."

I explained to her what Cole and I had experienced.

A clucking came across the line. "Oh, dear. Would you like me to send your father over with the trap?"

"That'd be great."

"It's unusual for raccoons to be under the house. They like attics and high places. Are you sure they're raccoons? Can you see how many animals are there?"

"No, we barely walked near them, and one growled like it came from the underworld. The other sounds were more screechy."

Cole pulled out his phone, presumably searching for exorcism techniques.

"Definitely sounds like a mama raccoon and her babies." There was pride in her voice at being an authority on all things trash panda.

"That was my thought."

Cole stared at me, awaiting the end of my conversation.

"Okay, Mom, thanks. Tell Dad the sooner, the better." I ended the call.

"So?"

"My father's bringing his raccoon trap."

Cole blinked slowly. "Your father has his own personal raccoon trap? Do you guys like, uh, eat roadkill?"

"This isn't *Deliverance*. Geez, Cole. They've had raccoons a few times, plus 'possums. My dad bought a trap instead of waiting on Fish and Game to deal with it. The question is, what do we do with them once they've been captured?"

My imagination envisioned opening the cage door in a meadow filled with wildflowers where the mother raccoon and her adorable babies look at me gratefully before scampering off to a blissful life. The reality would likely be closer to a scene from *The Ghost and The Darkness*.

Holden looked at his phone again. "It says here raccoons aren't usually found under the house. They like to give birth up high to protect their babies. Finding info on getting a mama and her babies out from under the house is proving nearly impossible, since it almost never happens."

"What do we do with them?"

"This says you have to euthanize them."

"I'm not killing them!"

"It's legally mandated."

"Why can't we relocate them?"

"I have no idea."

"Unacceptable," I said. "I'm calling Fish and Game right now." Several rings trilled before a woman's voice came on the line. "Hi, I have a question regarding raccoons. Are you who I need to speak with? With whom I need to speak, I mean."

The woman sounded wary and tired when she replied. "Depends, what's your question?"

"Say, hypothetically, one discovered a family of raccoons under their house…"

"You wouldn't find a family of raccoons under your house. Raccoons give birth up high," she interrupted.

"Yes," I said through gritted teeth. "I'm aware. But let's imagine a mama couldn't get to the attic and gave birth under the house. And let's say, again hypothetically, one was able to cajole the little family into a metal cage, by baiting it with marshmallows or cat food. What then should a person do to relocate said family?" I utilized all the patience and composure I typically reserved for conversations with my mother.

"You can't trap them," she said. "It's illegal under Washington State law to trap without a license. Do you have a license?"

"Of course not. So, what do I do? Hypothetically."

"I have the names of a couple licensed companies who can come out. They'll remove 'em for you according to regulation."

I got the impression she couldn't care less what happened to the critters living under my house.

"Alive, right?"

Silence.

"They won't kill them, will they? I can't bear the thought of someone bashing this mama and her cubs over the head because they had the misfortune of being born here."

More silence.

Finally, she said one word. "Kits."

"Pardon?"

"Raccoon offspring are called kits, not cubs."

"Whatever, it's not okay to kill a mama and her babies."

"Ma'am." Her voice dripped with disdain. "Raccoons are harbingers of disease, particularly rabies. There's a slight possibility the animals can be relocated, but it would need to be at least ten miles from the property. Once a female raccoon has nested someplace, that's her place, and she will be back. It's important to cover whatever entry point you think they may have used. The best thing you can hope for is they'll leave of their own accord. Once they've vacated the premises, it's vital you block the access point."

Cole waited for me to finish hollering my frustration after I'd ended the call.

"So?"

"So, I need to text my mother to inform her my dad's trap is illegal."

She sent back a poop emoji in response.

I called the first number the woman at Fish and Game gave me. "I'm not killing 'em. I want 'em to go away."

"We prefer the term euthanize, and I hope you're referring to a rodent and not your husband." After the situation had been fully explained to him, he clucked sympathetically. "Raccoons don't typically nest under the house."

I grimaced. "I've heard. However, these raccoons are non-conformists."

He said the soonest he could come was a week from Tuesday, and this whole thing was going to cost around $500 without any guarantee of success. I explained I couldn't wait that long, not to mention I didn't have an extra $500 lying around to remove raccoons from what was technically someone else's house. I didn't have high hopes Renee would cough up the money, either.

While dialing the next number and waiting for someone to answer, Tony appeared in the doorway and made a *what's happening* gesture with his arms out and his palms facing up. Cole walked over to him. I couldn't hear what they were saying, but he appeared to be filling Tony in on what was going on because Tony laughed and shook his head before beckoning me to come over to the front stoop.

"Hang up the phone, Audrey. I got a guy," he called out to me.

"You got a guy? What does that even mean?" I walked over to them.

"I got a cousin who owns a pest control company. He owes me a favor. I'll have him send one of his guys over."

Sure enough, less than fifteen minutes had passed before a white pickup truck arrived sporting a giant cockroach painted on the door. I'd been waiting inside with Tony and Cole, who'd cracked open a couple beers and made themselves comfortable.

I headed outside to greet the man. He lumbered out of his vehicle with great difficulty. He plodded toward me, flustered and sweaty from the short journey up the walkway. His top three buttons were undone on his white polo, gaping open to display ample chest hair.

"You think you got a raccoon?" he asked. "I haven't dealt with raccoons before. I only been with the company five months."

This was not reassuring information.

"I hear, though, that raccoons don't usually give birth under the house. They like the attic."

"You don't say." My desire to scream was tempered by my desire for him to solve the problem. "It's over here."

I lead him to the spot where demonic growls had previously been emanating. Of course, now it was quiet. I pointed to the area near the back corner of the house. He worked his way into a squatting position, an awkward endeavor, before popping up quicker than a jack-in-the-box. I wouldn't have thought he was capable of such nimble movement if I hadn't seen it with my own eyes.

"Yep! There's raccoons under there!" He said this like he was providing me new information.

"I know."

"I been called out on raccoons twice before, never found any. But you definitely got raccoons! She was lookin' at me!"

"Yes. I know." Deep breath.

"Well, see, the problem is, my boss, Nicky Bianchi; he's the only one licensed to deal with raccoons, and he's leaving on vacation tomorrow." Blink. Blink.

My silent stare must have made him uncomfortable because he shifted his substantial weight from one foot to the other.

"Let me call the home office, see what they say."

"Good idea."

Based on his side of the phone call, he had nothing good to tell me.

"Yeah, so, what happened was, and he's real hesitant to say this, but, uh, you're gonna hafta call someone else."

Funny, I'd already come to that conclusion.

Setting aside my pride, and fully prepared to beg, I called the first company again. Unfortunately, the answer didn't change.

"Sorry, this has been a crazy month. Lots of ants, late wasps, and now raccoons *under* a house. They never give birth under the house."

I swore under my breath the next person who uttered those words to me would find him or herself with a rabid raccoon problem of their own. I'd trap 'em and drive 'em to their house myself.

"Why do people keep saying that? It's obviously not true, because right now, I'm dealing with a mama raccoon who doesn't give two shits about where she's supposed to give birth. She's only trying to protect her babies."

"I understand this is stressful for you. Let's get you scheduled for Tuesday. I'll try to talk to Travis and see if he can squeeze you in between appointments tomorrow. I doubt it, but I can try. In the meantime, try a predator spray."

"Predator spray?"

"Like coyote urine. It'll make her think there's a predator in the area, so she might move the babies. Have you seen how many there are?"

"No. I haven't seen them, only heard them. The other pest control guy who was here said he looked right into two beady little eyes."

"She might not move 'em until their eyes are open."

"Which is?"

Three weeks. The answer was three weeks. I walked back into the house to find Cole and Tony huddled, whispering in the kitchen.

"Tony, your guy was useless. I called the first company back, and that guy suggested predator spray."

"Predator spray?" Cole repeated.

"Coyote urine."

"Where are we supposed to find coyote urine?" Cole's face scrunched in disgust.

Tony wheezed with laughter while I searched for predator spray on my phone.

"It isn't easy to acquire. I could track a coyote and get it to pee in a cup in less time than it'll take to get the strong stuff shipped here."

My statement caused Tony to lose it all over again. My phone rang in my hand.

CHAPTER TWENTY-ONE

"Hey, Dad, did Mom give you my message about trapping wildlife?"

"Yes, and I don't care; it's a stupid law. However, because you're there with the Chief of Police, it's probably best to play by the rules. I had a thought. Ever heard of Operation Nifty Package?"

The clandestine tone of his question caused me to giggle. "It sounds like a porno."

I now had both Cole and Tony's rapt attention. I put my father on speaker for them to hear.

"A while back, Operation Nifty Package was the U.S. government's attempt to flush out Panamanian dictator Manuel Noriega from his refuge and hiding place in a church. Navy SEALs shone spotlights and blared rock music to get him to leave the church in surrender. I believe they also played the *Howard Stern Show*. That's gotta be a violation of the Geneva Convention's approved tactics of torture."

"So, what are you proposing? Blasting music under the house to get her to leave?"

"Exactly. And lights, strobe lights would be best, to make the environment uninhabitable."

"The complete Morrissey collection should do it. She'll put on a black trench coat and slump away wearing a morose expression."

"I don't know who that is. Give me a couple hours, and I'll come set it up."

He seemed surprisingly unbothered by the idea of rousting rabid varmints out from the crawl space of the home I was renting from the widow of my ex-boyfriend. On the contrary, he instead sounded quite excited at the prospect.

"Now, gentlemen," I said to Cole and Tony. "Are you ready to hear what I've been trying to tell you all day?"

Chapter Twenty-Two

"Lemme get this straight," Tony said when I'd finished filling them in on what I'd discovered. "Our weekend receptionist Charlotte Murphy's husband, Kyle, the one you call the...?"

"Weasel."

"Weasel. You saw him hanging around with Fred Harper and Levi Scott?"

"Yes, but it's not only that they were hanging around together. Fred was yelling at Levi while the weasel, Kyle, stood by. I know Kyle does subcontracting work for Fred, but this didn't look work-related. He looked like Fred's henchman."

Cole inhaled a deep breath and slowly released it. "I'm not questioning what you saw. I'm questioning your interpretation. Did you actually hear them discussing anything specific?"

"No, but right after that, I ran into Chet. He and Fred made eye contact. It didn't look friendly. The weasel and Levi, who'd just finished being chastised by Fred, both mean-mugged Chet also. Which, when you think about it, made no sense until Chet wound up dead."

"How do you figure?" Cole tilted his head, causing his cowboy hat to go askew.

I resisted the urge to adjust it.

"Chet was the ringleader. He was the head of CROCCC, and he's had all these little minions running around, doing his bidding, and stirring up trouble. So, for Fred, Levi, and the...Kyle... can I just call him the weasel? It would be easier if I could stick with that."

Bianchi chortled. "I certainly don't care. You can call him whatever you want."

Cole gestured for me to continue without commenting on the nickname.

"For those three to be turning on Chet, something had to have happened. Maybe they're upset because Chet started the Brandt fire. Zeb was beloved in this town, even if some people were mad at him for selling the land."

"And, at a premium, I might add," Tony said.

"But he didn't need the money. He said he did it because the town needed it. I don't think he did it for the money at all."

Cole was quiet for a moment. He twisted his mouth to the side. "Maybe I've been looking at this all wrong. Let's say Chet is directly responsible for the graffiti and the fires. If that's the case, he'd escalated a political fight to arson and murder. Manslaughter, at the least. They probably didn't sign up for all that. They joined CROCCC because they wanted to keep city government accountable to its citizens, for the benefit of Chattertowne, not to heap destruction upon it."

"I see where you're coming from," I said. "But I'm not sure I agree with your premise. Sure, they're invested in their view of how Chattertowne should operate, and maybe in their minds, they have good intentions, but that doesn't give them the right to harass and malign Margarita and the city council. To me, they come across like toddlers throwing tantrums because they aren't getting their way. Frankly, I'm not sure I'd put anything past any of them."

Bianchi leaned forward and rested his hairy forearms on his thighs with his hands clasped together. "I think we have to consider the fact all three of us are outsiders. Cole is from Wyoming. I'm from the East Coast. Even though you grew up here, Audrey, you left for quite a while, and you think more like an outsider than a townie. We need the perspective of someone on the inside."

"You know who's been unusually quiet these past few days?" Both men looked at me expectantly. "Hiram Kaiser. He's Chet's—*was* Chet's right-hand man. I don't think I've seen him since the night of the city council meeting. I got the impression he wasn't an independent thinker, that Chet was the one pulling his strings. I've heard rumors Chet had plans to get Hy elected to mayor as a political puppet, since he was unable to run himself. He might be a good resource for understanding the heart of CROCCC and its members."

Cole raised his eyebrows and nodded his head. "You make a very good point." He looked at Bianchi. "What do you say? You wanna ride over to the Kaiser place and have a chat with him?"

Bianchi scowled. "Can't. I've got dinner at my in-laws tonight, and before that, I've gotta get down the Halloween decorations from the attic. Pia's been harping on me for a week."

Cole looked at me. "Audrey?"

"Let me get my coat. And I need to text my mom so she can tell my dad I'll be gone when he gets here with the raccoon relocation gear."

"Why not text your dad?"

"He's got a flip phone. My mom bought him a smartphone a couple years ago. The first day he had it, he'd dropped her off at a baby shower. She called him to come pick her up, but he couldn't figure out how to answer it. The phone's been in a drawer ever since. He went back to his old phone which has the sound quality of two tin cans and a string."

"I don't blame him. I feel like smartphones have made everyone a little dumber. At least he has an excuse for why he doesn't use social media. I'm constantly having to justify it." Cole finally adjusted his hat.

"You don't have any social media?"

"I've got enough people showing up at my office telling me how I'm failing this town and should go back to where I came from. The last thing I need is another place to be insulted on a regular basis."

Tony chuckled as he stood near the door. "Hate to tell you this, man, but that ship has sailed. Just because you're not showing up to your own roast doesn't mean it ain't happening."

* * *

We rode in Cole's car over to Hiram's place in the northwest part of town, what one might call the other side of the tracks, except trains hadn't rolled through town in more than thirty-five years. There was a newer rail trestle that cut across some of the Brandt fields south of the river.

Hiram and his wife Anna had no children. She did the scheduling for his plumbing business and ran a ballroom dance studio out of their home, a chocolate brown 1970s split level with a steep driveway.

Cole and I parked on the street and trudged up to their front porch. In the driveway was a blue minivan that had seen better days, Hiram's work truck, and a newer model sedan. The sedan looked out of place, with its tan leather interior and lack of dents.

Cole knocked on the door, as the doorbell was clearly out of order and looked to have been for some time. From within the house, classical music was being played at nearly full volume.

"I didn't take Hiram for a man with sophisticated musical taste," Cole mused.

"I don't think he is. Anna teaches ballroom dancing, mostly to engaged couples who don't want to look foolish at their wedding reception when all eyes are on them for the first dance."

"Makes sense." Cole knocked louder, and the music paused.

Heavy footsteps were punctuated by the opening of the front door. Hiram stood in the entryway wearing coveralls. He wiped his hands on a dishrag which looked long overdue for a wash.

"Afternoon, Chief Loveland." He looked at me and then back at Cole. "What can I do you for?"

"Do you mind if we come in? We wanted to speak with you about Chet Buchanan."

I wasn't keen on going inside, as the smell of some sort of animal—wet dog, perhaps—had wafted toward me. Hiram gave a slow nod and jerked his head to indicate we should follow him. The living room was tidy, but not clean. The rust orange and brown floral sofa harkened to an era when design trends were geared toward a more earthy yet gaudy style. The carpet was also brown, a practical shade to cover whatever messes were made by whichever creature was responsible for the smell.

"Have you lived here long?" I eased myself onto the sofa which, upon closer inspection, also featured rustic barns among the flowers.

"About four years." Hiram sat in a coordinated wingback chair across the ornately carved coffee table from me. "I inherited the place from my grandmother, along with her car."

"Ah." Bingo.

"Hy, I'm not sure if you heard…"

Hiram interrupted Cole. "About Chet. Yeah." From another room, the music began again. "Sorry about that. My wife has a young couple in there learning to waltz."

"No problem. I can imagine this news has been pretty tough on you. You two seemed quite close."

Hy sighed and scrubbed his cheeks with his palms. "We were, yes. He was like a brother to me."

"Hy."

He turned to look at me, his eyes red-rimmed. His face sagged with grief.

"What do you know about CROCCC's involvement with the graffiti?"

"I'm sorry, Chief, but why is she here? Is this an interview for the paper or for the investigation into the murder of a political martyr?"

"Martyr!" I couldn't withhold my scoff.

Hy's chin jutted out in defiance. "Yes, martyr. He had a righteous cause, and it cost him his life."

Cole leaned forward. "Tell me about the cause. I want to understand."

He looked earnest, but I suspected he was manipulating Hy into revealing more than he intended.

Hy frowned. "You're kinda putting me in a tough spot."

"How so?"

"Any information I provide to you in order to solve Chet's murder may be used against CROCCC, which was his baby. It's like I'm betraying him no matter what I do."

Cole nodded sympathetically. "I get that, but if helping find Chet's killer exposes CROCCC, maybe CROCCC wasn't as much an ally to Chet's cause as he believed."

I had to give it to Cole. He was handling the situation with skilled deftness.

Hy's face revealed his inner conflict. He looked tortured, pulled in multiple directions. I shifted on the sofa and felt something brush against my ankle.

"Ack! What the heck was that?" I pulled my feet up onto the cushion and tucked them underneath me.

Hy, still mired in his distressed processing, said, "Probably Laverne or Shirley," like that explained anything at all.

"Excuse me?"

"I guess it could be Squiggy," Hy said.

Cole looked at me in complete bafflement. "Do you have any idea what he's talking about?"

"Well, I know they're characters in a seventies sitcom my mom used to put on. She has a penchant for old TV shows and movies. I'm guessing that's not what he means."

Even though he hadn't appeared to be listening to us, Hy looked up at me with surprise. "Usually, when people hear their names, they've never heard of that show. I'm impressed."

Knowing retro pop culture was a point of pride for me, so his validation would typically make me preen a bit, but I still didn't know who *they* were.

"Hy, are Laverne and Shirley—"

"And Squiggly," Cole inserted.

"Squiggy. Not Squiggly. Are they…cats?"

"Ferrets."

I closed my eyes and took a slow, deep breath. My nostrils punished me with the musky scent of rodent. The music shut off again, leaving the living room silent except for the tick of a clock. Only it couldn't be the tick of a clock because it wasn't regular enough.

"Hy?"

"Hmm?"

"Are you telling me there are three ferrets underneath me right now?"

"Probably. Sometimes, they sneak into the dance studio, but they like the dark warmth the couch provides."

I closed my eyes again. I knew better than to take another deep breath. I reopened them to find both men staring at me.

Pull yourself together, Audrey. "Sorry. I'm not really an animal person, and

I've spent the past couple hours dealing with a mama raccoon who gave birth to a bunch of babies under my house."

"Really?" Hy grunted. "Raccoons usually prefer the attic."

Cole interjected before I completely lost it. "Where are we at, Hy? Are you going to help us solve this thing?"

Hiram sighed. "If it were me, I'd be looking at Fred Harper."

Cole and I exchanged looks, both of our eyebrows raised.

"I thought Fred and Wanda were active members of CROCCC, Wanda especially," I said.

Hy's mouth collapsed in on itself in a pucker. He nodded. "Wanda especially is right."

Cole tilted his head, and once again, his hat shifted but didn't come off. Maybe he used some sort of adhesive.

"Are you saying something was going on between Chet and Wanda?"

"Look, Chet was my best friend, but he wasn't an angel. He had a certain charisma that drew people to him. I have no doubt if they'd have let him run for mayor, he'd have won. He was passionate about reforming Chattertowne's city government, and he knew how to get people on board with his vision. You could say he developed a bit of a messiah complex, and with that, there will always be some who become fully devoted to the leader."

"You're being kinda cagy." Cole narrowed his gaze at Hiram. "Why do I get the feeling there's more to this than what you're saying?"

"Probably because there is. I reserve my right to keep things to myself that I deem irrelevant to your investigation. I will say this, though. He treated CROCCC like his own personal harem. He had his pick of the crop, married or not."

"You mean pick of the CROCCC." I was the only one who laughed at my joke.

"Hy, do you believe Fred had any knowledge of the affair?"

Hy grunted a laugh. "He'd have to have been blind not to know. Wanda fawned over Chet like he was the second coming. And if Fred had found out how...*committed* to the cause his wife had become, it stands to reason he might have confronted Chet about it, don'tcha think?"

"It does stand to reason." Cole nodded.

"What about Jenna?" I asked.

Hy wrinkled his forehead. "Jenna Doyle? What about her?"

Cole cleared his throat and sent me a look that told me he didn't want me to continue with my line of questioning, so I adjusted my tack.

"Would she be a good source for information about Fred?"

"Maybe. Dunno. She's not involved with CROCCC at all. In fact, she's anti-CROCCC. Chet kicked her out of the group within a day after she'd joined for trolling all his posts."

"Trolling?"

"Cole doesn't do social media," I explained to Hy and then turned to Cole. "Trolling is when someone comments on each post, heckling the OP and the other commenters."

"Like an online gnat." Hy nodded.

"I understand what trolling is. I'm curious how she trolled. Also, what's an OP?"

"Original poster." I turned back to Hy. "It seemed like Chet posted most of the content. Is there some unwritten rule that other people weren't allowed to post?"

"He was the admin of the group, so he had full control over what posts were approved or not. He had it set where every post required him to accept the posting. If he chose not to, they'd vanish. It was how he kept the group on message."

"I've seen you comment on stuff, but rarely post. As his right-hand man, I'd think you'd be a more visible participant."

A glimmer of scorn passed across his face. "I don't know what you're trying to accomplish here, Audrey, but Chet was my friend. I won't have you sowing seeds of division between us, even with him gone. He valued my opinion."

"I didn't say otherwise. So, you were more of the man behind the curtain?"

"I guess you could say that."

Cole stood and held out his hand. "Well, Hy, I appreciate you taking the time today."

Hy got to his feet and shook Cole's hand. "Of course, Chief. Anything I can do to assist in bringing Chet's killer to justice."

I looked up at both of them. "I guess that means we're leaving." I began to stand, and something furry skittered across the back of my legs and ran across the room. I jumped up and yelled. "Ahh!"

The critter stopped, as if surprised by my outburst, and stared at me with its tiny dark eyes.

"They won't hurt you, Audrey. They don't bite. Usually."

I didn't wait to find out and rushed toward the doorway. Cole followed behind me but turned to face Hy as we reached the front stoop.

"One more thing, Hy."

"Yeah?"

"Now that Chet's gone, who's in charge of CROCCC? I'd think you'd be next in line."

Hy rolled his shoulders back and lifted his chin. "It'll be up to our members to decide who Chet would have wanted to replace him, but I have no expectations about it. If they do indeed choose me, I'll humbly accept."

"Right." Cole touched the tip of his hat. "Well, thanks again. I'll be in touch if I have any further questions."

Hy nodded and shut the door behind us.

As I hoisted myself into the seat of the SUV, Cole said, "You hungry? I was thinking maybe we could hit the drive-thru at Julia and Jack's for burgers."

"Can I get a raincheck? I just wanna go home and wash the ferret off my ankles."

Chapter Twenty-Three

"So, what's the plan?" I asked.

Cole hadn't said a word since we'd left Hiram Kaiser's house. "What do you mean, what's the plan? My current plan is to drive you home like you asked me to do."

"I changed my mind. We should go see Fred Harper."

"I've already visited him once today."

"Yes, but that was before Hy spilled the beans about Wanda and Chet. Do you think spray painting hateful graffiti turned them on? Like, 'Ooh, Chet, I love how you wrote nasty stuff about the mayor. Kiss me, you fool!'"

We were stopped at a red light, which allowed Cole time to turn his full body to look at me bemused. "Have you considered therapy?"

"Yes. That doesn't mean my point is invalid."

"Your point being?"

"When you talked to Fred this morning, was it because of Wanda? No. It was because Fred had left the game at halftime with no explanation, which also means he doesn't have an alibi for the time of Chet's murder. Now we know he has a pretty strong motive as well. Means, motive, opportunity."

The light turned green, and Cole began driving again. At the next intersection, instead of going straight toward my house, he made a left.

"Does this mean we're going to talk to him?"

"It does, but I'm gonna need your help on something."

"What's that?"

"While I'm chatting with Fred, I want you to see if you can get any indication from Wanda about the situation with Chet. Anything at all. Just please be subtle. I know that's going to be a challenge, but try."

"You think I can't be subtle?"

"Audrey, you're about as subtle as a rodeo clown."

"So, what you're saying is, you find me immensely entertaining?"

Cole shook his head and chuckled. I took that as a yes.

The car turned into a long gravel driveway about a mile and a half out of town.

"Cole."

"What."

"The Harper property is awfully close to the trail's rest station. In fact, I think this may be the driveway that SUV entered that day I came out to take photos of the graffiti and got spooked."

Cole's expression turned serious, with his mouth tightly set. At the end of the driveway, a giant two-story four-bay garage stood to the left, while on the right was a craftsman-style home. The garage doors were all closed. In front of the garage were several trucks that listed Harper Construction on the side. We pulled to a stop, and two golden retrievers bounded out to Cole's side of the car. The dogs barked, but they were more barks of enthusiastic greeting than intimidation.

Cole got out and rubbed the head of one of the dogs. "Hey, boy. Did ya miss me? Good boy."

"I see you made a friend."

"Dogs aren't as judgmental as people. If you're kind to them, they accept you just as you are."

"Sounds like somebody should get themselves a dog."

"I will, eventually. I've only been here six months. I'm still settling into my job and my house."

A figure appeared on the front porch. It was Wanda, and even from a distance of twenty feet, it was obvious she'd been crying. Her face was splotchy, and her eyes were red-rimmed. She looked like she'd aged five years since I saw her sitting in the stadium the night before.

"Back again so soon?" Her voice was hoarse, like the inside of her throat had been rubbed with sandpaper.

"Yeah, I had a couple things come up today that I need a little clarification on. Mind if we come inside?"

Wanda didn't answer; she just turned her back on us and went inside. The only hint she'd left was an open door, which we took to indicate she was inviting us into the house.

The kitchen was fairly small, with only a two-person dinette situated in the corner. The countertops were yellow tile, and the cabinets appeared to be original. A lace valance hung above the only window, which was positioned above a wide porcelain apron sink. The appliances were modern in contrast to the rest of the kitchen.

Wanda leaned against the sink with her arms crossing her midsection. "Fred just got home. He should be down in a minute."

The three of us stood silently in the kitchen as an awkwardness permeated the air. The only sound was water running through the pipes above us, and the click clacking of the clock, a black and white cat whose eyes flicked from side to side to the rhythm of its swishing plastic tail.

It looked paranoid and suspicious. I could relate.

There was a thundering on the stairs and then Fred appeared in the doorway. He jerked back at the sight of us.

"Why didn't you tell me we had company, Wanda? Nice to see you again, Chief Loveland."

Fred held out his hand, and Cole responded in kind.

"Sorry to bother you again, Fred. I was hoping maybe we could have another quick chat."

Fred nodded. "Let's go out back. I've got a man cave out there." He looked at me. "How about you two ladies stay here and have some tea or something." He walked through the doorway and gestured for Cole to follow him.

I swallowed the indignation at his dismissive misogyny that rose in my throat. No point in throwing a fit when my intention was to talk with Wanda alone anyway. Still, his attitude did not sit well with me, and I couldn't resist throwing a quick jab. "Sure thing, Fred. I'd hate to have my brain get overwhelmed and confused by all that manly talk."

Fred glanced over his shoulder like he was unsure how to take my statement. Cole patted him on the back and nudged him outside.

I lowered my chin and gulped down the irritation I felt toward Fred. Whether Wanda had been romantically involved with Chet or not, Fred was still her husband. I needed to keep her talking, and insulting him could make her defensive.

"Sorry about that." Her voice was timid. "Fred can be a little…insensitive."

Her tone certainly wasn't what I expected from the author of those inflammatory online CROCCC posts. Gone were the aggressive, angry barbs she'd lobbed at anyone who'd dared to challenge Chet. Gone was the menacing glare I'd seen her direct at Chet and Susan. In their wake was a broken, sad woman who couldn't even meet my gaze. I had to wonder if Chet's murder had sapped her of her ferocity, or if she was just another example of a keyboard warrior who had little fight when she wasn't hiding behind a computer screen.

"Wanda, I can tell that Chet's death has hit you hard. I wasn't a fan of his, but I know you two were close."

Her gaze cut to mine. "What are you talking about? What have you heard?"

She jerked her head to look in the direction of the back doorway where Fred and Cole had exited. Her attention turned back to me, and I caught something in her eyes that looked a lot like fear.

"You've been an active member of CROCCC. I assume your husband was as well?"

Wanda's gaze darted around, seemingly waging a battle within herself, trying to figure out what she should and shouldn't say. "Fred doesn't really do Facebook. He got himself added to the group, but he never really participated. I think he was more of a lurker."

"So, even though he wasn't posting, he was aware of what was going on in the group?"

"Yes. I found that out one day when he came home from work and mentioned some comments I'd made on some of Chet's posts."

"Do you think Fred was jealous of Chet?"

"I know what you're doing, Audrey, and I don't like it one bit. You are trying to pin Chet's death on someone in CROCCC, just like you tried to pin the graffiti and the fires on us, but you're looking in the wrong direction. The person you should be investigating is Margarita Guzman."

"From what I've been told, CPD has yet to rule anyone out as a suspect. I'm curious, though, why you would point the finger at Margarita."

Wanda said nothing, but she pulled her cell phone out of her pocket. She entered her password and began sorting through, looking for something.

"Here it is. Blakesly's latest article."

She thrust her phone screen into my face.

When reached for comment, a Chattertowne Police Department spokesperson said that they hadn't determined whether all these incidents had been committed by one person, or multiple people. Here at the Chattertowne Clarion, we believe that the responsibility for the rash of criminal activity can be placed squarely on the shoulders of our maladroit mayor, Margarita Guzman, whose sheer ineptitude is eclipsed only by her propensity for playing the victim. If Chief Loveland truly wants to discover who's behind these acts, he need only climb one flight of stairs to find her.

She let the hand holding her phone drop. It hung at her side as she stared at me, waiting for some sort of response.

"That's quite a take. Does Blakesly have anything to back up her accusations?"

Wanda looked at her screen. "And I quote, 'I've spoken with a reliable witness who claims they saw Mayor Guzman driving out of the Chattertowne High School parking lot just before the end of halftime at Friday night's homecoming game.' End quote."

"That's strange. I didn't even see Margarita last night."

"I'm telling you. Margarita Guzman is diabolical."

"That seems a bit harsh. Regardless, I have a question to ask, and I don't think you're gonna like it."

"This day just keeps getting better. What is it?"

"There have been some rumors that perhaps you and Chet were…closer than the other members of CROCCC. Last night, I saw Chet with Susan Prendergast, and you didn't look very happy about it."

"Get out."

"Wanda, I—"

"I said, get out!" She pointed at the door. "Now!"

"I'm only trying to get to the truth."

She screamed at the top of her lungs, so I skedaddled out of there. Cole and Fred appeared in the gap between the house and garage.

"Everything okay?"

"I think I've worn out our welcome."

Cole shook his head.

"Thanks a lot, Ms. O'Connell. Now I get to deal with a hysterical wife." Fred grimaced at me.

I gave both men a sheepish look.

Cole and I piled back into his car. The dogs whimpered at the driver's side, so he rolled down his window and reached out a hand to pet them goodbye. He drove back along the gravel driveway until we reached the highway.

"I'm sorry. I was being subtle, but then, I guess I wasn't subtle enough."

"It's fine."

"I did get her talk a little about CROCCC. I guess Blakesly has a new post up on her site, accusing Margarita of doing all this to make herself look like a victim. I tried to talk to her about Chet, and that's when she blew a gasket. I shouldn't have pushed her."

"Audrey, it's okay."

"Why are you being so calm and nice about this?"

"Because, while you were riling up Mrs. Harper, I was slow-walking Mr. Harper to a near-confession. I think we're on to something here."

Chapter Twenty-Four

Sunday morning, I slept until nearly nine-thirty. Being someone who needed a good eight to nine hours of sleep per night, the week's events, which had brought with them a lot of late nights and early mornings, had taken their toll.

As I stumbled downstairs to the kitchen to make coffee, I scrolled through all my unread emails. Most touted Columbus Day sales.

"Why is that still a thing?" I grumbled.

I set my phone on the counter and tried to concentrate on measuring the correct amount of grounds into my French press. I'd been a Keurig drinker for years, which had made my life much easier, but the coffee never gave me the boost of a steeped pot. I needed the strong stuff.

The phone buzzed with a call.

"Morning, Viv."

"I didn't wake you, did I?"

"No, I'm making coffee."

"Wanna walk the trail today? I hear the humpies are running."

"At the end of September? Isn't that a little late?"

Humpies were a type of pink humpback salmon that showed up every other year in Puget Sound tributaries such as the Jeanetta River, which ran along the south end of Chattertowne and jutted north along the trail at the east end of town. On some years, as many as two million humpies entered the river, but typically, that was in late August or early September.

"I don't know. Maybe it's because of climate change. I heard some guys at the station talking about how they'd planned to be in their fishing boat all weekend, and their wives weren't super happy about it."

"Remember how dad used to pack a picnic lunch and take us down to the river so we could count how many jumped out of the water as they went by?"

"Yeah, only I'd usually lose count after a hundred."

"Give me an hour. I need to shower, and then I'll pick up some sandwiches on my way to your apartment."

"Sounds good. I'll have an Italian grinder. Extra meat and cheese."

I poured my coffee and added four drops of liquid stevia. I followed that with a large dollop of whipped cream because life is about balance.

"What's it like to have a metabolism that allows you to eat whatever you want and not gain an ounce?"

"I've never given it much thought."

"Exactly. See you at ten-thirty."

After my shower, I pulled on my warmest yoga pants, a long-sleeved shirt, and my favorite burgundy plaid flannel because it made my eyes look greener and less of a muddied hazel.

I grabbed my purse, my keys, and the overflowing trash bag from the kitchen. On the side of the house, I flung the bag into the garbage can and heard a familiar growl.

My father had set up a floodlight on a tripod and aimed it under the house. He'd called me the night before to say the mama raccoon hadn't left as a result of the songs he'd played from the list I'd sent him. I'd created a Spotify playlist of my least favorite music, but it turned out she'd been unbothered by it.

There was no accounting for taste.

I crouched down until we were eye-to-eye. The light shone in on her and her babies. Her eyes glowed, but the babies' were still sealed shut.

"Hey there." I used my most gentle voice.

She growled again.

"Look, I don't want to cause any issues for you, but I can't have you growling at me every time I come to take out the trash."

She blinked back at me.

"What's your name, Mama? I feel like if we're gonna be housemates for the time being, I should at least call you by your name. Rachel? Rebecca? Ruby? How about I call you Ruby?"

She blinked again.

"Alright, Ruby, it is. I'm going out for a bit. If you decide to take your babies and move along, I promise it won't hurt my feelings."

I stood and waited for another growl, but she remained quiet. It felt like a truce.

"See ya later, Ruby. Or not. Your call."

* * *

"Looks like we weren't the only ones with the idea to come walk the trail." Viv adjusted the straps on her backpack.

On my way to Viv's, I'd stopped to pick up the sandwiches and water bottles she now carried in her bag. Her apartment was only a couple blocks from the trailhead, so I'd left my car there, and we'd walked. It wasn't sunny, but it also wasn't raining. In Washington, that was considered a good weather day, so the trail was filled with pedestrians, joggers, strollers, and cyclists.

"I'll bet things will clear out soon. The Seahawks play at one. Are you sure you don't want me to carry your backpack? It's gotta be heavy."

"This is nothing. I did Mike's Maniacal Bootcamp a couple weeks ago. He made us trudge up Paradise Hill with two ten-pound dumbbells in our packs."

"Why would you pay someone to put yourself through that kind of torture?"

"I need the distraction. Keeps my mind from counting the minutes and days until Lacey's first parole hearing."

A cyclist whizzed past us, nearly clipping my left arm.

"Remind me to tell Cole he needs to start patrolling this trail. One of these days, those cyclists are gonna run someone over. They go highway speeds where families walk, and they never call out 'on your left' like they're supposed to."

"I'm sure he'll put it on his list of priorities somewhere between trying to stop a string of vandalism and arsons," she said drily.

As we reached a shaded area underneath the overpass, I pointed at the river. "I think I just saw a fish jump. Come on, let's check it out. This seems like as good a spot as any to eat."

We walked past the edge of the trail, across the grassy area with a picnic bench, and snaked our way down the dirt path to the rocky area below. A fallen tree provided the perfect natural bench for us to sit and watch the fish making their way upstream.

"Did you remember to tell them no tomatoes?" Viv asked as she handed me my sandwich.

"I don't think it comes with tomatoes."

Viv sighed. "It does. You have to ask them not to put them on."

She unwrapped her giant meat-and-cheese-filled sandwich, opened the bread, plucked the tomato out, and flung it into the water.

"Viv!"

"What?" She took a bite, filling her cheeks.

"You can't just throw things into the river."

"It's natural. Biodegradable."

I shook my head.

About thirty yards downstream, an aluminum fishing boat appeared. Viv and I were somewhat hidden by the brush, but we had a clear enough view of the three familiar faces.

Fred Harper, Levi Scott, and Kyle Murphy, aka the weasel.

"Let's drop anchor here," Fred said.

I turned to look at Viv.

"What?" she asked at full volume.

"Shh. I don't want them to see me."

We sat quietly and observed the scene.

"Kyle, did you bring marabou jigs, hoochies, or buzz bombs?" Fred asked.

"What?" The weasel's voice echoed down the channel.

"Shh!" Levi scolded. "You're gonna scare the fish."

"Kyle, are you saying you didn't bring the lures?" Fred said.

CHAPTER TWENTY-FOUR

"I brought salmon eggs."

"You brought salmon eggs…to catch salmon." Levi threw his hands in the air. "Geez, Kyle. They're not cannibals."

"Deke at the bait shop said salmon eggs or sand shrimp."

Fred shook his head. "Deke at the bait shop is notorious for giving bad advice to newbies on purpose."

"Well, look, how was I to know? You guys never told me what I was s'posed to bring. You said we're gonna have a meetin' about Chet, and we're goin' fishin'."

"Shhh." Levi hushed the weasel again. "Keep it down, will ya? The whole point of comin' out here was so we could talk without pryin' ears and eyes, like at Abigail's."

Viv took too big of a bite of her sandwich, and it caught in her throat. She covered her mouth and gave a muffled cough. I looked through the brush and saw Levi staring in our direction with his hand out, telling the others in the boat to stay quiet.

He seemed to be scanning the shoreline, but the brush provided us enough cover to stay hidden from view. We were stock-still, frozen in place.

"Whatcha see, Levi?" The weasel asked.

His gaze darted around, and I thought of my encounter with Ruby, the raccoon, and Laverne and Shirley, the ferrets. I'd certainly had more than my fair share of beady-eyed encounters for one week.

After a moment of holding our breaths, Levi turned back to the other men in the boat.

"Nothing. Must've been a bird or something."

"Look, I don't have long. Wanda wants me back in time to go watch the game at her sister's house. What are we gonna do about this little situation we've gotten ourselves into?" Fred asked.

Levi shook his head. "I dunno, man. I mean, I say we just lay low for a bit, see what shakes out."

"What about Hy? Something's gotta—"

Up on the trail above us, a noisy family passed by, making it difficult to hear what Fred was saying. I leaned farther back on the log, hoping to get enough of a visual that perhaps I could read his lips. Unfortunately, my propensity for clumsiness sent me ass over teakettle down the embankment, and an unintended squawk flew out of my mouth as my legs flung into the air. There was a quiet stillness while everyone around me processed what had just happened.

"Audrey?"

I looked up to see Levi standing grim-faced in the fishing boat with both hands on his hips. Behind him, Fred was crimson from the neck up, and the weasel stared at me with beady little eyes and a sneer on his face.

Chapter Twenty-Five

"Oh, hey, Levi. Out fishing for humpies?" It wasn't easy to play it cool when your feet were above your head.

"What are you doing?"

"Viv and I were just having a picnic." I turned to my sister and gritted my teeth. "Say hi, Viv."

She waved. "Hi, Levi. Long time, no see."

"Seems kinda strange, Audrey, us running into each other twice in one week after not seeing each other for years."

"Isn't it funny how that happens?" I scrambled my way into an upright position.

"You sure you aren't following me?"

I sucked in a breath and was about to protest when he laughed.

"I'm kidding. Maybe it's just fate telling me to ask you out again."

Viv made a snorting squeal akin to a pig stuck in the mud. Fred's face furrowed, and the weasel's eyes grew larger than I'd ever seen them.

"Oh, uh, you think so? What'd you have in mind?"

"What are you doing?" Viv hissed.

"I've got a plan," I said under my breath.

"Dinner tonight? How about Martini's at six?"

"Sounds good. I'll meet you there."

"Lookin' forward to it."

As that felt like a dismissal, I gathered up the bag of sandwiches and stood.

Viv looked up at me. "I guess that means we're done here?"

"Apparently, I've got to get ready for a date."

Viv returned my wry smile with a scowl.

* * *

The phone rang twice as I stepped out of the shower. By the time I got to it, it had stopped ringing. I had four missed calls from Holden.

"What's so urgent?" I asked when he answered my call.

"Your sister has informed me you plan on going out with Levi Scott tonight."

"Jealous?"

"Concerned."

"About?"

"I'm one hundred percent certain you're not dating him for his wit and intelligence. You're up to something."

"What if I am? It's not like he's gonna throw a fit in the middle of Martini's."

"He's taking you to Martini's? That's a bit above his pay grade, isn't it? Does he even own a collared shirt?"

"How would I know? We were sixteen when we dated. His entire wardrobe consisted of jeans, t-shirts, and Speedos."

"Speedos?"

"He was the captain of the swim team, remember?"

"We didn't run in the same circles. And you're avoiding the question."

"Levi knows something. Maybe a little food and wine will get him to tell me what he knows."

"No offense, but I've seen you attempt to use your feminine wiles to elicit information before, and it didn't work. What makes you think it will now?"

"Actually, it did, but let's not get into that. Levi and I have history, which means I know effective tactics to utilize."

Holden stayed quiet a moment and then cleared his throat. "I'd rather not hear about that. Also, Levi may not be the guy you used to know."

"I guess I'll find out. I need to finish getting ready. I'll talk to you later."

"Audrey."

"What, Holden?"

"Stay safe."

"I will."

* * *

I arrived inside the restaurant just after six to find the lobby full of waiting guests. The area was separated from the dining room by a long glass-enclosed fire feature. Levi was nowhere to be seen. Memories of being stood up on Valentine's Day flitted through my mind, but I pushed them away. A lot had changed since then. I wouldn't want to be held to account for every dumb thing I did in high school, so I needed to afford him the same grace.

I checked with the hostess, but she said Levi hadn't yet checked in for his reservation. She informed me they had a strict fifteen-minute hold policy before releasing the reservation, and they wouldn't seat me unless all members of the dining party were there. Planning had never been his strong suit, so the fact he'd made a reservation at all was surprising to me.

I wedged myself against a pillar in the corner near the firebox and watched, mesmerized, as the flames licked the metal coil, twisting across the glowing faux coals. My mind drifted to the events of the past week, beginning with the first graffiti incident at the parking lot and culminating in Chet's murder.

It didn't make sense. How had the prime suspect ended up a victim? Had I gotten it all wrong from the beginning? Had I allowed my bias against Chet's ideology, tactics, and personality to taint my view of the evidence? Possibly, or perhaps, he'd lost control of the monster he'd created, and it had turned on him.

I checked my phone. Sixteen minutes past six. Levi had officially entered the rudely late zone. The red heart-shaped box with the orange discount sticker flashed unbidden in my mind. I'd have been more annoyed if it weren't for the pit I felt in my stomach. The way things had been going recently, someone not showing could be a very bad sign.

At six-twenty, I decided to leave. That's when Levi rushed into the restaurant.

"Audrey, I'm so sorry! I got held up on a project I'm working on, and when I went to call you, I realized I didn't have your number." His face was flushed, his hair damp, and his gaze wide.

"Everything's okay, I hope." I hadn't yet decided if I was going to punish him for his tardiness or let him off the hook.

He furrowed his brows and shook his head. "Yeah, Fred just wanted to go over some things." He paused. "On the condos, we're putting up over on Madeleine Ave."

I'd once watched a documentary about human lie detectors. One of the easiest ways to determine if someone was being truthful was by watching to see if their body language matched what they said. His affirmative statement, coupled with a negative head shake and expression, led me to believe that, no, everything was not all right.

Levi lying to me wasn't a dealbreaker for this date. However, it gave me greater motivation to figure out what he knew.

I checked my phone and gestured to the guests waiting in the lobby. "We've missed our reservation, and this place is packed. The last walk-ins were given a forty-five-minute minimum wait time. Wanna go somewhere else?"

Levi's shoulders slumped. "I'm sorry. This is so lame. Not getting things off on the right foot, am I?"

"How about this? We can walk over to Julia and Jack's, grab some burgers and fries, and take them to the gazebo."

"I'd like that. Thanks for being so chill about it."

Levi's chocolate eyes seemed to melt, and I felt a twinge of long-dormant spark, that indelible mark young love tends to leave on our hearts. No matter how badly things ended, he'd been my first love.

We walked the four blocks to the burger stand and then back down to the gazebo overlooking the river. I sat crisscross applesauce on one bench, and Levi sat adjacent to me on another.

"Do you remember that swim meet in Portland?" He took a bite of his deluxe burger.

"Of course. That was when you first hinted you might want to ask me out."

CHAPTER TWENTY-FIVE

"Meryl was pushing me to do it, but I wasn't sure."

"Because you didn't know if you liked me?" I popped a fry in my mouth.

"No. Because I always felt dumb around you. You liked to throw out these seventy-five cent words that I'd have to look up in a dictionary if I wanted to know what you were talking about."

"Can I let you in on a secret?"

He held his chocolate shake in the air to indicate for me to continue.

"That was a coping mechanism for my own insecurities."

"What did you have to be insecure about? You were popular and pretty and smart. You were a cheerleader."

"I didn't feel popular. I became a cheerleader because I wanted to be involved, but I had major imposter syndrome the whole time. I'm not terribly coordinated. I felt less pretty, less skinny, and less…enthusiastic than the other girls. In case you haven't noticed, I'm not exactly the kind of girl one might call perky. I was smart, so I played it up—to the point of obnoxious at times, or so I've been told."

Levi blew out a slow whistle. "I had no idea you felt that way. I was too busy trying to play it cool."

"It worked. I thought you were super cool."

"Really?"

"Absolutely."

Levi bobbed his head to the left with a bemused expression.

"That is until you broke my heart." I slurped my milkshake through the straw.

"That's not how I remember it."

I shrugged my shoulders. "No matter." I inhaled a deep breath. "Levi, I gotta ask. What are you doing, hanging around guys like Chet and Fred and the-we—uh, Kyle Murphy?"

He narrowed his gaze. "What were you gonna say?"

I looked at him wide-eyed. "What?"

"You were gonna say something about Kyle."

I mumbled a verbal shrug.

"Audrey."

"I've kind of taken to calling him the weasel."

Levi threw his head back and laughed. "Oh, geez." He wiped a tear. "It's actually perfect. He's pretty much a rodent. I certainly wouldn't want him anywhere near my hen house."

"So, why all the huddled meetings?"

Levi appraised me. "Am I talking to reporter Audrey or girl I used to stick my tongue down her throat Audrey?"

I closed my eyes and grimaced.

"Oh, come on, it couldn't have been that bad."

I opened my eyes and blinked at him. "I guess I'm always going to be both."

He spun a fry in the air. "I'm not hanging with Chet. No one's hanging with Chet because, well, you know."

"People are getting hurt. Two people are dead. This isn't a joke, Levi."

His expression hardened. "Trust me, I understand the seriousness of this."

"Do you know who killed Chet?"

"I can think of a dozen people or more who'd want to get him out of the picture."

"Is there going to be a power play for CROCCC?"

"Audrey, if you think this is about being the public face of some online forum for whining, you really haven't been paying attention."

Chapter Twenty-Six

When I got home from my so-called date with Levi, I drew myself a bubble bath and grabbed the latest Chesapeake Bay mystery by Judy L. Murray. I was so ensconced in the book at first that I didn't pay much mind to the rattling sound coming from outside.

I turned off the faucet and crooked my head to listen.

There it was again. It was a clicking mixed with a whoosh.

My first thought was it was coming from the side of the house near the trash cans.

"It's probably Ruby and her babies making a midnight escape." My trembling voice was unconvincing, even to myself.

Another noise. This time, it sounded like metal bouncing against cement.

I pushed the bathtub stopper to drain the water and wobbled to my feet with water and bubbles cascading off me. I grabbed a towel from the rack and wrapped it around myself. Gripping the edge, I gracelessly stumbled out of the tub, slipping a bit on the wet floor.

My phone was in the bedroom on the nightstand. I tiptoed over to it, feeling foolish but also terrified.

"I'm off duty." Cole's groan was muffled like he'd been awoken from a deep sleep with a pillow over his face.

"Look," I whispered. "I'm sorry to call so late, but it seemed silly to call nine-one-one over something that may turn out to be nothing."

"If that's the case, you shouldn't be calling me either."

"I was in the bath reading and I started hearing noises on the side of the house."

"It's probably just the raccoons."

"Maybe. Or maybe whoever conked Chet on the side of the head like a boat being christened has decided I'm getting too close to the truth and wants to shut me up. Permanently."

A heavy sigh snaked through the phone. "May I ask what book you were reading?"

"What difference does that make?"

No response.

"It was a mystery novel, if you must know."

"This is probably just a combination of feral animals and an overactive imagination."

"Would you please just come over here? I'm freaking out, and I know I won't sleep at all."

"The least you could do is put on some coffee for dragging me out of bed."

* * *

Cole knocked on the door following his investigation of the perimeter of my house.

"You didn't have to knock again." I swung the door wide open and ushered him inside.

"I wasn't going to barge in here."

He wasn't wearing his typical cowboy hat, and since he'd been in bed when I'd called, his dark blonde hair was mussed on one side. He rubbed his head self-consciously with one of his gloved hands like he sensed me looking at it.

"Anything?"

He gestured toward the sofa. "Mind if I sit?"

"Be my guest." I sat in the barrel chair across from him and swiveled back and forth, awaiting his assessment."

"Tell me again about what you heard."

"I had the bath water running so it was hard to tell at first, just racket of some sort. The last noise sounded like metal clanging against concrete."

Cole reached into his coat and pulled out a can of neon pink spray paint.

My mouth gaped. "Holy sh-nikes!"

"If I had to guess, our resident tagger came to give you a message, but ran off when greeted by your growling raccoon."

"Ruby."

"Hmm?"

"Her name is Ruby."

"She sounds like the chick from *The Exorcist*. What was her name?"

"Linda Blair?"

"Not the actress. The character."

"Dunno. Never seen it."

He looked at me with incredulity. "You've never seen *The Exorcist*? It's a classic!"

"I don't like scary movies." I shrugged.

"You were literally reading a scary book right before you called me."

"No, I was reading a cozyish mystery. It's intense but not scary. I did hear a hissing sound. Maybe that was Ruby scaring off my intruder."

"More likely, it was the spray can."

"What did it say?"

"Like I said, they didn't finish."

"What did it say?" I repeated.

He pulled his phone out of his pocket and swiped the screen to unlock it. He turned it to face me. The photo was dim, but the pink letters glowed.

You're ne

"You're ne? Lemme guess. They weren't trying to say I'm neat."

"Maybe *you're neurotic.*"

"Hardy har. It could be *you're neighborly.*"

We both stared at each other for a moment before breaking into laughter.

"You're Nebulous."

"Surprising choice. You think so? I've always thought I was pretty easy to read."

"I have a theory." He leaned back and crossed his arms, observing me.

"Do tell."

"Audrey, I believe you give the impression you're an open book, but that's a diversion so people can't read what you're really thinking and feeling."

My breath caught. A shiver came over me. I rubbed my arms with vigor.

Cole must have sensed my discomfort with the conversation because he shifted gears.

"I have a question about something you said earlier. What makes you think you're getting close to the truth?"

"For one thing, today I spotted Levi, Fred, and the weasel at the river."

"They didn't happen to be fishing, did they?"

"Yes, but I think they were also plotting. They acted suspicious when they spotted Viv and me."

"Anything else?"

"Is that not enough? Am I boring you? I don't appreciate the dismissive tone."

He arched his eyebrow but said nothing.

"Did they teach that technique in police school?"

"What technique is that?"

"The not responding thing."

"Something like that."

I shut my mouth and jutted my chin in a weak attempt to stonewall him back. Under his blazing scrutiny, I faltered.

"Tonight, when I was talking to Levi—"

"Tonight?" He sat upright and leaned forward. "You were with him tonight? Or were you talking on the phone?"

"I was with him. I ran into him at the river, and he asked me on a date."

"You went on a date with a murder suspect?"

"In your world, he's a suspect. In my world, he's a source."

"So, this wasn't about romance; it was an interview?"

"We may have reminisced a bit, but I don't want to go down that road again with him."

Cole's gaze flickered. "Again?"

"You didn't know we dated in high school?"

"How would I know that?"

"You seem to know things."

CHAPTER TWENTY-SIX

He cleared his throat. "Were you able to get any information?"

"I asked him why he's been hanging out with Fred and the weasel. He pretty much avoided the question. He did say that this isn't really about CROCCC."

"How could it not be?"

I shrugged. "I don't know. I asked him if he thought there'd be a power play for Chet's replacement, and he acted like I was being naïve."

"How so?"

"He said if I thought this was about CROCCC, I haven't been paying attention."

Cole rested his knuckle under his chin and squinted. After a few minutes, his eyes opened wide, and he sat up straight.

"What?"

"I gotta go." He slapped his thighs and stood.

"Something just occurred to you. What is it?"

"I don't want to speak on it until I've checked a couple things."

"You're just gonna leave me here alone with the mad tagger running around?"

"You've got Ruby here to protect you."

I launched myself out of the chair. "So much for my tax dollars at work."

Cole flinched and then slowly shook his head. "You really are naïve." He walked toward the front door and opened it. "Don't forget to lock the door and deadbolt it."

I leaned against the doorframe. Halfway to his car, he stopped and turned to face me.

"You don't have to worry about wasting your tax dollars, Audrey. I didn't come here tonight as Chief of Police."

With that, he turned on his heel, got in his car, and drove away.

Chapter Twenty-Seven

I passed Joan at the reception desk and gave a quick wave. She was on the phone, so she returned my greeting with a head nod and a smile.

Vivienne was seated behind the glass in the shared waiting room of CPD and the passport office, talking to a gangly teen. I recognized him as the boy in striped overalls from the homecoming game.

"Gabrielle was responsible for bringing it to the stage, but she accidentally left it at the fountain. It's got to be here."

My ears pricked at the mention of Chet's murder scene.

"I don't know what to tell you, Joey. I've checked with both Sergeant Bianchi and Chief Loveland. We don't have it. Go back to school, and if we locate it, we'll let you know."

"Hello."

Joey whirled to face me, flushed and bug-eyed.

"I couldn't help but overhear. Something that belongs to you went missing?"

Joey postured the way teen boys do when trying to act cool. "Yeah, uh, sorta. I mean, it's definitely missing, but it doesn't exactly belong to me. Just temporarily."

I tilted my head to look around his tall, thin frame, and Viv came into view. She shrugged in response.

"See, I won the spirit award. I get my name on it, and I get to keep it at my house until graduation. But Gabrielle was making out with her boyfriend before the game and forgot about it until we were looking for it during halftime when I was supposed to be presented with it. By the time she realized where she'd left it, the whole area was blocked off 'cause of that guy being dead. I kept asking if anyone had seen my spirit award, but they told me they had more important things to deal with, and I get it, but this is important to *me*."

"Hmm. Yes. Joey, is it?"

"Yeah." He jutted his chin.

"My name is Audrey O'Connell, and I work at the *Chattertowne Coastal Current* Newspaper. I'm going to look into this and get back to you. If you can think of anything else that might help, give me a call over there, okay?"

Joey nodded.

"Hey, Viv, any chance I can get buzzed in to see your boss?"

"Yeah. He's extra grumpy today. I'm just warning you. I don't know what's gotten under his skin, but it's not super pleasant."

I held up a bag from Abigail's. "I brought treats."

"I'm not sure that'll work on him, but you're welcome to try." She pressed a button to unlock the door to the back offices of the police station. "Okay, Joey, here's the form to file an official police report."

I scurried down the hall and thrust myself into Cole's office. He looked up with alarm but quickly covered it with a blasé expression.

"I see your sister is shirking her duty to keep out the riff-raff."

I plopped into the seat across from his desk and threw down the bag. "You don't strike me as someone who's got a sweet tooth, so I took a chance and picked up three different kinds of bagels."

"Oh."

"Oh?"

"I wasn't expecting a peace offering."

"It's not a peace offering. It's breakfast. That's what normal people call it when they share a meal in the morning. And I come bearing news."

Cole peeked into the bag. "Is that an everything?"

"It is."

He pulled out the bagel and a napkin. "Thank you."

"You're welcome. Do you wanna know my news?"

He grabbed a packet of cream cheese out of the bag and tore it open with his teeth. A little bit of cream cheese stuck in the stubble on his upper lip.

"You've got…" I pointed at his mouth.

He attempted to wipe it away but missed.

"No, there." I pointed again.

He missed again.

"At the risk of being cliché…" I reached over the desk and dabbed the cream cheese from just above his lip. "Got it."

"Cliché?" He made another swipe with his napkin to make sure it was gone.

"You know, the old 'you've got something on you lip' schtick that happens in every rom-com."

"You're assuming I watch rom-coms?"

I shook my head. "Never mind. You wanna know or not?"

"Of course." He spread the cream cheese across his bagel and took a bite. "Pretty good."

"The trophy."

"What trophy?"

"The spirit award."

He looked at me with his eyebrows knit together. "The spirit award is a trophy?"

"Yes."

He slammed his palms on his desk. "That's it! I thought that kid was squawking about a plaque! It's a trophy?"

"More like a statue. It's a bronze cougar, a miniature version of the one Chet was riding side saddle."

He flung his hands in the air. "All this time, it was staring me in the face. We've got to find that trophy."

"We?"

"We, as in Chattertowne PD."

"Ah. Do I at least get to tag along?"

"It's the least I can do, considering you brought breakfast." He indicated the bag. "Aren't you going to eat?"

I pulled another bag out of my pocket.

"What's that?"

"Unlike you, I do have a sweet tooth, and I didn't want your garlic and sesame seeds all over my pumpkin spice scone."

Cole grimaced. "It might be an improvement."

* * *

Cole, Bianchi, and I arrived in the courtyard of Chattertowne High right as the bell rang to dismiss students from their second-period classes. The area around the fountain still had yellow crime scene tape, but it was sagging in some places and broken in others.

Some of the kids dawdled and gawked as they passed. I recognized a few, mostly from the Cavalcade and the homecoming game, Blakesly's daughter Regan among them. She broke away from the group she was walking with and approached us.

"Sheriff." She smiled and fluttered her lashes at Cole but ignored the rest of us.

Her flirting had a surprising effect on the usually unflappable Cole. Pink crept up his neck from his collar to his forehead.

He cleared his throat. "Uh, it's chief, not sheriff."

"Oh, sorry." Her voice was barely above a whisper with the thin tinkle of laughter. "I guess it's the hat. Makes me think of that sheriff from *Riverdale*."

Bianchi made a guttural sound.

"Don't want to be late for class." I gave my best hall monitor impression.

Regan barely glanced over her shoulder at me. She once again directed her comments only to Cole. "I may have some information which may be useful to your investigation. Perhaps I could come by after school, and I can tell you all about it."

Cole rolled his shoulders back. "Sure. About three?"

"Can't wait." Her sly smile spread as she flounced off toward the math building.

Bianchi covered his mouth with his hand and imitated the squawking and static of a police walkie. "Danger. I repeat. Danger."

"No one's in any danger." Cole shifted his gaze toward the fountain and back. "I mean in this particular case. She's just a kid trying to get attention."

"She may know something. Her parents are right in the thick of everything. Maybe she overheard something."

Bianchi folded his arms and leaned back on his heels. "Why would she rat out her own parents?"

"Because she's a teenager. Kind of a bratty one at that."

Cole twisted his mouth to the side. "Probably wouldn't be a bad idea to have someone in the room when I talk to her. Just for appearance's sake."

Bianchi shook his head. "I got a scout meeting for my kid at three."

Cole looked at me and arched his left brow.

"I can be there. I don't think she'll be thrilled to see me, though."

"Great. Now, let's broaden the perimeter for where this cougar statue might have been tossed. I'd say the whole campus should be searched."

"I'll take the stadium area." Bianchi pointed to the north and began to walk away.

"Let me know if you find anything." Cole turned to me. "What about you?"

I thought for a moment. "Seems to me if a person wanted to toss a murder weapon, they'd throw it in the bushes or a trash can."

"It certainly would be the most expedient place to stash it. I'll check out the shrubs. You take the trash cans."

"That's not what I—"

The bell rang, and he pretended not to be able to hear what I was saying. I stuck my tongue out at him as he walked away, laughing.

Since Cole was searching outside, I decided to start inside. Much of the school would have been locked during the game. The homecoming festivities would have meant a lot of people coming and going into the marching band building, the gym and locker rooms, and the bathrooms.

I gave cursory glances into the trash cans in the hallway outside the gym, but they were nearly empty. Up ahead, a janitor's cart was positioned outside the boys' locker room. A man with gray curly hair came out carrying a roll of paper towels and a spray bottle.

"Ozzie?"

CHAPTER TWENTY-SEVEN

The man looked up at me. "Yes?"

"It's me, Audrey O'Connell. I used to be a student here."

His eyes twinkled with delight. "Audrey! How are you? I didn't know you were back in town."

"A couple years now. I work for the *Current*."

He nodded his head. "Come to think of it, I do recall your series on Kupit and the whole city hall debacle. What are you doing here?"

"I'm investigating Chet's death."

Ozzie took on a somber posture. "Yeah. I didn't like what the guy stood for, but nobody should be killed over their political opinions. Also, I'm not sure I'll ever get the blood off the cement."

"There's a good chance the murder weapon is still here. I noticed the trash cans are pretty much empty."

"Yeah, I took them out first thing this morning."

"Any chance the spirit award could have been in one of the bags?"

He grimaced. "You think that's what took him out?"

"It's one of the theories."

Ozzie stared at the floor for a moment and then shook his head. "Nah, I don't think so. I did the trash on Friday afternoon. Mostly, what was in 'em were posters from homecoming. ASB came and pulled them down right after school. The paper and cardboard took up a lot of space, which is why I emptied 'em, but they were all pretty light."

I gave a deep sigh. "Well, I can't say I'm too disappointed not have to dig through garbage, but finding the statue may help solve this."

"I'll keep an eye out. Maybe someone stashed it somewhere in the gym."

"Oh! What about the towel bins?"

Ozzie shook his head again. "Did 'em already."

"Ah, well, it was worth a shot."

A walkie-talkie beeped from his cart.

"Ozzie, we got a cleanup request from room 214. Someone tossed their cookies."

He grabbed the radio and pressed the button. "I'm on it." A melancholy smile crossed his face. "Only eight months 'til retirement."

"I'd love to do a celebration piece on you when the time comes."

"That would be very nice. Thank you."

He gave me a half salute and pushed his cart down the hall toward the exit. I wandered toward the entrance to the gym. Along the wall, several glass display cases held various artifacts from the school's impressive athletic history. While it had been a while since CHS dominated its conference, it had more than a hundred years of accomplishments to celebrate. I scanned the memorabilia feeling a sense of pride to have been a part of that tradition. Just past the doors that led into the basketball and volleyball courts, one more case stood on its own. The top shelf held wool pennants with holes where moths had eaten away at them and old pom poms from various eras. The second shelf held photos of cheer squads, mine included. I was at the bottom of a pyramid.

What I saw on the bottom shelf caused me to catch my breath.

The spirit award stood proud in its normal spot like it had no idea it was supposed to be missing.

I crouched to look into the bronze eyes of the Chattertowne Cougar.

"Hello there."

I pulled my phone out of my pocket and called Cole.

"I hope you washed your hands before touching that phone."

"Turns out, I didn't have to dig through garbage after all. Right now, I'm staring into the face of one spirit-filled cougar statue. And Cole, he's got what looks to be blood around his mouth."

Chapter Twenty-Eight

Cole placed the bagged statue on his desk when we got back to his office at the police station.

"Hiding in plain sight. I gotta give it to whoever did this; it was pretty clever." He dropped into his chair and leaned back with his hands clasped behind his cowboy hat.

I resisted the urge to correct his grammar. "And, to the clever woman who found it…" I nodded my head at him.

"Good job."

I made a face at him. "You can do better than that."

"Very good job."

I blew my hair out of my face. "Whatever. I know you're impressed by me."

A hint of a smile played across his face. "Now we just need to get this processed, check for prints, and verify it's Chet's blood."

"Who else's blood would be on it?"

"You never know. Wanna do lunch? Something about progressing on a case makes me hungry."

"Can't. If I'm gonna come back at three for the meeting with Regan, I gotta go to the paper and do some writing."

"If it's too much, I can ask Viv to sit in with us."

I tapped my hands on his desk. "Not at all. I'm curious about what she has to say."

"Raincheck on lunch, then?"

Something about the way he looked at me caught me by surprise. Was he flirting with me?

"Rain check. Absolutely."

As I hustled out of the police station, I threw Viv a wide-eyed look. She returned it with one of her own. I mouthed that I would talk to her later. The truth was it was one of the rare times in my life I didn't know what to say.

* * *

Just before three, I parked my car across from the City Hall Building. I mentally patted myself on the back for being early. As I crossed the street, I noticed Regan and Blakesly in a heated conversation over by the entrance to the marina docks.

Blakesly grabbed Regan's arm, but she yanked it away. She reached for her again, but Regan marched toward City Hall. I caught up with them right in front of the door.

"Everything okay here?"

"Mind your own business," Blakesly snarled.

Regan tipped her head back in defiance. "She just doesn't want me to blow the lid off her precious CROCCC's nefarious activities."

"Regan!"

Blakesly made another attempt to grab Regan, but she shrugged her off.

"Do you mean the graffiti or the fires or Chet?"

"All of it. They want everyone to believe they care about this town, but it's a lie. A scam. Chet was the worst of them all. He's no martyr." Regan's cheeks reddened, and a flash of rage crossed her face.

"Regan Kennedy Whitehead, that's enough!"

"What, mother, are you afraid I'll reveal the true character of your venerated saint?

Blakesly took hold of Regan by the waist and ushered her away.

Regan looked over her shoulder at me and mouthed, *Fred Harper Construction.*

* * *

"Right on time, I see." Cole checked his watch. "And by right on time, I mean ten minutes late."

I eased into the chair. "I don't suppose you've noticed Regan isn't here."

"I expect it from teenagers."

I gripped the armrests. "Well, I wouldn't hold your breath."

"Why's that?"

"She's not coming. That's why I'm late."

He pressed his lips into a fine line.

"Believe it or not, I was going to be a couple minutes—well, probably more like thirty seconds, but still—I was going to be early. Then I ran into Regan and Blakesly outside."

"Blakesly?"

"Yeah. I don't know how she knew Regan was coming to talk to us, but she was here to stop her. And she was successful."

Cole rested his forearms on the desk. "Did either of them say anything useful?"

"Regan called CROCCC's purposes nefarious, and then she mouthed Fred Harper's name. I take that back. She mouthed Fred Harper *Construction*."

"Hmm. Fred's been on my radar, but more so because of his wife's questionable relationship with Chet. According to Holden, there have been informal meetings at Harper's current job site with some of CROCCC's most prominent participants, but why would she specifically mention his company?"

We both sat silent for a few minutes.

I sat up in my chair. "We must be looking at this all wrong."

"Speak for yourself."

"Are you telling me you haven't been thinking in terms of anti-government vigilantes trying to terrorize and bully the mayor and the council into getting their way?"

"That's one aspect. I haven't ruled out other motives."

"Such as?"

"I'm relatively new to this town, so I don't feel as invested in preserving its archaic culture in the same way others do. I don't look at progress as inherently evil or a threat to what makes Chattertowne special."

"That makes you an anomaly around here."

He intensified his gaze. "You sure about that?"

"What are you getting at?"

"While Chattertowne's residents as a whole want to keep things the way they've always been, that doesn't mean they're a monolith, even the old guard like Fred Harper. He's a businessman, first and foremost. That means his priorities are profits, growth, and progress."

"Okay, so Fred wants to grow his business, which means more construction."

"It also means getting permits and re-zoning some areas of town."

I clucked my tongue. "Wouldn't it be wild if all this hubbub about protecting the quaint integrity of the town was really a front for moving us into a more commercialized version of Chattertowne?"

Cole shook his head. "Doesn't sound wild to me at all."

I checked my phone. "I'm gonna run home to throw in a load of laundry and get dinner before the meeting tonight. You going?"

"Which meeting? There are two."

"The heritage commission meeting. What's the other one?"

"I got a message this morning. The economic and zoning commission moved their meeting up a week. They're starting at five-thirty, and then the heritage meeting is at seven."

I gave him an intense stare. "That's not a coincidence."

"You think?"

"I never really considered it, but the two groups have diametrically opposed mandates. One is to preserve Chattertowne's heritage, the other is the mow it down in the name of prosperity and progress."

"I'm not sure those things are mutually exclusive."

I blinked at him. "Do you know who's on each committee?"

Cole turned to his computer. "Let me pull up the website. Okay. There are six positions on the heritage commission. Position one is held by Mildred

CHAPTER TWENTY-EIGHT

Driscoll. Two is Ingrid Norvald. Oh, three is Claudine O'Connell, your mom."

"All long-standing citizens of Chattertowne committed to preservation. Now look at who else."

Cole blew a long, slow whistle. "Zeb Brandt, Wanda Harper, and Chet Buchanan."

"Two of those people will be unable to attend tonight's meeting due to being, you know, dead."

"So, you think they may have been killed to rebalance the committee in favor of economic development and growth? That might make sense if Zeb hadn't been collateral damage, not an intended target."

"We've assumed that, but maybe whoever set the fire knew he was in there."

Cole sighed. "It's a possibility."

"Now look at who's on the economic development and zoning committee."

Cole typed on his keyboard and leaned back in his chair. "Abigail Ferguson. I'm guessing she's the owner of the bakery?"

I nodded.

"Dave Stokes."

"He owns Chuck's Chowder Grotto."

"I thought some guy named Chuck owned Chuck's Chowder Grotto."

"He named it after former Seahawks head coach Chuck Knox."

"Hmm. You learn something every day. Okay, position three is Giuseppe Martini. I know that one. Ah, here we go. Fred Harper, Don Whitehead, and—" He paused and gave me a befuddled look. "Hiram Kaiser?"

I tsked and nodded my head. "The question is, whose side is Hiram really on?" I made a face. "On whose side is Hiram, really? On whose side really is Hiram?"

Cole laughed and shook his head. "You tie yourself in knots trying to avoid dangling that preposition when ninety-nine percent of people you're talking *to*," he placed heavy emphasis on the word to, "don't care at all."

"I care."

"I know you do. I suggest you care less, particularly around me. I wasn't an English major, so I don't need you correcting either of our grammar."

"I'll try to restrain myself. I can't promise anything. As for tonight, if I'm gonna get back for the first meeting, I'd better skedaddle."

I heard Cole's low, rumbling laughter as I hustled down the hall. I waved to my sister as I sped by her desk and shouted, "Gotta go! I'll call you later!"

Vivienne merely shook her head.

Chapter Twenty-Nine

Unlike the city council meeting the previous week, the economic development and zoning commission meeting was sparsely attended. Specifically, in addition to the six members, there were only six people in attendance, including Cole who sat next to Margarita in the second-row center. Jenna Doyle sat in the front row on the right side, while Blakesly Whitehead and Gabe and Tammy Milner sat on the left.

I caught a slight narrowing of Fred Harper's gaze as I slid into the chair next to Cole.

"Sorry I'm late. I'd try to make up an excuse, but the truth is, I just didn't leave on time."

He leaned over and whispered, "You didn't miss much. Fred insisted on everyone standing and saying the pledge of allegiance, and then Joan read the minutes from the last meeting."

Fred banged his gavel and glared at Cole and me. "Next on the agenda, we will open the floor to public comments."

Jenna raised her hand.

Fred smiled at her and nodded. "Jenna Doyle."

Jenna stood and practically curtsied at Fred. "Thank you, Mr. Chairman. In light of recent events, most particularly the untimely deaths of heritage committee members Zeb Brandt and Chet Buchanan, it seems to me it would be more efficient to combine the heritage and development committees. As it stands, the two groups have been at odds with each other for months over the construction of a six-story mixed-use complex over by the old buffalo field."

Cole whispered in my ear. "Did she say buffalo field?"

I nodded. "Technically, it was American bison. Over by the wetlands there used to be a field filled with them. About twenty-five years ago it was sold to developers who've been fighting to get something built on that land ever since. Between Fish and Wildlife and the heritage commission, it's been one long battle."

"What happened to the buffalo?"

"Bison. I believe they were sent to a farm upstate."

Cole was unable to completely choke back his laugh, and a gurgle emanated from him. "You mean they were slaughtered."

"No, I think the herd was actually relocated about forty minutes north of here."

Jenna scowled in our direction and shushed us before she continued.

"Rather than keeping them separate and undergoing the process of finding replacements, I propose this committee absorb the heritage committee and its members." With that, she sat in her seat.

Fred clapped once. "Sounds good to me. Thank you, Jenna." To Joan he said, "I'd like to add a vote on this to new business."

The Milners grumbled, exchanging confused looks. Blakesly sat up in her chair and whipped her head to look at Don. He ignored her.

Margarita jumped to her feet. "You can't do that!"

Fred banged his gavel. "Mayor Guzman, you are out of order."

"This is a kangaroo proceeding."

He banged it again. "Sit down and raise your hand like a civilized person if you'd like to be recognized. For someone who's accusing us of running a kangaroo proceeding, you are certainly not abiding by the parliamentary rules."

Margarita glared as she sat and raised her hand.

"Mayor Guzman, would you like to express an opinion on this matter?"

Margarita took a deep breath to compose herself. "This is completely out of line with your authority and jurisdiction. You can't just take over another committee by coup."

"Actually, this thought has occurred to me before. These past few months we've been at loggerheads with the heritage commission, and it's been a massive waste of time and taxpayer money. I looked into it, and there's nothing in our town charter which prohibits it. As a matter of fact, the port commission was temporarily absorbed by the public safety commission following the smuggling scandals of the nineteen eighties. It's established precedent. We have a motion on the floor. Do I have a second?"

Don Whitehead raised his hand. "I second."

Margarita opened her mouth but closed it without speaking. She shook her head and scanned the panel. "Abigail, Dave. You can't possibly be okay with this."

Both committee members appeared uncomfortable but stayed silent.

"I say we put it to a vote now." Fred banged his gavel again. "Let's start on the end. Abigail, aye or nay on the absorption of the heritage commission?"

Abigail knit her brows together. She looked at Margarita and then at Fred. "Nay."

Jenna booed. The Milners clapped. Fred waved a dismissive hand at them. Blakesly stared daggers at Don, who continued to face straight ahead.

Bang! "Dave?"

Dave shook his head. "This isn't right, Fred. Nay."

Another negative murmur from the front row.

"Giuseppe. Surely, you've been frustrated with the lack of progress the last several months."

"I have. However, I've got to side with the mayor on this one. Nay."

Margarita breathed a sigh of relief.

I leaned across Cole and patted her leg. "It's gonna be okay. By my count, it will probably go 4-2 against."

Bang! Fred glared at me. "I vote aye. Don?"

Don looked at Blakesly with a nearly imperceptible smirk. "Aye."

From my angle I could barely see her face, but she appeared stoic, not celebratory. Apparently, they weren't on the same side of the issue.

"Hy?"

Hiram's face was unreadable.

I whispered to Cole, "Here we go."

Cole cleared his throat.

Hiram jerked his head to look at us and then looked at Fred, who gave a slight nod. Hiram set his mouth tight.

"Aye."

"The ayes carry." Bang!

Jenna gave a celebratory whoop. Margarita gasped. Blakesly stood and walked out of the room without a word.

Cole tilted his head and raised his hand.

"Yes, Chief Loveland?" Fred raised one superior eyebrow

Cole stood and tipped his hat. "With all due respect, Chairman Harper, but I believe if my math is correct, we have a tie."

"Indeed, however, as chairman, I break all ties. I say double yay."

I leaned toward Margarita. "This can't be legal."

Margarita's shoulders slumped. "He's right. Chairman gets a second tiebreaking vote. It's a dumb rule, but it's legitimate."

"The motion to dissolve and absorb the heritage commission is passed." Bang!

"What did you just say?"

We all turned to face the woman at the back of the room. Wanda's face was purple with rage.

"What did you do, Fred?"

Fred ignored his wife and addressed the committee. "Do we have any other new business? If not, I ask for a motion to dismiss so we can inform the heritage commission their meeting has been cancelled."

Abigail raised her hand. "I move that we end this travesty of a meeting right now."

Fred made a dismissive gesture. "Second?"

"Second." Dave scowled. "I won't stand for this. You all should be ashamed of yourselves."

Bang! "Motion to dismiss seconded. All in favor?"

Three sullen ayes and three gleeful ayes brought the meeting to an official close. Hiram stood and began to leave.

"Hy!"

He ignored me and kept walking, so I followed him.

I caught up to him and grabbed his arm. "Hy!"

He whirled to face me. "Audrey, stay out of this."

"This isn't what Chet would have wanted."

"Oh, so now you care what Chet would have wanted?" He flashed a disgusted snarl and stormed out of the room.

A commotion at the front caught my attention. Wanda was shrieking at Fred and poking him in the chest with her finger.

"I will never forgive you for this. Never!"

"Fine by me. Come on, Jenna."

Jenna Doyle popped out of her seat and followed Fred through the doorway like a puppy following its master.

Wanda turned her scathing expression on me. "Are you happy now?" She stomped after Fred and Jenna.

I looked at Margarita and Cole, who returned my gaze with surprise.

"Audrey, what did you do?" Cole was teasing and looked to be attempting to suppress a smile.

"I have absolutely no idea."

Chapter Thirty

Something looked strange when I pulled into my driveway, but it took me a minute to figure out what it was. All the pots that lined my walkway filled with geraniums, making their last gasps before the first frost, were scattered and broken across the concrete. I looked around to see if the person responsible was still nearby, but the street and sidewalks were quiet. Still, I couldn't shake the feeling I was being watched. I pulled out my phone and, as I waited for the call to connect, tried to rub the goosebumps off my arms.

"Hey, whatcha doin'?" My attempt at a casual tone was thwarted by shivers and a quivering voice.

Holden groaned like he was stretching. "I'm watching the Mariners blow their final chance of the season to get a wildcard spot, so, just a typical Tuesday night in early October. What about you?"

"Oh, nothing much. Just got back from the zoning and development committee's meeting where they staged a rebellion and overthrew the heritage committee to find some angry little elf has destroyed all my ceramic flowerpots."

"I didn't understand half of what you said. I'm a visual learner. I'll be right over, and you can show me."

Less than fifteen minutes passed before Holden rang my doorbell.

He motioned toward the debris field. "I'm sorry about your pots, but from what I can tell, whoever did this did you a favor."

I crossed my arms and leaned against the doorframe. "How do you figure?"

"Somebody had to put those poor plants out of their misery."

I swatted at his shoulder and tried to ignore the electricity that zapped between us.

"So back up a bit and tell me what happened at City Hall."

I gave him the short version.

"I never would have thought Hy would side with that plan. You're saying Fred, Hy, the Milners, and the Whiteheads all were in favor of disbanding the heritage commission in order to end the standoff over Fred's construction project?"

"Wait. The buffalo field development is a Harper Construction project? Isn't that a massive conflict of interest?"

"That's the Chattertowne way. Ignore conflicts of interest and nepotism unless perpetrated by outsiders." He walked down the front steps and squatted to get a closer look. "What makes you think someone from the meeting did this? Couldn't it have been the mama raccoon?"

"I had someone attempt to spray graffiti on the side of the house last night, and then tonight, I got dirty looks and nastiness thrown my way by several people, including Wanda Harper, who, for some unknown reason, blames me for Fred's actions tonight."

He picked up a broken piece of pottery. "This certainly seems like an act of rage. She couldn't be happy with Fred. That move goes against everything Chet believed."

"That reminds me. Hy seemed kind of under duress tonight. He barked at me for saying that exact thing."

Holden stood and looked up at the cloudy sky. "As someone who's been coerced into doing things I don't want to do, it makes sense Hy would vote the way he did. His business depends on the work Fred throws his way."

"I hadn't thought about that. There is one more thing."

"What's that?"

"I don't think Blakesly was very happy about Don's affirmative vote either."

"I've read some of Blakesly's 'articles.'" He made air quotes. "She's kind of all over the place. Her views aren't consistent, and her logic is often deeply flawed. However, she never once wavered in her support of Chet Buchanan."

"Maybe she was another in Chet's harem."

"Could be. Do you want me to look around a bit before I leave, make sure no one's lurking?"

I gave a nervous laugh. "Would you? I feel stupid for asking, but I'd feel better."

Holden walked the perimeter of the house. Other than some growling as he passed Ruby's lair and the truncated attempt at graffiti, he found nothing out of place. He gave me a quick hug goodbye.

I waited on the front stoop until he drove away. As I turned to walk into the house, a car engine started halfway down the block. I whipped around just in time to catch a glimpse of glowing red taillights and the back of a dark SUV.

* * *

"I need you to run a search on all the dark SUVs in Chattertowne." I plopped into the chair across from Cole's desk.

"I'm really going to have to speak to your sister about letting you barge in here without warning."

"I'm a taxpayer. I pay your salary."

"Now you sound like Chet and Hy."

I pulled my mouth into a grimace. "Don't like that comparison. At all."

"What's this about a vehicle search?"

"Remember how I felt like I was being stalked when I went to check out the graffiti at the trail?"

"Yes. Something about a slow-moving SUV, which could belong to hundreds of people around here. This is Chattertowne. We're basically fifty percent pick-ups, forty percent SUVs, and ten percent Subaru Outbacks."

"I don't doubt that, but if it belongs to someone on our short list of suspects, then we can narrow it down."

"What's this we stuff? You got a mouse in your pocket?" Cole snickered at his own joke.

"Haha. My Dad says that all the time. Don't think you're breaking any comedic ground."

"The task you're asking me to do isn't as simple as you're making it sound. Why the sudden resurgence of interest in the SUV?"

"I think they broke all my flowerpots on my front walkway and then sat watching me."

Cole stiffened and sat upright in his chair. "Why didn't you call me?"

"I didn't want to bug you. It's not like a major crime; it's more annoying than anything else. Holden checked out the side and back yard. Everything was clear. Right after he left, though, I heard another vehicle start its engine and when I looked, it was a dark SUV like the one by the trail parking lot."

Cole played with his chin hair as he listened to my account. "Holden was there?"

"I called him. Like I said, I didn't want to bug you with something so trivial, but I did have the sense I was being watched. I just didn't want to believe it."

Cole picked up his desk phone and pushed several buttons. "Chen, I need you to do me a favor." He paused. "Yeah. See if you can get me a list of all the black SUVs registered in town. I'd say 2010 and later."

"Dark."

"Hold on," he said into the receiver and then covered it with his hand. "You said black the first time you brought it up at the trail."

"I said black*ish*. Super dark tinted windows. Last night, it looked like it could be more of a dark gray, but that may have been the lighting."

Back into the receiver, Cole said, "Make that dark-colored SUV." Pause. "Yeah. I know." Pause. "See what you can find and let me know. Thanks." He hung the receiver back onto the hook.

"Thanks for doing that. I'll feel better when I know who's watching me."

"Glad to do it. There's a good chance the owner of the SUV has some involvement in this case."

"Did you know Fred Harper Construction has the contract to build the contested buffalo field project? The one he basically just ensured will get approval by his actions last night?"

"I had an inkling. I also believe he ensured the implosion of his scheme."

"How do you figure?" I asked.

"Wanda and Blakesly. They're both married to committee members and have also been privy to the plans of Chet and CROCCC. My suspicion is they both harbored romantic feelings for Chet, whether they were consummated or not I'm not sure, but I believe it's possible he was playing them to gain access to the plans of their husbands. Likewise, Don and Fred were using Wanda and Blakesly's access to Chet to obtain information on his agenda."

"It's all pretty gross when you spell it out like that. Everyone has nefarious motives."

Cole nodded. "Which is why they're devouring themselves from the inside out."

"The weakest links in this chain are the women who are now discovering they've been pawns in a game they didn't know they were playing."

"It's the old checkers versus chess analogy."

"We should go talk to Wanda."

"There's that we again."

"I know for a fact you don't have the resources to investigate this as fully as you'd like. I'm a good investigator. This," I gestured between us, "is mutually beneficial."

Cole gave a sigh of acquiescence and stood. He grabbed his jacket off the coat rack. "I need to stop at Abigail's on the way."

"So we can drill her on what she knows about what happened at the meeting last night?"

"So I can get a scone and some coffee."

* * *

"Last night was bonkers. I'm trying to decide if I want to quit or if I should stay so they can't run roughshod over all the rest of the committees." Abigail used tongs to grab two caramel apple scones from the case and placed them in individual bags, which she handed to Cole and me.

"I hope you stay." I broke off a chunk of scone and popped it into my mouth. "Someone's gotta keep them accowhumble."

Cole grimaced at me. "A cow humble?"

I swallowed my bite. "Sorry, shouldn't talk with my mouth full. My mother would be horrified. Accountable."

Abigail slumped her shoulders and released a heavy sigh. "I joined the development commission because I wanted to bring a level-headed approach to growth in this town. At times, I've been frustrated with the draconian measures some on the heritage commission have tried to enforce on business owners, but I also see the importance of maintaining Chattertowne's charm. Our reputation as a place where antique meets modern convenience is what draws people here. That's why I was in support of the parking lot."

"I wasn't here when everything went down with the government corruption scandal, but I've been here long enough to understand the sentiment people have expressed about wanting more transparency. Many felt that transaction between Zeb Brandt and the city was shady. Why do you suppose people feel that way?" Cole sipped his coffee.

Abigail leaned against the glass display case. "Well, for one thing, there's a divide in this country right now that has nothing to do with facts. It's all about perception and an immediate rejection of ideas coming from anyone who might have a different political bent. Add in Chattertowne's recent scandals, and Chet's failed political run, which played on the idea anyone associated with the running of this city is corrupt, you've got a large portion of citizens ripe for manipulation. That's what CROCCC is all about, twisting good intentions into some plot to fleece the populace with authoritarian actions. Chet was the ultimate pot-stirrer, and he made getting anything done nearly impossible."

"It's a bit hypocritical for him to do that while also serving on the heritage commission," I said.

"I think in Chet's mind, everything he did was in the town's best interest. He trusted himself to make sound decisions on the committee, but no one else."

I weighed my next question carefully. "Abigail, what's your take on Hy voting for the dissolution of the heritage commission last night? He all but sealed his fate to not be chosen as CROCCC's next leader."

Abigail shrugged. "If I had to guess, it's a matter of survival. There were several times Chet would show up to meetings and appear to be watching

Hy to make sure he voted the way Chet wanted him to vote. On the parking lot vote, Hy indicated he was leaning toward a yes, but at the break, Chet cornered him and gave him an earful. I couldn't hear what was being said, but Hy's position shifted when we reconvened. It still passed, but Hy was a no-vote."

Cole held up his coffee cup. "This is good stuff. Thanks for the info. If you can think of anything else that might be helpful in sorting this whole mess, give me a call." He handed her his card and a twenty-dollar bill.

"Oh, this is too much!"

"It's a really good cup of coffee."

He smiled at her, and she blushed. I looked at her more closely and determined she was younger and prettier than I'd noticed. She was older than Cole and me, but not by much. And she was single. I didn't enjoy the strange feeling that gurgled in my stomach. I chalked it up to hunger pangs and broke off another chunk of scone.

"Did you wink at her?" I asked as we climbed into his car.

Cole guffawed. "No, why would you think I winked at her?"

I buckled my seatbelt. "You were definitely flirting."

"I was not."

"Hmph."

Cole looked at me with amusement but returned to the task of backing out of his parking spot without a word. We drove to the Harper home and pulled into the driveway. One of the four garage bays was open. Inside was a black Chevy Suburban SUV with dark-tinted windows.

Chapter Thirty-One

I pointed wordlessly at the black SUV in the Harper's garage. Cole put the gearshift into park and unbuckled his seatbelt. We climbed out of the car and walked to the garage entrance.

I pointed at the car. "This is it."

"You're sure?"

"It has to be. The trail isn't far from here; it looks just like the car that passed me, and it belongs to a couple of our top suspects."

Cole snapped a photo of the license plate with his phone. "Something doesn't sit right with me, though."

"What?"

"This morning, you insisted it was dark. You've never claimed it was black."

"Well, I didn't want to rule out the possibility it was dark blue or gray."

"You believe it was black, though, right?"

I gave a more assured nod than I felt. "I'm almost positive."

Cole walked toward the house. I heard him grumble the word *almost* under his breath. He knocked on the front door, but there was no answer. He rang the doorbell. Still nothing. I followed him around to the side of the old farmhouse. He peeked in the kitchen window.

He held out his arm and pointed at me. "Call 911!" He raced around to the side door and yanked on a pair of blue rubber gloves before rattling the knob. Locked.

"What's happening?" I pulled out my phone and dialed the emergency number with trembling fingers.

Cole banged his shoulder against the door. "Tell them we need an ambulance."

"Nine-one-one, what's your emergency?" The dispatcher's calm voice did nothing to quell my terror.

"Um, yes, I'm at—wait, what's the address here?"

Cole began to kick at the door to break it down. "Just tell them Fred Harper's place off Pioneer Road."

I repeated the information and requested an ambulance. As I disconnected the call, Cole managed to get the door open. He rushed inside.

"Audrey, don't come in here!"

I paused in the doorway.

Wanda Harper lay on the kitchen floor in an unnatural position. Fred was slumped over the table. Next to his hand was a coffee cup which had tipped and spilled some of its contents.

He crouched to check Wanda's pulse. "I think we're too late." He stood, red-faced and grief-stricken. He checked Fred's pulse. "Dammit."

I slapped my hand over my mouth to suppress a yelp. "What…happened here?"

Sirens sounded in the distance.

"I have no idea. I need you to stay outside, though. This looks like a crime scene. At best, it's an accident scene."

Even though I couldn't go inside, I scanned the room, looking for any indication to explain what might have happened. I sniffed the air. "Doesn't smell like a gas leak, does it? It would smell like rotting eggs. Natural gas isn't detectable, but the utility company adds something to it that smells like sulfur, so people are alerted to it."

"I don't smell anything like that." Cole walked over to a part of the kitchen I couldn't see from my angle. "Oh."

"What is it?"

He leaned into view, held up a box of rat poison, and shook it.

"Oh, my gawd. Do you think…oh geez." My gaze cut to the coffee cup on its side.

"There's also a note on the fridge. It looks to be Wanda's handwriting." He snapped a photo with his phone and brought it over to show me.

I read aloud. "'He that has eyes to see and ears to hear may convince himself that no mortal can keep a secret. If his lips are silent, he chatters with his fingertips; betrayal oozes out of him at every pore. Sigmund Freud.' What do you think it means?"

"I believe we're looking at a murder-suicide here."

"You think Wanda killed Fred and then herself? Because of last night's vote?"

"I'm not sure we'll ever know. There's plenty of betrayal to go around. Fred's vote, his possible affair with Jenna, Wanda's siding with Chet against Fred's project, her possible affair with Chet."

An ambulance, two firetrucks, and a police car pulled into the driveway, one after another. I ducked out of the way as the first responders made their way into the kitchen. I wandered over to the open garage bay and walked alongside the SUV, careful not to touch it in case it was considered part of the crime scene. The windows had been tinted to near-illegal darkness. While I still wasn't one hundred percent certain, I felt confident it was the vehicle that stalked me at the trail so it must have also been the one outside my house the night before. Just as I was about to walk outside, a half-empty box of bright pink spray paint canisters hidden in the corner of the garage caught my eye.

* * *

After I discovered the spray paint cache, I went to grab Cole. Unfortunately, it was at that moment Daphne Pierce, the county coroner, arrived. She examined both Fred and Wanda and authorized the EMTs to transport their bodies to the hospital, where autopsies would be performed. It took over an hour for the scene to be processed.

Now, standing in front of what I believed to be incontrovertible evidence of Wanda's guilt, I felt frustrated Cole didn't see things the same way. I was also getting hangry.

Cole stood with hands on his hips and stared at the box of pink spray paint cans. "I mean, he did own a construction company."

"None of his other construction stuff is here."

"True, but this is only a small piece of the puzzle. We can't jump to conclusions no matter how it looks. Four people are dead. The stakes are too high to get this wrong."

"You mean you're not ready to say with finality Wanda was responsible for all of this."

"I'll never say that. There's no way she could've pulled it off on her own. We know there were at least two, if not three, graffiti artists. We know someone was tagging the pool while someone else was setting fire to the Brandt's barn."

"One of them had to be Chet."

Cole shrugged. "Maybe. There's something else."

"What's that?"

"Daphne says the time of death for the Harpers was last night, not this morning as I'd assumed. I figured they were drinking their morning coffee. Turns out they often drank a cup before bed. Not sure how they ever slept after that. Anyway, if they were dead last night, there's a good chance someone other than Wanda or Fred was driving the vehicle you saw leaving your neighborhood."

"It could have still been one of them."

"Sure, it could have. It also could be unrelated to the vandalism. Maybe it really was the mama raccoon who destroyed the pots, and the SUV you saw belonged to a cautious-driving neighbor or someone visiting a neighbor."

"You don't really believe that."

"My job is to gather facts without inserting too much of my own beliefs."

"If there is someone else, they probably think they've gotten away with it. Now, with Wanda, Fred, and Chet gone, they'll be lulled into a false sense of security."

Cole rubbed his whiskers. "Good point, and not a bad strategy."

I allowed the wave of pride from his validation to wash over me. "Thanks."

He gave me a sly smile out of the corner of his mouth. Just as he was about to say something, his walkie beeped.

"This is Chief Loveland."

"Hey, Cole, it's Vivienne. Is my sister there with you?"

"Viv, I'm not her receptionist. Why don't you call her directly?"

"I figured this was the easiest way to get ahold of both of you at the same time."

Cole and I exchanged baffled looks.

"Both of us?"

"Yes. I just got an urgent call from a man named Todd Wainwright."

"That's Chet's lawyer," I whispered loudly. "*Was* Chet's lawyer, I mean."

"Audrey? Was that you? I can't hear you."

"Yes, Viv, sorry. I was reminding Cole that Todd Wainwright is the lawyer Chet preemptively hired right before I went to visit him in Tacoma. He said because of attorney-client privilege, he had to cut our meeting short."

"Well, he must have changed his mind, because he'd like to see both of you in his office tomorrow morning. He says it's very important and can't wait."

Chapter Thirty-Two

"The drivers here are ridiculous." Cole changed from the left lane into the middle lane of Interstate 5 and glared at the oblivious woman going just under the speed limit. "It's a combination of the most inept and most aggressive drivers I've ever experienced."

"You're not used to driving on the freeways here, are you?"

"I try to stick close to home."

We were over an hour into our journey to Tacoma to meet with Todd Wainwright, who acted kind of cagey about why it had to be in person and not over the phone.

On our way out of town, we'd stopped at Abigail's for coffee and pastries. Almost like a scene in a movie, everyone stopped talking when we walked into the café. A few murmurs skated across the room, but it wasn't until we were halfway through the doorway that conversations resumed at full volume. I wasn't sure if they were observing us for insight into the investigation, or because we arrived together and it kind of looked like a date.

It definitely wasn't a date. If it were, Cole would've allowed me some say in the music selection. Instead, when I whimpered about his choice of early nineties pop, he muttered something about "my car, my radio," and turned up the volume. If I didn't particularly appreciate the music stylings of cheesy one-hit wonders at normal volume, I certainly didn't love it at peak volume.

Thankfully, as one of the worst offenders hit an off-key crescendo in the chorus, we pulled into the strip mall where Todd's office was located. Once again, the lot was nearly empty, and once again, Lottie's Union Jack Mini

Cooper was parked in front of the door.

"You sure you entered the right address into the nav?"

"I've been here before, remember? Believe it or not, this is it."

Cole followed me into the office.

Lottie looked up from filing her stiletto nails. "Hello again, luv! How can I—" She must have caught sight of Cole because her next words came out in what could only be described as a cockney purr. "Well, hello, officer. You here to slap those cuffs on me?" She held out her limp wrists and gave a playful pout.

Cole jerked his head back and shook it. "N-no. We have an appointment to see Mr. Wainwright."

Lottie let her hands fall to the desk in disappointment. She picked up the phone and pressed a button. "Todd, there's some people here to meet wif ya. A lady from before and an officah." She paused. "Yeah, she called an' said she comin' in layah. Affah lunch." Pause. "Okay." She replaced the receiver and looked up at us with her overly long false lashes practically touching above her brows. "He says you can go back."

I led Cole down the same hallway crammed with file cabinets I'd navigated five days prior. Todd stood in his doorway and waved us inside his office.

"C'mon in, guys."

We entered the office and took a seat opposite Todd.

"That's for making the trek down here, and sorry for the clandestine nature of this meeting, but I'm up against some tough legal and ethical parameters, and I've gotta tread carefully."

Cole crossed his legs and clasped his hands in his lap. "Audrey tells me when she met with you last Wednesday, you had to cut the meeting short due to a conflict of interest."

Todd vigorously nodded his head. "Yeah, yeah. The law, it's a tricky mistress."

I had no idea what that meant, so I waited for him to offer further explanation. He didn't give one.

"When Ms. O'Connell was here, I'd just that morning been retained by a client she mentioned by name."

"Chet Buchanan."

"See, that's the thing. I can neither confirm nor deny that I ever had such a client."

Cole stood and threw his hands in the air. "I don't know what kind of games you're playing, Mr. Wainwright, but I didn't drive all the way down here in rush hour traffic to be told you can't say anything. You called us."

Todd made a calm-down motion. "Now, now, Chief Loveland. I didn't mean to rile you. I'm merely trying to squirm my way through a set of regulations that could get me disbarred if it's found I've violated them while aiding in your investigation. Please, have a seat. I promise this will be helpful to you."

Cole lowered himself back into the chair. This time, he didn't cross his leg. He leaned forward with his hands clasped between them while his right knee bounced up and down.

"It has come to my attention that a few days ago, one of my clients was murdered. While I am bound beyond his death to maintain our privileged conversations, I do believe I can offer some insight that will shed light on the situation. I'm trying to maneuver this conversation in accordance with the standards to which I am held as an attorney in the state of Washington. However, as an officer of the court, I cannot in good conscience withhold information I believe pertains to this case."

Cole blew out a long breath, possibly mustering patience with his exhale.

I raised my hand.

"Yes, Ms. O'Connell?"

"You know anything you say to us will also be held in confidence. We won't report you to the Bar for sharing information."

Todd's rejection of my statement was swift and aggressive. He slammed his hand on the desk and pointed at me. "Just because I'm a divorce lawyer in a strip mall doesn't mean I don't take my duty to my clients very seriously. How else could I have built all this?" He waved his hands in the air.

I scanned the room, looking at the 'all this' he referenced, and found it lacking. However, insulting him wasn't the way to obtain the information we needed him to share.

Cole leaned even further forward. "Let's cut to the chase. What *can* you tell us?"

Todd looked at me. "I need you to give me a dollar."

"What?" I thought for a moment I misheard him.

"You came here last week to discuss case law and to possibly retain my services. Now, do it. I'm charging you a dollar retainer fee."

"But I thought—"

"Last week, I had a conflict of interest. This week I no longer represent the client which presented that conflict." He held out his hand.

I dug in my purse, to no avail. I did, however, locate a smushed tootsie roll, a lipstick that had gone missing six months ago, and two tampons.

"Oh, for the love of—" Cole reached into his back pocket and pulled out his wallet. He tugged a crisp dollar bill from the money clip and thrust it toward Todd.

Todd waved him off. "Nope. Gotta come from her."

Cole grunted. He handed me the note, which I examined.

"Do you iron your money?"

He indicated for me to hand it to Todd.

As I passed the dollar across Todd's desk, I murmured, "That's the kind of fresh cash you get from robbing a bank."

Cole glared at me and then returned his attention to Todd. "So, what now?"

Todd carefully folded the bill in half and then in quarters and slid it into the sagging breast pocket of his polyester button-up that was only buttoned up just north of his navel. He ran his hands through his slicked red hair and clasped them at the back of his neck.

"Audrey, you came to me asking about the culpability of online instigators as it pertains to the commission of crimes by others within their sphere of influence. I'd like to present you with a," he cleared his throat and looked pointedly at us, "*hypothetical* scenario."

"Okay."

Cole nodded.

"Let's say someone feels quite passionate about an action their local government had taken. Several actions, actually, which have left them frustrated about their voice not being heard in the process. They attempt to get involved in an official capacity, but are denied that opportunity, so they adopt an if you can't join 'em, beat 'em approach. They use a grassroots campaign to recruit like-minded individuals because one voice is easily ignored, but a chorus of voices protesting a policy or action gets noticed. Now, they are, by default, the leader of the movement. Follow me?"

I nodded. "I'm tracking."

"Perhaps in their zeal, our leader fails to recognize that some in the group may be taking things a bit too far. For example, a secret told in confidence about an elected official to one of the members ends up spray painted on a public wall."

I leaned over to Cole and whispered, "Margarita."

"Yes, I get it."

Todd covered his ears and hummed. "I can't hear you!"

I waved my hands in front of his face. "Continue."

Still with his hands over his ears, he yelled, "What?"

I gestured for him to continue.

"Oh!" He removed his hands. "It's important to note that leaders often draw obsessive types who fantasize about the attention they receive being romantic."

"Wasn't it?"

Todd's ears turned pink. "*Hypothetically*, it may have been flirty, maybe a little sexual, but no promises were made."

"And this leader manipulates their obsession to his advantage?" Cole tilted his head.

"Who's to say what's manipulation and what's delusion?"

"Give me a break." A half-scoff, half-gurgle escaped my throat.

Todd looked down his nose at me. "I don't have to do this, you know. I could keep it all close to the vest."

"Don't mind her."

Todd pursed his lips into a scowl. "Anyway, unbeknownst to our dear leader…"

"That's what they call the dictator of North Korea. It's kind of fitting, actually."

"Audrey." Cole's tone held a warning.

"Sorry."

"One of his followers decides the best way to stand out from the crowd and get his attention is to do something dramatic."

"Like what?"

He looked at me with an intense stare like he was willing me to read his mind.

"Like…arson?" I gasped and looked at Cole. "Chet didn't start the fire. Wanda did it because she had an unrequited crush and wanted him to pay attention to her!"

"Dammit, Audrey!" Todd glared at me. "You have to warn me when I need to cover my ears."

"Come on, this whole thing is a charade. You may be technically keeping privilege, but there's not a court in the land who wouldn't see what you're doing here."

It was the wrong thing to say.

Todd stood and calmly spoke his next two words. "Get. Out."

Cole jumped to his feet. "Mr. Wainwright, Audrey didn't mean to—"

Todd pointed at the door. "Get out of my office, both of you. It would be quite an embarrassment for Chattertowne to have another police chief arrested in such a short time after Chief Kimball."

Cole pulled me to my feet. "Come on, Audrey. You heard the man."

He dragged me into the hall.

I called over my shoulder. "It's assistant police chief Kimball! And she's a lovely woman when she's not murdering people!"

We climbed into Cole's vehicle, and he turned to glare at me.

"What?"

"You just couldn't keep your mouth shut for five more minutes?"

"He's a sleazeball. No matter how much he wants to act like he's super ethical, he represents scum like Chet and soon-to-be ex-husbands trying to avoid paying child support. Besides, we got all the information we needed."

Cole set his mouth into a grim line and out the gear shift into reverse. "We'll never know, now, will we?"

Chapter Thirty-Three

"Are you really not gonna talk to me all the way back to Chattertowne?" I yelled this over the music, which he'd turned up to an uncomfortable volume.

"What's there to say?"

I turned down the radio.

"Hey! I like that song."

"Nobody likes that song. Not even his mother. Now, listen. I know you're mad at me. I get it. I just felt like Todd was playing a whole lot of games. I couldn't bear him acting like Chet was a saint."

"I didn't take that from what he said at all. He was trying his best to convey to us what Chet told him without violating privilege."

"He was justifying Chet's behavior and villainizing Wanda."

"If she burned down two buildings and killed three men, she is a villain."

"I don't accept that he has no culpability in her actions."

"You don't have to accept it. There's no case to prove. They're all dead."

* * *

Cole's words echoed through my mind that night as I soaked in a bubble bath.

They're all dead.

Were they, though?

Zeb Brandt was dead, probably because Wanda got a rush from the old mill fire and wanted to impress Chet. Unfortunately, she didn't know Zeb was in the barn. If she were still alive, it most likely would have been classified as second-degree murder because it was an accidental death occurring in the commission of a felony.

Chet was dead. The motive for his murder remained unclear, but it wasn't an accident. It might not have been premeditated, but it was intentional. Perhaps Wanda flew into a jealous rage when she saw Chet with Susan. I hadn't yet ruled out the possibility Fred killed Chet because he believed Chet and Wanda were having an affair.

Which brought me to Fred. All indications were Wanda poisoned Fred's coffee and then took her own life so she wouldn't have to face the consequences of her actions. The quote on the fridge in her handwriting wasn't exactly a suicide note, but it was an indication of her state of mind. Whether it was Wanda's betrayal with Chet, Fred's betrayal with Jenna, Fred's betrayal of Chet, or Chet's betrayal with Susan, it was too convoluted to determine. It could be one or all. Did it even matter anyway?

Like Cole said, they were all dead. Except...

Jenna and Susan.

I sat up in the bath and picked up my phone.

"Pissing off my boss doesn't make my job easier, Audrey." Viv sounded tired.

"I know. I'm sorry. Come over, and I'll pour you a glass of wine to make it up to you."

"Why do I get the feeling this invitation isn't solely altruistic?"

"I may have a couple questions for you. Why not answer them while sipping a Portuguese Alicante Bouschet?"

"Since when do you drink Portuguese wine?" Viv gasped. "Have you been secretly seeing Holden?"

"No! I mean, we've hung out more in the past week than we have in the past year and a half, but not drinking wine together. He may have mentioned it, is all. I thought I'd try it out with my very best sister."

"I'm your only sister."

"Come over. I'm getting out of the bath now."

***

By the time Viv arrived, I was bundled in a robe on the sofa with a fire blazing in the fireplace, sipping white wine.

"I think Holden's trying to kill me, "I announced when she plopped onto the sofa next to me.

"That's an unexpected twist."

"That wine he recommended is a red." I indicated the open bottle on the coffee table next to an empty glass with pink residue.

Vivienne threw her head back in laughter. "He knows you're allergic! Maybe he is trying to kill you to get revenge for the time you accused him of murder."

"That must be it."

"Good news is *I'm* not allergic to red wine." Viv tucked her platinum blonde hair behind her ear and poured the contents of the bottle into the glass. She held her glass in the air. "Here's to no more murders now that Wanda's dead!"

I absentmindedly clinked her glass and sipped my Riesling. "I hope you're right."

"Why wouldn't I be? Cole said all signs point to Wanda setting the fires to impress Chet, but when he rebuffed her advances, she killed him in a fit of rage. Then she took out Fred and finally herself."

"Maybe."

"That's not convincing."

"Because I'm not convinced," I said. "I think it's possible Fred killed Chet because of Wanda's obsession."

"Well, that doesn't change anything, because even if he did, he's not committing any more crimes." Viv did a wonky sign of the cross. "Rest in Peace."

"We aren't catholic."

"I know. I just feel like I need to do something to absolve my guilt when I talk trash about dead people."

"Could Jenna have killed Fred and Wanda?"

Viv scrunched her face. "Why would she do that?"

"The other night, after Fred led his mini-revolution, he left with Jenna. I'm almost positive they were having an affair. Then Wanda stormed out after them. Maybe there was a fight."

"You think Jenna killed them out of jealousy? That makes no sense. They were poisoned. That's not a crime of passion. It's a dispassionate deliberate act of murder. Plus, how would she sneak rat poison in their coffee?"

I sighed and sipped my wine. "True. And it was sitting on their kitchen counter." I sat upright. "I have an idea."

Viv called after me as I ran up the stairs. "What now?"

I shuffled back downstairs, holding my laptop. "I'm going to post a quick update to the Current's website indicating my skepticism that the crimes can all be attributed to Wanda. That way, if someone else is out there with a guilty conscience, they'll try to figure out what I know."

"You're making yourself bait."

"If there's someone to lure, this should do it."

"Audrey, you're trying to lure a murderer, not a humpie. One may put up a fight; the other might get you killed."

* * *

The next morning, I woke to the sound of my phone buzzing before dawn.

"This better be an emergency, Cole."

"Are you out of your mind?"

"I don't know. Call me after eight when my brain normally turns on."

"Audrey, I saw what you posted last night. That was reckless and dangerous. You're lucky someone didn't show up and murder you in your sleep."

"That was kind of the point."

"Excuse me?"

"Viv stayed the night. We took turns keeping a lookout in case anyone took the bait. Unfortunately, we didn't get any action."

Cole's frustrated sigh blew through the phone. "I've hardly slept in more than a week. The last thing I need is to be worrying about you putting yourself in harm's way just to get a story."

"Aww, you're worried about me. We've come a long way since you dubbed me the enemy press."

A grunt came through the phone. "Tell your sister I need her to be on time today." He hung up the call.

"Nice talking to you, too," I said into my disconnected phone.

Since I was already semi-conscious, I meandered downstairs to find Viv already awake, dressed, and sipping coffee.

"Your boss just called. He says don't be late."

Viv scoffed. "I'm never late." She must have noticed my skepticism because she added, "Ten minutes isn't going to kill anyone."

Later, she would tell me how that statement came back to haunt her.

Chapter Thirty-Four

Throughout the morning, I read every comment left on my article. Some complained the investigation had been slow and Cole hadn't been forthcoming enough about what he planned to do to stem the sudden tide of crime which had swept across Chattertowne over the past couple weeks. Some posted their condolences for the victims, while others gave *I told you so*'s and *serves you right*'s like that was helpful in any way.

None of the comments raised my antennae or indicated a knowledge of the crimes beyond what had been made public. So far, my plan was a bust.

Then the doorbell rang.

Still wearing the clothes I'd slept in and not having yet run a brush through my hair, I said a quick prayer that neither Holden nor Cole stood on my front porch. I should have broadened that prayer to include the man who was, in fact, standing on the other side of my front door when I opened it.

"Hy? What are you doing here?"

Hiram looked more haggard than I'd ever seen him. His hair was more mussed than mine, his jowls sagged even more than normal, and his eyes were bloodshot.

"We need to talk." His gruff voice added to my impression he hadn't had much sleep. "Can I come in?"

"Uh."

With only a rickety aluminum screen door between us, any feeling of security was an illusion, but still, I felt better with him outside and me inside.

"I was just about to get ready to meet Cole at the station."

"Audrey, I know you're lying. Don't play games with me."

Damn my terrible poker face.

He opened the screen door and pushed past me into the living room. I considered running outside to call for help, but something about his demeanor stopped me. Instead of coming at me, Hy paced in a circle in front of my fireplace.

Even though it was about forty-five degrees outside, I left the door ajar and walked over to him. He stopped in his tracks and looked at me with surprise, like he'd forgotten I was there, or even where he was.

I stared into his eyes. They weren't red from lack of sleep. They were watery.

He'd been crying.

I touched his upper arm. "Why don't you sit and regroup for a minute, and then you can tell me what's going on. Would you like some coffee?"

He grunted, nodded, and collapsed onto the sofa.

I went into the kitchen and turned on the single-cup coffee maker. "Creamer?"

"Black."

After I made his drink, I set the mug on the table in front of him. He picked it up, took a sip, and placed it down again.

"I'm not gonna lie, Hy, you kinda freaked me out."

"Sorry. I didn't know where else to go."

"Why are you here?"

"I saw your article or whatever on the *Current*'s website. You said you don't believe Wanda was responsible for all of this." Hy dropped his head and let his hands hang loose between his open legs.

I observed him for a moment. "This is about Wanda."

He raised his gaze to look at me. I saw deep pain.

"You were in love with her."

His head dropped again. "I only acted on it once. That didn't go too well." He threw out a sad laugh. "She was in love with him."

"Fred?"

This time, his laugh was bitter. "That SOB? He was a serial cheater and abuser. Maybe not physically, but mentally, for sure. One night after a

CROCCC meeting I saw her crying in her car. She just sat there, without the engine on, without the radio, just sobbing. Fred had 'accidentally' messaged her something intended for his girlfriend." He used air quotes. "I think he did it on purpose to mess with Wanda. I tried to comfort her, but when I moved in for a kiss, she made it quite clear she wasn't interested in me that way."

"You both were married."

"Unhappily."

I let that pass without comment. "So, the message was meant for Jenna?"

He looked at me with surprise. "He wasn't trying too hard to keep the secret, but I had no idea it was that well known."

"I began to suspect when she was the first person he called after Cole visited him following Chet's death. It was a Saturday morning. Then, at the meeting Monday night, he didn't even try to hide it."

Hiram gave a sad nod. "That must have been the final straw for her. Not only had he humiliated her by walking out with his girlfriend, he did it right after voting to disband her precious heritage commission."

"You voted the same as Fred."

"I didn't have a choice."

"How so?"

Hiram rubbed his hands together. "Fred threatened to pull all my contracts and block me from any future deals if I didn't side with him."

"Couldn't you have reported him?"

"Only if I never wanted to work in this county again. He's got politicians in his pocket from the lowest levels of Chattertowne government to the state legislature."

"Had."

"Huh?"

"He *had* politicians in his pocket."

"Oh. Yeah. It didn't matter, anyway. If I'd voted against him, Wanda still had no interest in me, even with Chet dead."

"It seems weird Wanda would have killed Chet out of jealousy and then also Fred for the same reason."

CHAPTER THIRTY-FOUR

"Wanda didn't kill Chet." His tone was resolute. "I know that for a fact."

"Why do you say that?"

"Because I saw Wanda and Fred arguing during the second quarter of the homecoming game. They were headed to the parking lot. I texted her to see if she was okay, but she said she had a migraine and insisted on Fred driving her home. I saw Chet a couple minutes later walking through the courtyard. Susan had dumped him, so he was moping."

"Why didn't you say anything about any of this when Cole and I came to your house?"

"I couldn't give Wanda an alibi without giving Fred one, too. I didn't wanna do that."

"You hear how petty that sounds, right? You pointed us right at Fred, knowing he wasn't guilty."

Hiram shrugged his shoulders. "He was guilty, just not of that."

"Even if she didn't kill Chet, Wanda definitely killed Fred."

Once again, Hiram shrugged.

"I can't believe you're being so nonchalant about murder."

"I'm not being nonchalant. I'm numb. In the past week, I've lost my best friend and the woman I loved—whether she loved me back or not. To make things worse, I betrayed them both for money."

"If Fred didn't kill Chet, and Wanda didn't kill Chet, who did?"

Hiram shrugged again. "Dunno. Wasn't me, I can tell you that much."

"Hy, you have to tell Cole."

"What difference does it make?"

"Well, for one thing, it's not insignificant that you were the last person to see Chet. For another, that means Chet's killer is still out there somewhere."

Hy's head reared back, and he grimaced. "I wasn't the last person to see Chet."

"You just said—"

"I said I saw him walking in the courtyard after Fred and Wanda left."

"Right, the courtyard where he was killed."

"He was alive when I left him. And he wasn't alone."

"Who was with him?"

Hiram tilted his head. "He was pulled into a dark corner by Blakesly Whitehead."

Chapter Thirty-Five

Viv looked up from her desk with surprise. It wasn't so much because of my unexpected appearance at the station—as I'd become a regular visitor—but likely due to the man standing next to me with my arm gripped tightly around his.

She stared at our arms linked together. "Hiram, this is a safe space. Has she brought you in here against your will?"

He grunted a laugh. "Citizen's arrest, more like it."

I swatted at him with my free hand. "That's not true. I'm merely accompanying him to make sure he does what he said he would do."

Viv tilted her head. "Which is?"

I nudged him.

"I'm here to amend my statement to Chief Loveland regarding the murder of Chet Buchanan."

I gave Viv a triumphant look. "He in?"

She never broke eye contact while picking up the receiver. "Hey, Cole, you have some visitors." She paused. "I'm aware, but this is urgent." Another pause and an impatient sigh. "Come to the lobby, and you'll get all those answers." She hung up the phone and plastered on a fake smile. "He'll be right out."

I dragged Hiram over to the chairs facing Viv's glass enclosure. She mouthed, *what the hell,* and I responded by puckering my lips. Cole burst into the lobby and took in the sight of Hiram and me.

He turned to Viv and pointed at us. "This is your idea of something worth interrupting my weekly planning session with Bianchi?"

Viv glared in response.

I yanked Hiram to his feet. "Hy has something he'd like to tell you."

Cole planted his feet shoulder-width apart and crossed his arms. He turned his attention to Hiram. "What's this about?"

Hy dropped his chin, barely making eye contact. "I wasn't completely forthcoming about Chet's murder."

"Okay. This sounds like a conversation we should have in my office."

Hiram nodded. Cole marched toward the locked door and entered the code. He waved his hand for us to follow him…or I thought he did. I got to the door, but he blocked my entrance.

"Not you."

"I'm sorry, what?"

"Audrey, this is still a police investigation. You're a reporter, not a detective."

"I already know everything he's going to say. He spilled his guts at my house."

"Even more reason you don't need to be in there. I need to make sure everything is clean and above board. After what happened before with the assistant chief, it's imperative I protect the integrity of the process."

I threw a glance at Viv, who winced at the mention of her incarcerated girlfriend.

"Go home. I'll call you later." His voice held a finality, and his mouth was firmly set.

My shoulders slumped, and I made an exaggerated pout. "Fine, but please call me as soon as you're done."

Cole led Hiram into the interrogation room where I'd once sat with a forensic artist sketching out Peter Chatterton's portrait.

I turned to Viv. "Make sure he calls me."

"What's this about?"

"Long story, but the gist is he could have cleared the Harpers of Chet's murder, but he didn't because of an unrequited love for Wanda and hatred for Fred. He also may hold the missing piece of the puzzle as to who did kill Chet."

"Who?" Viv whispered.

I looked around to make sure no one was listening and lowered my voice to a volume just above hers. "He says the last time he saw Chet, he was with *Buh-lakes-ly Wah-hite-head.*" I enunciated each syllable of her name and added an extra couple for emphasis.

"Really!"

I nodded emphatically. "Really."

"Why would Blakesly kill Chet?"

"I don't know that she did, but without the info, Cole would have had no reason to look at her too closely."

"All I know is I hope this string of violent crimes is finally over. I was telling Lacey about it on our weekly call last night and she couldn't believe how crazy things have gotten."

I chose not to mention the chaos Viv's girlfriend had wrought on this town not long ago.

She lowered her voice. "Wanna hear a little gossip?"

"Always."

"Lacey says she went out for drinks one night a few years back with Margarita, you know, just as friends. Margarita had a few too many—"

"Margaritas?" I bobbled my head, pleased with my joke.

"Cosmos, actually. Focus, Audrey."

"Sorry."

"Lacey told me Margarita confided in her that she's trans!"

"Ohh."

She narrowed her gaze. "You knew."

"I just found out."

"When?"

"Last week."

"And you didn't tell me?"

"It wasn't my secret to tell."

Viv's mouth gaped. "Since when are you so tight-lipped?"

"Since I witnessed firsthand what people are capable of doing in the name of keeping their secrets."

"You're a reporter. Your entire job is to pull back the veil and reveal what's underneath."

"Margarita's secret hurts no one. I have a feeling, though, that Chet's death is the direct result of a secret someone didn't want revealed."

"You think he was killed because he was blackmailing someone? Like Marcus did?"

"Maybe. I don't know. There are so many moving parts to this I'm still trying to figure out on which side everyone is aligned. I used to think it was Chet, Hy, the Harpers, the Milners, and the Whiteheads versus Margarita. Now I don't know what to believe."

* * *

Instead of heading to my car, I took a left out of the City Hall building and walked toward the marina. I had no intention of going onto the docks, but I needed some fresh air to clear my thoughts.

I leaned against the railing and closed my eyes, allowing the crisp autumn air coming up from the river to wash over me. Unfortunately, it smelled less like my favorite ocean breeze fabric softener and more like stale pond water mixed with bad sushi.

I opened my eyes and took in the view. Most of the boats had been buttoned up in anticipation of the inevitable stormy weather, which often hit mid-October and didn't let up until spring. Some boats still appeared to be in regular use, such as my boss Nicholas Anderson's year-round liveaboard.

At the far edge two people—a man and a woman—stood in a tight embrace. One seemed to be comforting the other, as his hand caressed her long, dark hair. They released, and the man wiped the cheek of the woman. He put his arm around her shoulder, and they walked toward the gangplank.

I gasped audibly.

It was Levi Scott and Jenna Doyle.

Levi caught sight of me and gave me a feeble smile. Jenna, still upset and crying, had her face buried in the crook of his arm. They walked up the ramp and down the street.

CHAPTER THIRTY-FIVE

How long had those two been an item?

* * *

I stopped by the *Current* to show my face in case anyone wondered if I still worked there. Tasha, the receptionist, was on the phone when I walked into the lobby. She gave a smirk and a flourishing wave with her left hand, something she did on a regular basis to show off her engagement ring from Sandros, our IT guy.

I ducked into Anderson's office, but it was empty. He still taught a couple English classes at the high school.

Everyone else seemed to be absent or busy.

My stomach growled. When had I last eaten?

I waved to Tasha as I hustled back out of the office.

I was standing over my kitchen sink shoveling a deep-fried taco from Alberto's into my mouth when my phone buzzed a text from an unknown number.

Meet me @new pking lot @6

Who is this?

I hv tip abt Chets death

The text was punctuated with a skull emoji.

Can't you just tell me?

No cops or I wont show

I stared at my phone screen. I started to sweat, and it wasn't just from the hot sauce on my tacos.

This was either exclusive information that could lead to solving the case and putting me on the local journalistic map, or it could be the killer using my own baiting tactics against me.

Either way, I was going to the meet.

At 5:45, I opened my front door to leave.

"Oh! You startled me! I was just going to leave these under the mat." Standing on my porch was my neighbor.

"What do you have?"

She thrust a stack of mail at me. "Victor accidentally delivered these to me by mistake."

I took the envelopes and flyers from her and shoved them into my satchel. "Thanks, Nancy."

She looked at me expectantly.

"Oh, I, uh, I'd invite you in, but I was just on my way out. I have a meeting down at the new parking lot."

"Always so busy. Raincheck then?"

"Of course."

As she scuttled back across my yard, I got into my car and flopped my satchel on the seat beside me. The sun wouldn't set for another forty-five minutes or so, but because it was cloudy, the sky had started to darken.

I drove out of town and into the outskirts, where homes became fewer and further between. I passed two horse ranches and an alpaca farm before turning into the entrance for the lot. Up ahead, I could see the remains of the Brandt barn and, next to the newly laid asphalt, which still sported the bright pink graffiti that started this whole fortnight of chaos, the ashes of the old mill.

I pulled into a corner spot facing the river, although I had my pick since the lot was empty. I put my car in park but kept the engine running for heat. The doors automatically unlocked. I was uncharacteristically on time, but the person who'd sent me the cryptic messages hadn't yet arrived, causing me to wonder if it were someone who knew me—and my habitual tardiness—well.

I needed to let someone know where I was. Not Cole, though. He'd be annoyed I'd gone alone without telling him, no doubt. Besides, I was still irritated with him for shutting me out of the interview with Hiram, so I shared my location with Viv instead.

I drummed my fingers on the steering wheel. I chewed the inside of my cheek. I craned my neck to look at the road about a dozen times. Finally, I yanked the stack of mail Nancy had given me out of my satchel.

Mostly it was junk, a couple utility bills, and a free sample of laundry detergent. I got pretty excited about the sample.

Amidst the stack was a small light pink envelope with my name and address on the front, but no return address. I tore it open and pulled out a piece of paper—two, actually—and unfolded them. The letter was dated Monday and, judging by its content, was written the night of the meeting where Fred disbanded the heritage commission.

The night Fred and Wanda died.

Wanda's perfect cursive was like a voice from the grave.

I pored over her words, taking in all the revelations and surprises, along with confirmation of several working theories. The entire picture became clear: CROCCC, Chet and the women of CROCCC, the plan, the counterplan from Fred and his cronies, the graffiti, the fires, and the murders. It was in that moment I knew who killed Chet Buchanan.

Hiram was right. It wasn't Wanda.

I texted Holden and Cole in a group text.

I know who killed Chet.

Once again, I scanned the letter, verifying everything I thought I had read. I was so absorbed in it the world around me faded away.

I guess that's why I didn't see the dark gray SUV pull into the lot, blocking my car. I also didn't see its driver coming around to my window until I heard a tap. I jumped a bit and yelped when I saw what the hooded figure had used to tap on the glass.

It was the barrel of a rifle.

Chapter Thirty-Six

In the span of thirty seconds—which felt like thirty minutes—I debated whether to open the door or lock it. My car was blocked, so I couldn't drive away, and I had little faith in my ability to outrun anyone. With only one pathetic lesson at the gun range with Holden a couple years before, I also didn't have enough experience with guns to know the power or capability of the rifle, but I suspected it could shoot me through the closed window.

I shoved the letter into my satchel, opened the door, and got out with both hands in the air.

I'd have to bank on my wits to get out of the situation with my life. "Regan, you don't want to do this. I'm not your nemesis. I can help you."

She pulled her hood down. "You don't seem very surprised to see me."

"I know what Chet did to you, and I understand why you felt the need to take action."

"You know nothing." She slammed my car door. "Give me your phone."

I hesitated, but when she pointed the rifle at my face, I complied.

"Before she poisoned herself and Fred, Wanda mailed a full confession to me." I softened my voice, hoping she would see me as an ally. "She explained everything, how Chet preyed on all of you, how he pitted you, your mom, and Wanda against each other."

"It's worse than that." Her pretty, sullen face clouded. "What kind of sicko, when an eighteen-year-old confronts him, begging him to leave her mom alone so her parents don't end up divorced, seduces her and…" She stopped, breathing heavily. She touched her mouth with her fingertips, trying to suppress a gag.

Another horrifying piece of the puzzle clicked into place. "Chet got you pregnant, didn't he?" She was just a little girl. I wanted to kill him myself.

She doubled over and vomited, gripping the rifle at her midsection.

"Oh, Regan, I'm so sorry."

She stood and wiped her mouth on her sleeve. "Come on." She poked the rifle into my shoulder.

"Come on, what?"

"Move." She poked me again.

"Where are we going?"

"Down to the river."

My shivers weren't only because of the wind, which had picked up in the past few minutes. "Regan, I have a pretty serious case of aquaphobia. Can't we just stay up here?"

She jutted her chin side to side. "Oh, I know all about your fear of water. That's one of the reasons I asked you to meet me here. I'm in Mr. Anderson's English class. He's made us read all your articles. That's how I found out about your latest post, the one where you gave all the reasons you didn't think Wanda or Fred were Chet's killers. He had us read it in class today."

So, my plan had worked. Too bad I hadn't fully thought through what came next.

Regan poked me again with the rifle, this time in my kidney.

"Ow!"

"Then move."

We scampered down the rocky berm to the riverbank. I slid halfway, scraping my palm on a jagged rock. Regan was nimble, likely due to years of cheerleading and tumbling.

"Did you know I was also a cheerleader at Chattertowne High?" I wiped my dirty, bloody palm on my jeans.

She smirked. "Like a million years ago, I'm sure."

"More like half a million. I was on the squad with Onyx Carpenter."

Regan's mouth gaped. "You know Onyx Carpenter?" Her tone was hushed with awe.

I nodded. "I do. Of course, I haven't seen her much lately. She's too busy with her talk show, promoting her skincare line, and she also travels quite a bit when her husband's band is on tour."

"I love Bonzerkind! I went to their concert last year. Meacham Fields is so hot."

For a moment, the hard-eyed killer holding a gun on me dissolved into a wide-eyed teenager who probably still had stuffed animals on her bed, celebrity posters on her wall, and wore a retainer at bedtime.

"She's supposed to be in town next spring. Maybe I can set it up for you to meet her."

A brief glimmer of excitement crossed her face but darkened just as quickly. "Next spring, I'll be almost nine months pregnant." Her voice was barely audible over the sound of the river rushing past us. Heavy rain in the foothills overnight had it running high.

"Regan, what happened? Between you and Chet, I mean."

She looked lost and sad and small. "I hated him. I know it sounds crazy now, considering…" She waved the rifle in front of her stomach. "He was tearing my family apart. I don't know what it was about him, but my mom was under his spell. Same with Wanda. They were always fighting to see who could lick his boots better. By the end of it, I'm not even sure it was about him anymore. Wanda would comment on his posts like he was the savior of Chattertowne, and then my mom would go write an even more disgusting blog, praising him. He ate it up. Chet loved having them at each other's throats, trying to get his attention."

Raindrops began to pelt my head. "I can't imagine your dad appreciated that too much."

Regan scoffed. "He hated him, too. Not at first, though. My parents invited him over for dinner. My dad liked his ideas about getting control of the mayor's office. Nobody likes Margarita."

"I like Margarita."

"That's because you're a journalist. You guys are all biased. My dad says you're a communist."

A squawk of laughter mixed with shock escaped me. "That's ridiculous."

"My parents say the media is just the government's way of controlling what people think."

"Regan, you're too smart to believe that."

Her face reddened. "Are you calling my parents stupid?"

"No…I…I'm sorry. I just meant—"

"Shut up. I don't want to hear anything from you. My mom is standing up for freedom of speech."

"And your dad?"

"He liked Chet okay when he was trying to stop Margarita and her corruption, but then things got weird."

"Weird?"

Regan's eyes began to fill with tears. "They started fighting. A lot."

"Your parents?"

Regan nodded, tears now streaming down her cheeks. "My dad liked the anti-government control stuff, but Chet was starting to behave like the people he was trying to take down. He was all about stopping the mayor or the city council from taking rights away, but then he acted like a dictator in CROCCC. My mom thought he could do no wrong, but my dad got mad when Chet started trying to block the buffalo building. He said Chet was putting sentimentality over progress. My mom said she felt used and betrayed by my dad teaming up with Fred Harper to take down CROCCC, because he'd used all the information that she'd shared with him against Chet."

"Were Chet and your mom having an affair?"

"Eww. No, gross. You think I'd sleep with a man my mom slept with? That's practically incest." She grunted. "It wasn't for lack of trying on her part. That's the funny thing. She was obsessed with him, but he wasn't interested in her. Not that way, at least. She told him what Fred and my dad were up to. He gave her enough attention to keep her loyal, that's all."

"So, how did you—"

She poked me again. "Keep walking."

We walked south along the riverbank, me in front with Regan behind. We were headed further from town, into farmland with few cars, fewer people, and larger distance between houses. It was getting dark, and the terrain was rocky. I slipped a few times on the rain-soaked pebbles. I lost my bearings.

"About two months ago, I showed up at his paint store to confront him. He thought I was looking for a job. At that point, I wasn't sure if something was going on between him and my mom, so I figured working for him was a good way to keep an eye on things. One night, my mom stopped by. She acted like she was there to see me, but really, she was there for him. After she left, I begged him to leave her alone. He laughed and said he could have her if he wanted her. Then he asked me how I could think he'd go after her when he'd made it clear he wanted me."

"How did you feel about that?"

"Conflicted. I didn't see him that way. I mean, he wasn't ugly, just old. He had a dad bod. I thought if I gave into him, he wouldn't mess with her." She sighed. "There was something about him, I can't even explain it, but I caught feelings. When I found out I was pregnant, I thought maybe we could be a real couple. Stupid me."

"He didn't feel the same?"

"He'd started seeing that bitch Madame Prendergast. Told me I needed to 'handle it' on my own because he was going to marry *her*, and he didn't want my little problem messing up his life." She used air quotes. "They'd only been dating like three weeks!"

"Your mom must have been furious with him when she found out about the baby."

"She doesn't know about the baby. I haven't told anyone else."

I stopped and turned to face her. "She knows."

"She doesn't. Why are you saying that?"

"In her letter, Wanda said she overheard your mother confronting Chet shortly before he died. She was screaming at him about defiling her daughter and taking responsibility for his child."

The white of Regan's eyes glowed in the darkness. "I—I didn't know that she knew." She gasped. "That must have been when I—I saw them together."

"At the homecoming game?"

"I'd seen him earlier that night with Madame Prendergast. *Susan.*" She spat the name like it was poison. "They were all smiley and he was acting all affectionate and romantic toward her. Not like he'd been with me. With me, it felt dirty and aggressive. Cold, almost like he was forcing himself to do it. Sometimes, it seemed like he was only doing it to manage me. With her, he was acting sweet. And not in a fake way."

"That couldn't have felt good."

"No. I realized I was nothing more than part of his agenda for saving Chattertowne from itself. That's what he liked to say, like he had all the answers and everyone else just needed to be handled. Managed."

"What happened? At the game?"

"I was going to change into my dress, and I saw Chet and my mom huddled up in a corner in the courtyard. It looked like they were making out."

"I don't think they were."

"Doesn't sound like it, but that's what it looked like. I was so mad that I stormed into the band building and started pacing, trying to figure out what to do. All those things I did to keep him away from my mom were for nothing. I can't remember the last time I was so mad."

Her face darkened with rage, and tears poured from her eyes.

"Someone had left the spirit award sitting on a table. I didn't think; I just grabbed it and marched into the courtyard. My mom was gone, but Chet was sitting at the edge of the fountain alone. He looked like he was pouting. He saw me coming, and he started to stand up, but I swung the trophy at his head. I must not have swung hard enough because he climbed onto the statue to get away from me. He was holding his head, and he freaked when he pulled his hand away and saw the blood. He yelled for help, but it must have been right after a touchdown because his scream was drowned out by the cannon. He snarled at me and called me names. He called my baby names. I jumped up and swung again. This time I gave him an uppercut and he flung backward. It was like I was a different person." She stared ahead like she was watching the replay of herself in an out-of-body experience.

Disassociation. It was common during and in the aftermath of severe trauma.

"And then I was myself again, and I saw what I'd done. I started freaking out. I rinsed the trophy and my face in the fountain and ran into the building with it shoved under my cheer sweater. I dumped it into a trashcan and then ran into the locker room before anyone saw me. I got into my dress, sash, and tiara and ran out to the homecoming ceremony like nothing had happened."

"I can't even imagine how traumatic all of that must have been."

"I think I was in shock, mostly."

She was quiet for a moment.

"I hate to ask, but what exactly is your end game here? You're not a murderer, Regan, not really. You're a girl who got in over her head."

She looked out at the black water. "I think you killed Chet, and then you tried to kill me, but I got away."

"Wait, what?"

She leveled her gaze at me. "You killed Chet because you didn't like what he stood for, and I witnessed it, so you tried to silence me. Lucky for me, I brought a gun to our meeting. Not so lucky for you. I'll make sure my mom writes a decent obituary for you."

"You'll never get away with it."

"Of course I will. No one knows any of this except you and poor Wanda. Pretty soon, you'll both be turned into ashes, along with Wanda's letter to you." Her pocket buzzed. She pulled my phone out and stared at the glowing screen. "Cole Loveland, hmm? He's sexy. You have a lot of texts and missed calls from him." She threw my phone into the river. "Sorry, Cole, Audrey's unable to come to the phone at the moment...or ever again." She directed the rifle at my chest.

I couldn't believe this was how it was going to end for me. Just as I was about to open my mouth to plead my case, a blinding light shone down on us from up on the berm.

"Regan, put the weapon down."

She jerked her head to look up at the disembodied voice behind the light. "I'm just protecting myself from her! Thank goodness you're here, Cole! She killed Chet!"

I took advantage of the distraction and tried to run. Regan was quicker, though. She tackled me from behind, knocking us both into the water. Besides being freezing, my aquaphobia kicked into high gear, causing my body to go into a state of paralysis. All I was able to muster was a tiny squeak.

Regan forced my head under the water, banging my head against a rock. She pulled me up out of the water and then thrust me down again. The last thing I remembered was the muted voices shouting from the shore before everything went black.

Chapter Thirty-Seven

"So, should I expect to see you unconscious on a gurney every couple years, or is this the last of it?"

I opened my eyes to find Holden's concerned face looming over me. I was in an ambulance.

"I'd like to say it won't happen again, but I thought the last time was the last time." My voice came out raspy.

"I'm strongly considering putting a tracking device on you."

"Haha." I struggled to sit up, but the back of my head throbbed. I grabbed it and winced.

"Actually, Holden, that's not a bad idea." Cole approached from the back of a police car with flashing lights. "Since Audrey doesn't seem to have enough common sense to not meet killers at night in secluded locations without telling anyone where she's going or what she's doing."

"I sent Viv my location. And I didn't know I was meeting a killer. Obviously, you found me somehow."

"I tried to call after you sent that text about identifying Chet's killer," Cole said. "When you didn't answer, I called Viv. She offered to drive by your place on her way home from work. Your car wasn't there, but your neighbor mentioned something about a meeting down here. That's when Viv noticed you were sharing your location."

Good old Nancy. "Where is Viv?"

"I told her to wait at the house in case you came home." Cole rocked back on his heels and crossed his arms. He looked distinctly uncomfortable.

Holden glanced at him. "I get it, man. Part of you wants to hug her with relief, and the other part of you wants to shake her for putting herself in a dangerous position."

"Something like that," Cole murmured. His pupils were so large his blue eyes looked black, and his expression was inscrutable.

Holden cocked his head to the side and observed Cole. He turned his attention back to me. "I'm gonna head to your house to hang with Viv until you're ready for us to pick you up from the hospital. Unless you want me to follow you there."

"You don't have to do that," Cole interjected. "I'll be there with her so I can bring her home."

They exchanged looks and posturing like they were having an entire conversation without using words.

"Do I have to go to the hospital?"

Cole nodded. "Yeah, you do. Cataloging your injuries will be an important component of the case against Regan."

I shook my head in disbelief but immediately regretted it when pain shot through my wound. "I still can't believe Regan did this. Blakesly's going to be devastated."

"That's what she gets for naming her kid after a Shakespearean villain."

I stared at Cole.

"What? You think because I grew up in Wyoming, I don't know King Lear?"

"You really are full of surprises."

Holden cleared his throat. "I'll, uh, I'll see you later at the house." He leaned down and kissed my forehead. "I don't know what I'd do if I lost you." His husky whisper nearly cracked with emotion.

Did he mean losing me to death...or to someone else? I stared into his eyes but couldn't find my answer.

And what would I do if the answer I found was that he was afraid of losing me to Cole? Probably laugh. It was laughable, wasn't it? I was the thorn in his side. The burr in his saddle. He barely tolerated me.

No way. Cole Loveland didn't see me in a romantic way. He couldn't possibly.

I stole a glance at him. Beneath the brim of his hat, his brow was furrowed with concern. He caught me staring, and his eyes pooled with an unexpected warmth.

Could he? What would I do if he did?

Once again, Holden cleared his throat.

"I'll, uh, I'll be there as soon as I can," I said.

Holden straightened and looked at Cole. "Make sure they look her over really well."

Cole gave a slight nod. "I'll take good care of her."

Holden's smile faltered just as he turned and walked away.

Cole came closer and looked at me with an intensity that caught my breath. A subtle wave of his cologne washed over my face.

"I'm going to follow the ambulance to the ER. As soon as they get you into a room, I'll come find you."

"Okay." I touched my fingertips to my forehead.

"What is it?"

"I feel a little dizzy."

He looked around for a paramedic, and when he spotted one shouted, "Let's get her out of here."

A flurry of activity had me thrust into the back of the ambulance and on my way to the hospital with sirens wailing and paramedics strapping various cuffs and monitors to me.

I was too embarrassed to admit to them I didn't think it was my head wound causing my lightheadedness, but a certain cowboy police chief with deep blue eyes and a crackling wit.

* * *

I spent four hours at the emergency room before they finally released me to Cole's custody with a few stitches in my skull and some heavy-duty pain meds I had no intention of taking. The last time I'd been given medication for an injury, I lost track of how much I'd taken and went into a deep sleep for nearly a full day.

We drove back to Chattertowne in silence, with nothing but the sound of his tires thumping against the pavement.

"I'm sorry about all the teasing I've done since you came to town. I never meant any of it in a malicious way."

Cole looked straight ahead at the road. He pursed his lips. "I never took it in a malicious way. Why would you think I did?"

I gave a soft laugh. "Because you took an immediate dislike to me, and it seemed to grow with each encounter. The less you liked me, the more I felt compelled to tease you. I guess I thought it would loosen you up, but instead, it seemed to make you despise me more. I regret that now."

He jerked his head to look at me and then returned his attention to the highway. "Audrey, I never despised you." He let out a baffled laugh and a whoosh of air. "Not even a little."

I observed his profile. "That's good, 'cause I never despised you either."

He glanced at me. "Well, there's that, then. Not exactly a ringing endorsement, but I'll take it."

"There's that." I sighed.

There was that. Whatever *that* meant.

* * *

Vivienne had a fire going and, from the smell of things, a pot of French press brewing when we walked into my house.

Holden sat adjacent to the fireplace in a wingback chair with his legs crossed like he was preparing to read a bedtime story. He gave Cole and me the once-over. "How'd it go?"

"Just a few stitches," I said.

"Seventeen." Cole grimaced. "Seventeen is not a few."

"Seventeen!" Vivienne shuffled into the living room from the kitchen. "You got seventeen stitches?" She hugged me and then whirled me around. "Gah! You're like Frankenstein!"

"Frankenstein's monster," I mumbled.

"Sit!" she ordered.

I dropped my satchel on the floor and plopped onto the sofa. Vivienne and Cole sat in the swivel barrel chairs across from me. Holden looked to be holding court, sitting perpendicular to us with his fingers tented and a serious expression on his face.

"I've heard bits and pieces," Viv began, "but can you tell me what happened?"

"It might be easier if I just read this." I reached into my satchel and pulled out the pink envelope. I waved it in front of them. The faintest whiff of what was probably Wanda's perfume permeated the air.

Vivienne pulled her brows together. "What's that?"

"This is the letter Wanda wrote and sent to me right before she, uh, died. I got it this afternoon."

Cole and Holden both sat upright in their chairs.

"I think you'll find it explains nearly everything."

Chapter Thirty-Eight

Audrey,

I'd like to give you the benefit of the doubt that you believe you're helping Chattertowne with your articles, so I hope you'll give me the benefit of the doubt as well when you write my story. You see, I love this community. I've lived here my whole life. My parents met and fell in love in the tenth grade at Chattertowne High. Their parents and grandparents lived here their entire lives. I believe in this place, and I believe in its people. I am not alone in my distrust of outsiders and those who want to alter our town. We have good reason to be wary.

Several years ago, things began to change. Outsiders moved in and brought with them new ideas, things they said would make this a better place. How can you improve upon perfection? Certainly not by plowing down the past to make way for tacky apartments and parking lots. As kids, my big brother and I would walk down to the old mill and cut across that field to fish at the river. He died, you know. My brother Wally, I mean. The city council approved the addition of that highway offramp to the Fodge Hill overpass after all those housing developments were built up there. Someone came barreling off at fifty miles per hour, not knowing they'd left the highway, and slammed into the side of my brother's car. He was nineteen. He had his whole life ahead of him, and it was taken away. And for what? Progress? Shaving minutes off someone's commute?

I went to school with Chet, all twelve years. Thirteen, I guess, if you count kindergarten. Same elementary, junior high, and high school. We reconnected when he started the Chattertowne nostalgia page. More like we connected for the first time. We weren't really friends growing up. We traveled in different social circles. His online group brought me back to a simpler time... a time before Wally's death and before the flood of Californians came in and tried to take over like an alien race seeking an unblemished planet after ruining their own. He posted stories of a bygone era, photos of parades, of football games, of the Kupit Festival, of beautiful Victorian-style homes before they were torn down or modernized. He valued the things I valued, and he valued me.

Not like Fred. Fred grew up in Chattertowne, too, but he only pretended to care about the things I did. He said he wanted to preserve the town's charm, and then what does he do? He puts together a deal for a giant housing complex on the buffalo farm! A million cookie-cutter houses squashed next to each other with no yard, no parking, and no charm. Him and his posse of troglodytes—Don Whitehead, Levi Scott, Kyle Murphy—all they care about is making money. Oh sure, they acted like they supported CROCCC's mission; all the while, they worked against us behind our backs.

Even Hiram, Chet's very best friend, betrayed him. One minute he's drawing porno stick figures on the new parking lot, the next he's voting to disband the Heritage Commission. Disgusting. I hope what he's done haunts him forever.

That was us, by the way. The graffiti. Chet and me and Hy. I'm sure you suspected, but since this is my last opportunity to get it all out, I might as well spill it. The graffiti was Chet's idea. He wanted to send a strong message to Margarita and the city council and Zeb. He was furious at Zeb. He felt he should have put his legacy as a Brandt above money.

Fred had a bunch of pink spray paint in the garage leftover from his last project. First, we hit her house, then the parking lot. It was kind of fun. I felt like a rebellious kid again, getting high behind the wood shop dumpster. Anyway, I passed the trailhead on my way home and stopped off to do a little more "decorating."

I saw you there, taking pictures the next day. I tried to be stealthy, but somehow you heard me. And then Chief Loveland arrived so I ran back to the house.

That night, while Fred was "working late" with Jenna, I decided to burn the mill down. I figured Chet would be pleased with me. The council would realize they had the makings of a revolution on their hands, and they'd shape up.

Unfortunately, I didn't get the chance to tell Chet right away. He texted that he wasn't happy with me about outing Margarita. She called him very upset after you and Chief Loveland visited her with the news. She accused Chet of doing it. He swore to her he'd kept his promise not to tell anyone, but she was really upset and said even if he hadn't done it himself, he'd instigated it with his online comments. She threatened to send the sheriff after him, maybe file a lawsuit. She mentioned some sleazy divorce lawyer in Tacoma who also apparently takes on whiny leftist politicians' frivolous lawsuits.

Chet knew it was me who had tagged the trail building because I was the only person he'd told, one night after a CROCCC meeting at Time's Up Tavern. He texted, saying he'd told me about Margarita's secret on accident, that he'd had too much whiskey, and I'd complicated things for him by what I'd done. He said he wasn't sure he could trust me anymore.

I asked him about the kiss we'd shared that night in the alley behind the bar, if that had been an accident on account of too much whiskey, but he never responded.

That's when I decided to tell him I burned down the mill for him. I didn't get that chance, though, because when I showed up at his paint shop, what did I find? Regan Whitehead in her tiny little cheer skirt, flouncing around, and Chet, looking like he wanted to devour her. He was talking her into tagging the old pool building. I don't think they even knew I was there. I left quietly, in tears. It was all too much.

I did mention Chet's plan for the old pool building to Fred, hoping he'd mention it to Don Whitehead and he'd stop Regan from doing it.

No such luck.

I needed to go bigger, to get Chet's attention off that child, and to prove I was all in. The next night I set fire to the Brandt barn. How could I know Zeb was sleeping out there? I never would have hurt him on purpose, please believe me. I didn't mean for anyone to get hurt. I've barely slept a wink since I learned Zeb had died. I'll be gone before his funeral, so I won't have to face Edna.

Of course, Chet was horrified by what happened to Zeb, as we all were. He confronted everyone at CROCCC, demanding to know who was responsible. I couldn't tell him. He'd hate me.

The fire at the Brandt farm was my last criminal act...until now, that is. I needed to lay low. Things had gotten way out of control. Zeb was dead, CROCCC was fractured, Chet was fooling around with Regan, and then he was with that witch Susan Prendergast. I felt like I was going to vomit watching them canoodle at the homecoming game. I decided I was going home, so I went to go get the car keys from Fred. He was making out with Jenna Doyle behind the announcing booth. I informed him if he didn't leave with me immediately, I was going to get the best lawyer in the state to take him for everything he owned. I was also going to report all the bribes he'd been making to grease the wheels of his development project.

As we left, I witnessed an argument between Chet and Blakesly. She was hysterical, hitting him and screaming about him taking advantage of Regan. He scuttled her to a dark corner, but I'd heard enough.

I felt like I'd been punched in the gut. I'd put all my faith in him, risked my marriage, campaigned for him, committed crimes for him, and he'd molested a young girl. Eighteen may technically be an adult, and she may think she's mature, but I babysat Regan just a few years ago, for goodness' sake.

Honestly, I'd have killed him if Blakesly hadn't. I don't know that she did it for a fact, of course, but it makes sense. She was in love with Chet also, and he'd violated her teen daughter. Or maybe it was Don. His wife didn't hide her admiration, so he barely tolerated Chet, and that was before he knew the man had relations with Regan. Either way, he deserved what he got.

It all ends tonight. I don't want to go through a divorce, and I certainly don't want to go to prison. I can't let my husband continue to destroy the legacy of Chattertowne, and I want his girlfriend to suffer for humiliating me. The way they strutted out of that meeting together... they had no shame.

It's just better this way. No loose ends to tie up, no long and drawn-out court cases, no more secrets.

When you tell my story, will you please tell the people of Chattertowne I did my best to protect the integrity of this wonderful town? I did it for them, to preserve our culture, our history. I made some mistakes, but my heart was in the right place.

Tell my friends and family I'm sorry I didn't say goodbye. I can't face them.

Tell Edna Brandt I didn't mean to bring her so much pain.

Tell Blakesly she should dump her jerk husband and tell Regan it's not her fault that the man manipulated her and took advantage of her.

Tell Gabe and Tammy Milner to keep fighting the fight, make our elected officials accountable.

Tell Margarita I regret revealing information that wasn't mine to share, but I hope she'll do a better job of listening to her constituents before making decisions that affect all of us.

Tell Hiram I know he was in love with me, and I forgive him for what he did in the meeting the other night. I know it's not easy to choose between your values and your ability to make a living.

Tell Jenna Doyle she's reaped what she sowed.

Tell Chief Loveland I'm sorry for making such a mess for him. I know he will be good for Chattertowne.

Finally, just a tiny favor. If you could, please ask Onyx Carpenter to play me when this story is made into a movie. I know she's younger and completely different complexion, but I think she understands what it means to be from Chattertowne, and I think she'd do me justice.

I hope this letter finds you well, Audrey. I wish you the best.
Wanda Harper
PS: When it comes to love, choose the one who chooses you. Otherwise, you'll spend your life chasing something that will never be yours, not really. I'm guessing you'll eventually share this with those closest to you, so I won't spell it out, but I hope you are picking up what I'm putting down.

Chapter Thirty-Nine

"I hope you're picking up what I'm putting down." I finished reading Wanda's letter aloud and set it, along with the pink envelope in which it came, on the coffee table.

Cole, Holden, and Vivienne sat in silence. The fireplace crackled a bit, but other than that, dead quiet.

Cole rubbed his beard, now nearly full. "I've never in my entire career heard that extensive of a confession. She laid it all out there."

Holden leaned back and crossed his giant biceps. "She didn't get everything right."

"No, but I'm not sure any of us could have imagined Regan could be responsible for Chet's murder. I knew for certain when I saw her face, though. I suppose the rifle pointed at me through the glass helped cement my theory."

"So, Audrey, when you texted Cole and me to say you knew who killed Chet, you weren't positive it was Regan?" Holden clasped his hands together behind his head.

"I was about seventy-five percent. I was willing to concede it could have been Blakesly, partly because she's been so nasty to me for no reason, but mostly because, as a mother, she had to be furious about the situation."

Viv tilted her head. "A protective mother makes much more sense. So, what skewed things toward Regan in your mind?"

"After I read Wanda's letter, where she talked about Chet having a sexual relationship with Regan, I remembered a couple things. First, at the Cavalcade, I saw Regan vomit into a trash can. Then, on Monday, when she was supposed to come give her statement at the police department, and I ran into her arguing with Blakesly in front of City Hall, she said something that caught my attention. She said, *he's no martyr*, and then this look flashed across her face. I can't explain it, but it was deep pain mixed with seething rage. She knew he hadn't died for the cause like a martyr, because she'd killed him for another reason entirely."

Viv sighed and shook her head. "She's just a kid. Will they consider that?"

Cole grimaced. He rubbed his chin hair. "Maybe. The District Attorney's office will look at the entirety of the case and make a determination. I can point out the mitigating factors of the case, but ultimately, it will be up to the D.A. to make that call."

Holden slapped his hands on his thighs and stood. "I gotta get going. Early day tomorrow."

I looked at him and cocked my head. "Who…do you work for now? Fred's dead."

He scratched his cheek. "I don't know. I guess I figure someone's got to show up and handle things. Might as well be me."

I rose from the couch. "I'll walk you out."

"Not necessary." Holden lingered near the front door, looking at Cole, waiting for him.

Cole must have gotten the hint because he stood and stretched. "I should go too. You need some rest."

"I'll stay and keep an eye on her for concussion symptoms." Viv got up and gave each of them a hug. "Thanks, guys, for looking out for my sister."

They both nodded.

Viv pointed toward the kitchen. "I'm gonna go straighten up." She gave me a tiny smile and an eyebrow raise before turning to walk away.

I followed Holden and Cole through the doorway and onto my front porch.

Cole gave me a hug, something I never expected, and before I could say anything, he'd jogged to his car. He gave a quick wave, got in, and drove away, leaving Holden and me alone.

He adjusted his shirt. "You, uh, you going to the football game at the high school tomorrow night?"

"It's not my beat, but I'll probably be there. It's a good place to hear everyone's thoughts and opinions about what's happened."

"Me too. I'll be there, I mean. Maybe I'll see you there."

I smiled at him. "Sounds good."

He opened his mouth like he wanted to say something, but then a ruckus behind me caught his attention. I whirled around just in time to see Ruby and her babies traipsing across my front lawn in a line. I gasped and she stopped. We made eye contact for a brief moment; she chittered, and then she scurried away with three baby raccoons—kits—waddling behind her.

I burst into tears.

Holden looked at me with alarm.

It was silly, but Ruby's departure brought all the sadness and grief over the events of the previous couple of weeks to the surface in a way I couldn't control. Tears streamed down my face, and sobs wracked my shoulders.

"Come here." Holden pulled me close and wrapped his arms around me. "It's okay," he whispered in my ear. "It's all gonna be okay."

He held me until I regained my composure. We rocked back and forth until my whimpers and cries became heavy sighs.

"You know what's crazy about all this?" I sniffled.

"What's that?"

"I wanted her to leave so badly, but now that she's gone, I'm really sad about it."

"You were her safe place when she needed one."

"I know."

"Now it's time to move on. It's best for everyone."

I sniffed. "Are we still talking about raccoons?"

Holden's only response was a long squeeze.

Chapter Forty

Chattertowne Coastal Current
Plea Agreement Reached in Chet Buchanan Murder Case
By Audrey O'Connell

Yesterday, three months after the murder of one-time mayoral candidate Chet Buchanan, a plea agreement of first-degree manslaughter was entered in Snohomish County Superior Court for Regan Whitehead, 18, of Chattertowne, who has acknowledged her role in the bludgeoning death of one of Chattertowne's most controversial figures. Prosecutors cited extenuating circumstances to Judge Angus McKinley in defense of their recommendation for twenty-eight months jail time–the minimum of the sentencing range—including time served, along with three hundred hours of community service and five years probation for Whitehead.

Mr. Buchanan was killed last fall during a confrontation between the defendant and the victim over their affair, which allegedly began when Whitehead was seventeen. The relationship resulted in a pregnancy, for which paternity tests have confirmed to be the late Mr. Buchanan's child. Ms. Whitehead is approximately five months pregnant.

Ms. Whitehead's attorneys provided text messages, which they claimed showed a pattern of grooming behavior by the deceased, manipulation, and verbal abuse. Prosecutors must have agreed, because they negotiated terms favorable to the defendant.

In a statement to the judge, Whitehead said:

"As a mother-to-be, I realize that one of the most important lessons I can teach my child is to take accountability for my actions. My youth is a factor, but it is not an excuse. I would like to apologize to the people I have hurt, mostly my parents."

Judge McKinley accepted the recommendation of prosecutors and wished the defendant well.

The child will be raised by its maternal grandparents until Whitehead is released. While she has twenty-five months remaining on her sentence, she likely will be released in as little as six months.

Acknowledgements

I am blessed to have so many amazing people in my corner. I couldn't do any of this without you. My husband, my kids, my parents, my siblings, my in-laws, my friends and extended family, my writing sisters, my crime fiction community, my editor extraordinaire Shawn, everyone at Level Best and my Level besties, my new agent Paula, and my former agent Dawn Dowdle, who championed my writing to the very end. Thank you.

About the Author

Kate B Jackson (KB Jackson) is an Anthony Award finalist and an Agatha Award winning author of mystery novels for grownups and mystery/adventure novels for kids. An alumnus of the University of Washington—go Huskies!—she lives in the PNW with her hilarious husband. They have four mostly-grown children. A part-time genetic genealogist, she loves to craft stories with elements of history and family dynamics. Her books are about secrets (Chattertowne Mysteries), sisters (Cruising Sisters Mysteries), and Sasquatch (Sasquatch Hunters).

AUTHOR WEBSITE:

https://KBJackson.com

SOCIAL MEDIA HANDLES:

https://www.instagram.com/kbjacksonauthor/
https://www.facebook.com/KBJacksonAuthor
https://www.goodreads.com/user/show/152007919-kate-jackson
https://www.tiktok.com/@generalkate?

Also by K.B. Jackson

<u>CHATTERTOWNE MYSTERIES (LEVEL BEST)</u>
Secrets Don't Sink (2023)

<u>SASQUATCH HUNTERS (REYCRAFT BOOKS)</u>
The Sasquatch of Hawthorne Elementary (2023)
The Sasquatch of Harriman Lake (2024)

<u>CRUISING SISTERS MYSTERIES (TULE PUBLISHING)</u>
Until Depths Do Us Part (2024)